GERANIUMS

GERANIUMS

MARLENE HAUSER

The Book Guild Ltd

First published in Great Britain in 2022 by
The Book Guild Ltd
Unit E2 Airfield Business Park,
Harrison Road, Market Harborough,
Leicestershire. LE16 7UL
Tel: 0116 2792299
www.bookguild.co.uk
Email: info@bookguild.co.uk
Twitter: @bookguild

Typeset in 11pt Minion Pro

Printed and bound by CPI Group (UK) Ltd, Croydon, CR0 4YY

ISBN 978 1914471 551

British Library Cataloguing in Publication Data.
A catalogue record for this book is available from the British Library.

If my grandmother, Emma Ewen, had not been placed in a plaster cast from head to toe at the age of twelve and left in it for two years, I like to think that a great many things would have turned out different – for me and my sister and brother, for my father, but most of all for my mother.

PROLOGUE

Far away, through the tall windows by her hospital bed, Emma could see the treetops and glimpses of Philadelphia beyond – on a good day, that is, when she had the strength to lift her head. Some distance below her, a black-and-white tiled floor seemed to skitter away, first to the left, then to the right.

Weights attached to her body cast pulled her deviating spine straight; one of the preferred treatments for spinal scoliosis, caused by childhood polio. Twelve-year-old Emma's clothes, toys and books had all been taken away and burned, standard practice in the 1920s to avoid further contagion. But why did they need to hoist her almost to the ceiling? she wondered.

She had no option but to hold still. Below her, nurses changed beds and wheeled patients, but Emma liked it best when they, as she saw it, flapped their wings, did the Charleston, the Black Bottom and the Lindy Hop, reeling across the checkered floor.

After two years of treatment and rehabilitation, Emma walked out briskly one breezy day. The doctors had done their best, and my grandmother did what any strong-willed teenage girl would: she closed the door on the past twenty-four months without looking back, the same way she had closed the door on the night when, aged six, she had witnessed her mother go to her death in a raging house fire. Her mother had run back into the burning family mansion when it was discovered that the youngest of her eight children had been left behind.

Emma had watched the flames lick the night sky as the largest house on the block collapsed, falling in on itself like a woman to her knees, fiery skirts billowing around her. Later on someone bundled up the young girl, cupping her cold feet in their dry hands. She woke lying in a strange house, under a quilt, watched over by a woman who told her, "Emmie" – no one called her Emmie – "your mother and baby sister are now far away in heaven."

It seemed that almost overnight a new mansion, a larger one, went up, and this new woman with her new baby came into their lives and presided over them. Emma was sent away to a convent boarding school. The nuns protested that she was too young, but her stepmother had decided that six children besides her own were quite enough for any woman to contend with.

Just before one school vacation, Emma was told that she would not be going to join her family. In angry protest, she lay down in the middle of the road, stopping the traffic. It took two Sisters of Mercy to haul the rigid child upright, and three policemen to sort out the jam she'd caused. It was one of those two nuns, while trying to soothe the tired, frightened young girl, sponging her back and calling her 'little bird', who noticed her once-straight spine was deviating to the left.

By then Emma was twelve. It was her stepmother who decided the unsatisfactory child should go to the Children's Hospital of Philadelphia. With each X-ray Emma felt more naked and exposed; with each month spent in plaster or in a wheeled cage, with each electric shock, she felt more sure that nobody in the world cared about her.

She walked out of the hospital a girl of barely fourteen, a

fledgling straight out of the nest, free! She closed the door on her spell of sickness wanting only one thing – to dance, the way the nurses did, maybe while smoking a cigarette.

But for Emma dancing remained an impossibility. My grandmother was a hunchback, imperfect, no matter what lengths she went to to prove she was not handicapped. While it would come as no surprise to me, it did to many others that a woman so tiny, so delicate, so tragically twisted, only four foot nine inches tall, could give birth to a giant of a man like my father Jack.

Emma Ewen never acknowledged her mistakes, would not countenance even the idea of being wrong. More than that, she felt compelled to show anyone who ever doubted her how truly mistaken they were. This conviction took on a new intensity when she married Jonathan Preston: the young man every girl wanted to catch, gorgeous, blond, blue-eyed – and very much from the wrong side of Philadelphia.

No one ever quite knew how they met. It could have been at a local football game, while ice-skating or maybe at the same dance where Emma claimed to have fallen, and forever after maintained that this was when she'd damaged her spine. "It was not," she would always make clear, "polio."

Jonathan and Emma eloped to Florida, and at a very young age Emma Ewen Preston came home pregnant. Her firstborn son was duly christened with his ne'er-do-well father's name.

Emma had been warned that she would be disowned by her family: for marrying a farmer's son and bearing his child.

The family lawyer explained the new reality to Emma: "A sum of money will be held in trust for you. For the rest of your life, you will receive an annual dividend of four per cent on the principal, but this will cease upon your death. I'm afraid, my dear, this is the sole provision that will be made for you. Apart from this, you are henceforth disinherited."

Jonathan Preston didn't leave Emma straight away but more

like four and a half years and two children later. She did not regret his departure for a single minute. Afterwards she acted as father and mother to her son and daughter and brought them up according to her own exacting code of behaviour. Her son, who called himself Jack to distance himself from his absent father, would become an officer and a gentleman, she had decided.

When he chose to go against her plans for military school and an officer's commission and instead joined the Navy at seventeen, intending to qualify as a pilot since flying was all he had ever wanted to do, she would not allow him to backtrack. Emma wanted to teach him to accept full responsibility for any decisions he took. After all, a Preston was a Preston, and they never made mistakes. They had to be right, to the bitter end. If he wanted to be a Naval pilot, she would shove him all the way to the top.

To illustrate the rank to which Jack Preston should aspire, she took him to celebrate his enlistment at the swankiest place in Philadelphia: the Waldorf Club. Since gentlemen did not wear a hat indoors, even a uniform one in time of war, his was consigned to the cloakroom. After they had eaten, Jack returned to claim it but the cloakroom attendant handed him a brigadier general's hat by mistake.

"No, that's not my hat," he said.

"Sorry, sir. Would you be so kind as to describe it?"

"It's white, it's small, it's round. Like that." He held out two thumbs and his forefingers to show exactly how small and how round.

The maître d' took over from the baffled attendant. He took the brigadier general's hat, with its abundance of gold braid, back to the closet and reverently presented another hat extended on a silver tray.

"No," Jack Preston said with exasperation, "that is not my hat. It's small, it's round, it's white."

"Jack," Emma warned her son, "calm down."

"I am calm! I told you I wanted to keep it with me. I could have tucked it right here inside my belt. Just like the other fellows do."

By now other men, officers, were lining up for their hats. Jack felt the heat. To the right and left hats were being passed out. The crowd behind him at the coat check became amused. They all wanted to watch, or so it seemed to Jack. Finally, one of the officers stepped out and whispered to the maître d'.

The maître d' returned with a small white sailor's cap, centred neatly on his silver tray. The men waiting behind Jack stood a little straighter, a little taller. It was a kind of salute, a show of respect for an ordinary seaman, the lowest-ranking hand on a ship. Jack's sort was fodder for the front lines. Last in, first out. Sailors of this rank had a life expectancy in service of thirty – maybe sixty – days, maximum.

Jack Preston snatched the 'Dixie cup' from the tray. Would his mother ever quit humiliating him? He hadn't wanted to eat at the Club – too many officers. He'd wanted to take her down to the harbour, show her the ships; he loved the snapping flags and the tinkle of the glass buoys against the swell.

Jack made his way out of the Waldorf Club, took a deep breath and cocked the 'Dixie cup' just so, a little off to the right. He resented the fact that despite the way she had set out to make him look small in that fancy place, he still felt sorry for his mother, or M, as he called her: no husband, no mother, cast out by her family. *God, I'm all she really has.*

He put her into a taxicab, deciding he would go for a stroll. Jack was as handsome as his father had been: blond hair, blue eyes, tall, well-built, with a natural swagger girls already swooned before.

He imagined himself a sort of Flash Gordon, a rocket man. He did the math. He would spend his eighteenth birthday on Okinawa. Japan! Jack let out a long, low whistle. It'd be just like going to the moon.

ONE

How do you describe beauty? Details of the hair, face, hands? Elegance? No. None of that counts for much beside something else, something far more remarkable.

My mother had a sort of radiance. It still beams out from the oldest photographs of her, the black-and-white ones, where she is forever dandling one or another of her younger siblings. Her jet-black hair seems to be constantly in motion, flying out from behind her. With eyes fixed on the camera, she gives her wide smile, from ear to ear, the one that some of us still wear today.

Not everyone had a mother like mine: beautiful, sweet, innocent, young, caring, not intellectual but generously warm and, most of all, sensitive. "Perhaps too sensitive," was what people came to say in time. She loved her children, all three of us.

The second oldest of three children, Lauren Rose Ryan, was her father's favourite. She used to roll her uniform skirt up at the waist on the way to school, down when she arrived and back up on the way home. She bought red lipstick at the five and dime, and shared it with any girl who asked. As soon as she'd smiled for the high-school yearbook she was off, gone to New York. Lauren Rose

1

became an American Airlines stewardess, a coveted job for which only the loveliest girls need apply. After every paycheque she brought home for her proud mother a geranium or two. In a few months, the entire backyard of the row house under the railroad bridge in Lower Darby, Pennsylvania, was filled with flowers: red ones, white ones, pink ones. Whenever the train passed by overhead, the clay pots rattled and petals scattered like confetti.

Lauren would give her mother Anna anything, everything. Mother and daughter both knew it, even if they never talked about it. Lauren's father was a handful. Typically Irish, a big lunk of a man but loyal with it, Michael brought his paycheque straight home from the car factory every week. That was the contract: Anna managed, Michael worked – and drank with the money that was handed back to him.

Lauren was first engaged to an Italian boy, someone from the neighborhood she had known for years. They both had big families, liked to laugh. They both loved the colour red. "We'll have a hundred children," they used to say, to each other and to anyone else who would listen. They both liked to cook, and they both liked to talk – and talk, and talk, and talk.

Compared to her girlfriends', Lauren's engagement ring was small. It held one little diamond, maybe a quarter carat.

"From the five and dime?" she used to ask.

"You bet!" her fiancé would laugh. "You just wait… Someday."

Someday came. It was a windy, bright May in 1951. The plane almost didn't take off. The stewardesses told each other to get ready with the 'barf bags'. As she served drinks, then meals, Lauren noticed the quarter carat on her ring finger. She did not care about having the biggest diamond in the world. She cared about family, friends, a church wedding and making people feel good. Tonight was her engagement party. She could hardly wait to touch down, get home.

"May I take your tray?" she asked a male passenger. "Anything else?"

"No… no, thank you," he said.

"Juicy Fruit?"

"Oh, yes, that would be great, thank you – thank you very much."

Lauren handed him the stick of gum and looked into his startlingly blue eyes. She caught her breath. His voice sounded so familiar to her, it was as if she had been hearing it all her life.

When he came down the aisle later and chatted with the stewardesses, she was mesmerised. South Philly? he said, singling out Lauren Rose. Imagine that, he was going there, too. He could give her a lift. He had spent his birthday on Okinawa in '45, he told her. It was on VJ Day after they dropped the atom bomb. A hundred thousand troops died, capturing the island alone, but Jack Preston came home.

Now he was back from Korea, where his plane had been shot down and he'd walked out on his own two feet. He had been a gunner since '49. "Boy," he said, "it was a bitch, excuse me, being balled up in the belly of the beast." He had not seen his mother in almost two years. Now he was an officer and a pilot. Had just been awarded his wings. He was a regular war hero.

They drank black coffee together in the galley, the new pilot and the stewardess, both of them eyecatching in their uniforms. The drone of the engines made them shout all the louder.

"Wait for me," he said, "and I'll take you home."

Jack remained after all the other passengers disembarked, and then, just as promised, he escorted Lauren Rose down the airstairs. A perfect match. The world stood at attention for the stunning young pair.

Emma Preston waited at the gate closest to the tarmac with her daughter Penny. *Where is my son?* Each vied with the other to see Jack first, and suddenly there he was, larger than life. Emma smiled proudly, and in the next instant gasped in shock.

"No," she said aloud at the sight of the woman with jet-black hair, "no… please don't tell me he's brought home an Oriental!"

3

TWO

A safety pin.

That was how Emma Preston knew for sure that my mother was the wrong bride for her son. How did she know? It was easy. On the day in question Lauren had come for a dress fitting. Emma had taken over all the preparations for the wedding. It would, whether anybody else liked it or not, be a society affair. She told everyone who would listen how she had taken the reins right out of the bride's family's hands, so that now the wedding, the reception, the honeymoon, all would be on a suitably lavish scale.

"You know," she told Anna Ryan, the mother of the bride, "we come from the other side…" Here Emma allowed her voice to trail off, gesturing vaguely to some imaginary other, better, side of the tracks that wasn't Lower Darby, Philadelphia. She lightly touched the string of pearls at her throat, then the back of her chignon, and straightened the raw silk jacket, tugging it slightly at the hem, before pressing her entire A-line skirt flat. Anna simply folded her arms over her large chest, across the grey cardigan, buttoned over the loose cotton dress splashed with ragged blue daisies, enjoying the scene, containing the flash of her dark eyes and wide smile.

4

The implication was that the Ryans could not afford to do things in the correct way. On the face of it Emma was acting generously, but the truth was that she had nightmares about the dress, the venue – *God forbid the backyard, under the viaduct* – and what sort of food the Ryans would serve, left to their own devices. Emma, disinherited daughter of one of Philadelphia's wealthiest businessmen, still had so much to prove.

"That will be fine," Anna Ryan said graciously, in her dining room that overlooked the back garden with its rows and rows of multi-coloured geraniums. Right then, the downtown train rattled loudly over the trestle bridge, causing petals to rain down.

"You just let me know where I can chip in," she said.

Emma explained it to her son, my father Jack, who explained it to Lauren Rose. "That's just the way it is because that's just who my mother, M, is," Jack told his fiancée, who went along with it all like the proverbial lamb to the slaughter because that was just the way it was and Lauren Rose was exactly who she was: a woman terribly in love.

Emma Preston, being generous with her money, magnanimous even, saved Lauren's parents a fortune. The dress alone would have cost Michael Ryan a year's salary. Custom designed by Emma's own tailor, the one who made her the clever dresses with the discreet pads to hide the evidence of her 'dancing accident'. While the tailor gave the bride's dress its final fitting he admired Lauren Rose up and down. "Perfect, exquisite," he said repeatedly as he measured, tucked, snipped and cut. In the fitting room, excitement mounted over tea and slim flutes of champagne until the mother of the groom noticed something shocking.

"Lauren Rose," Emma said as she put her teacup down, "is that a safety pin I see?" It had flashed just momentarily from the hem of the girl's pleated skirt as she undressed.

Lauren Rose smiled. "This is just a stopgap. I didn't have time to sew it up. My heel got caught in the hem as I was coming down the stairs and I didn't want to be late. It's all been such a whirlwind lately." She smiled again as she tried to explain the presence of the rogue safety pin to a woman who took these things very seriously.

Emma knew she should not begrudge Lauren Rose her beauty, but she did. She found it impossible to smile back, to return a genuine kindness. Inwardly she was beside herself, convinced this was a serious flaw they could not afford to ignore. Lauren passed for a suitable new addition to the family on many counts: make-up, hair, cleanliness, manicure, pedicure, fresh bra, panties, hosiery and, thankfully, a half-slip. But how could Jack marry her? After the fitting and before the wedding day, Emma tried incessantly to make her son understand he was making a dreadful mistake.

"Do you realise, she had a safety pin in the hem of her skirt?" she reiterated, when what she wanted to say was: Jack, it is about refinement, something your father never understood, until it was too late, of course. It's why I divorced him, chose to be a single mother, and you will divorce Lauren Rose, too.

"Oh, M," my father was reported to have said, "I love her and you will, too."

On the day of the wedding, though, Jack's feet, seemingly riveted to the floor, would not move. There were three hundred guests, and M. What would his mother do if he just upped and ran? Blinded by the sunlight splintering through the stained glass, the colours also playing over Lauren's dress, Jack felt he could barely see his wife-to-be. Organ refrains echoed in his head, hollow-sounding like shells exploding in a field, ringing in his ears, resounding in his helmet. He wanted to cut and run.

Instead, Jack lifted Lauren Rose's veil. Momentarily, he thought of other girls, different ones. In a flash, he recalled handholding, skating, hot chocolate, talk of other engagements, but that was long ago. This was his wife now, Lauren Rose, he affirmed. Yet he barely knew her. Could M be right? Arm in arm, they turned towards the priest, and the congregation knelt.

That safety pin, thought Jack, his sister Penny and his mother

6

M. Each silently wondered why they had ignored that telltale sign. Emma knew all about it: marrying the wrong kind.

Jack and Lauren Rose kissed.

A few days after the wedding Emma began to call herself Mrs Jack Preston. Sometimes she would add Senior: Mrs Jack Preston, Sr. Other times: just Mrs Jack Preston.

"I want to make quite sure," she told her son when he questioned her about it, "that everyone knows exactly to whom you belong." She laughed then, something he rarely heard her do. The pure, bell-like sound caught him off guard for a moment. He had meant to ask: *Mrs Jack Preston... shouldn't that be my wife?*

Oh, what the hell, he thought, *what could really be wrong with it? After all, she is my mom.*

THREE

After the honeymoon they moved to South Dakota. Jack had found the house himself and kept telling Lauren Rose, "You will love it, really love it… it's a steal."

"Plenty of space for a young couple like you." The realtor began her pitch as she met them at the door. "Thinking of starting a family?"

"Yes," Jack said as he swung open closets, doors, ran down and up the basement stairs, in and out of every room. "Great," he said, "so much light! We could put a bar right over there."

Lauren Rose walked slowly from one room to the next, trying them on for size. Did she fit? She stopped in the living room in front of the empty, flagstone fireplace. She stood at the edge of a large dark spot on the carpet.

"What's this?" she asked.

Jack and the realtor froze for a moment and then walked towards her tentatively, as if to the centre of a net.

"A stain… think nothing of it," Jack said.

"It looks like blood."

"It is," he answered.

"A woman died here." The realtor chose her words carefully.

"Who? How?"

"An accident—"

"A suicide," Jack broke in, impatient.

"Suicide?" Lauren Rose faltered.

"At least it wasn't murder. Why else do you think it's so cheap?" Jack laughed.

Lauren looked out the large bay window, at the last view an unknown woman had seen before her death. An expanse of grass, yellowing in the November light, fanned out before row after row of identical tract housing.

"Jack, let's go," she said.

"Excuse me," he said to the realtor, and led his wife of only days by the elbow into the next room.

"No," she insisted, "I don't want to live in a house where a woman took her own life."

"Lauren. You are making way too much of this. The house is a bargain. Dirt-cheap. I can replace the carpet, before we move in. There's nothing to fear."

"I'll be here on my own all day. This is where we will have our first baby." She held one hand to her lips, as if she had just let slip her deepest wish: children.

"Lauren, listen, I'm not taking this," he said through gritted teeth. "I found the house. It's right for us, and you are balking at a bit of blood on the floor?"

"Jack, please."

"No, don't talk to me. Get in the car."

The engine hummed as they drove back to the air base and their temporary quarters. Lauren Rose stared out at the flat landscape. She wanted to hold her ground. She ran her finger over the inside of the charm bracelet, the smooth part of the links around her wrist, the small letters that spelled out Atlantic City, where they had honeymooned. She clenched her teeth, had a little trouble breathing and then couldn't swallow. Her stomach ached.

What could she do? Jack wanted the house with blood on the floor.

A woman killed herself, Lauren Rose thought. *Had it been just a normal afternoon, had she felt lonely and afraid? Didn't she have a husband, a friend, a big family she could lean on, like me?*

Jack slammed the car into park. Lauren Rose accidentally sliced her finger on the base of her bracelet, the letter A. He did not say a word, but instead banged the car door closed. Pressing the flesh over the stinging paper-thin cut, Lauren Rose opened her own door. *Something,* she thought, *he hasn't done since the wedding.* What was wrong with him? He was hopping mad. She found herself afraid and far from home. Powerless. She had no money. She ran after him.

"Jack," she said, "do you really want it?"

"Want what?" He knocked her hands off his arm.

"The house?"

"Yes, I do."

So that was the house where my older sister, Margaret Anne Preston, Mags, was born on October 12th, 1953. The next child, they were certain, would be a boy.

"It has to be," Jack declared, and Lauren Rose agreed, "a son."

That, of course, would be perfect, would make everyone completely happy.

FOUR

Lauren Rose, pregnant again when the Mayflower van loaded up the last of their things for the long drive from South Dakota to Fort Belvoir, Virginia, wasted not one minute on goodbyes. She and Mags would drive with Jack in the new Chevrolet, stopping only overnight in Philadelphia to visit M and Penny, and then Lauren Rose's own parents, along with her brothers Sean and Danny.

Maybe they would stop in Atlantic City too, relax at the shore and celebrate the good news: Lauren Rose was sure that this time it would be a boy. Jack thought about it non-stop – *a son*. Lauren Rose wanted to name the baby Jack: "After you," she said, taking her husband by the arm.

He frowned. "No, not after me."

"Why not?"

"Because that is the worst thing in the world."

"Don't be silly," she said, pretending to tease him when in fact she was puzzled. She had learned to be careful around him. He took things personally; to him everything was criticism.

"What do you know? Who were you named after?" he snapped.

"Well, nobody…" She didn't finish. This was beginning to be

a habit with Lauren Rose. It infuriated them both, but sometimes, even if her initial thought started out on a high note, like the fact that her mother had seen her name in a dream, she would stop mid-sentence. Somehow it seemed irrelevant. She already knew Jack's response: "Stupid... that's pretty inane." Lauren Rose began to feel silly by comparison with a man who appeared so smart.

"I was named," he said, "after Jonathan, my father."

"So where'd Jack come from?"

"It's a nickname. I wanted a name for myself. I'm my own man. I am somebody," he finished, punching his own chest.

"I see," she said, which she didn't. She wanted to suggest they call the child Michael, after the father she adored, but instead she said, "Jack, you choose. You'll think of something just right."

They pulled up to Anna and Michael's little summer compound in Sandy Cove. There were two houses, an old one named Candy Lane after the board game and a modern one called Crew Cut because the roof was flat instead of tiled and pitched. Anna and Michael had built with plenty of room for three children and all the little ones they expected them to bring home. Lauren Rose, engulfed by Sean and Danny, allowed Anna to wrest baby Mags from her arms even before she had a chance to get out of the Chevrolet.

"You decide," she said, once again.

Darkness crept across Jack's face, something Lauren Rose thought she might dispel, something she could fix if she watched what she said and never opposed him. No one else knew, but in South Dakota, the place where, he would claim years later, he first heard her talking to people who were not there, Jack used to startle her from sleep. Semi-conscious and sweating profusely, he'd yell as if he were under attack, shouting, "Jump, you bastard, jump!"

Lauren Rose would gently touch him on the arm, saying, "Wake up, darling, wake up. You're dreaming, Jack. A bad dream."

She would be careful not to move too close because once he

pinned her to the headboard, ready to crack her skull, before he recognised she was not a Japanese soldier. She wanted to tell somebody how much it had frightened her, maybe even him, but she decided to keep it a secret. *After all, didn't everybody do their bit for the war? This might just be hers.*

It would have been better for us all if she'd spoken up as soon as she knew he had a problem.

"That's great," her family said, taking turns to pat her rounded belly, "another one on the way."

"A boy," Jack declared.

"Gotta be," Michael agreed, as they toasted one another, putting burgers on the grill.

"What if it's not?" Anna asked, tossing the potatoes in butter and parsley.

They all fell quiet. Some said Anna could tell by the look in a pregnant woman's eye what sex the child would be. Did she know something they did not?

"Gotta be," Michael said again, and they all started laughing. Only Lauren Rose did not laugh, and Jack thought: *What does Anna know anyway? Nothin'.*

"Arthur," he told his pregnant wife later. "I think I will call him Arthur – after the legendary king." He had looked at his mother-in-law throughout the visit almost defiantly and thought about the boy to come who would be free and magnificent.

They said their goodbyes and left. Lauren Rose grew quiet. She'd remembered how good it was to be around friends and family. Even M and Penny had proved friendly to her and Mags this time. They'd appeared to check their criticism, or at least kept it to a bare minimum. Why did Penny's young twin girls seem so stellar? M made a point of saying constantly, "Exemplary, just exemplary." And by comparison, she said barely anything about Mags. "No offense intended," she continually said to Lauren Rose. "No offense intended."

Lauren Rose and Jack bounced boys' names back and forth all

the way from Pennsylvania to Virginia, but Arthur stuck. Lauren Rose chose Gabriel for the second name.

"After the angel," she said, toying with her charm bracelet again.

"Are you sure?" Jack asked.

"Yes," she announced, "he was the topmost angel, chosen to announce the birth of Jesus." She'd thought of the name days before and kept it to herself, savouring it, because she knew this was special, this would please Jack, make him happy.

"Are you certain? I mean, we're not going to call him Gabby. This isn't some sort of Irish thing, is it?"

"No. *Arthur Gabriel.* I like it, don't you?"

"Yes... yes, I do."

They started buying baby clothes in shades of blue, and as he painted the nursery, Jack remembered his mother-in-law's warning. What was it she'd said: "What if it's not?" *What if it's not?* he asked himself. *What if it's not? An impossibility.*

Jack got on well at the Pentagon, which was an impressive assignment, especially for a kid who had not gone to the US Air Force Academy, but instead came up through the ranks. Deep down, even if he recognised this position was just to help ensure a speedy promotion from lieutenant to captain, Jack knew a desk job did not suit him. He wanted something else: to be in the sky, flying. A man could die like this, behind a desk, watching a clock.

Lauren Rose liked Virginia better than South Dakota. It was warmer, the houses were closer together and the people seemed friendlier. She had a beautiful baby daughter whom everyone said looked just like her. Truth was, Mags looked like her father, even without the blonde hair or the blue eyes. Her eyes, it could be argued, were like Lauren Rose's, brown, but in truth they were most like Aunt Penny's and her twin girls'. Mags could have been one of Aunt Penny's brood, though no one had the heart to tell Lauren Rose this.

14

One thing she had learned about her husband by now was that he was, more often than not, angry. He could lose his temper over the smallest of things. Not a single day would go by without something being wrong. No matter how hard she tried, something was always out of place, not right. Didn't she know anything? He had even made a fuss when she was nursing one morning. He was in a hurry and had lost a button from his uniform.

"Here, just use a safety pin," she said, as she tried to keep Mags propped up on one breast.

"Don't be stupid," he snapped, stepping closer towards her, as his arm swung up, his lip curled. "All right, if you're too busy, I'll just have to do it myself."

Jack pulled out a needle, then a thread, knotting it the way he had learned as a new recruit. *A safety pin...*

Something nagged at Lauren Rose. It seemed as if her husband had almost hit her, and then frozen. She'd been holding the baby. Why should he get so worked up about a safety pin?

FIVE

There were so many things Jack did not like. He was hard on himself, too. He was never good enough, and in consequence worked longer hours than anyone else in the office. He was never home, and any social life they had was dictated purely by him. Lauren Rose loved going out, meeting new people, potential friends – except for the aftermath, when Jack would fall into a grouchy mood after they came home. If they had a party at their house, after everyone left, he would nurse a drink and grill her. Who was that you were talking to, and what for? Why did they make you laugh? Am I not good enough? Why are you looking so happy? Do you not know that I could take all of this – he would demonstrate with one gigantic swipe of his hand – away from you any time I choose?

At these moments Lauren Rose would hold Mags closer. You'd never take my daughter from me, she would reply, but only ever in her mind, never aloud. Instead she would tell him, over and over, "Jack, I was just having fun, a few laughs. You know I only have eyes for you." She vowed to try harder, be nicer, more beautiful. And if that didn't work, she knew what would: the new baby, that longed-for little boy, Arthur Gabriel.

Sometimes in the shower, she would think about her son-to-come. What would he look like? Just like his father, she was sure. Lauren Rose already felt she knew every inch of her son by heart. He would have blue eyes, blond hair, be strong, a real fighter, nothing would get him down, ever. With a sparkle in his eyes, she added. Kind to strangers, too. Maybe she couldn't call him Jack out loud, but on her own and in secret she could call him anything she wanted.

Sometimes Lauren Rose went into the shower just to get away. Jack might be raging over anything. She would bring Mags and put her in her jumper seat on the floor. Maybe she would turn on the radio, sing along with Pat Boone to 'Ain't That a Shame?' or maybe 'All at Once You Love Her' with Perry Como or even 'Angels in the Sky' with the Crew Cuts.

Sometimes she would cry, leaning her head against the cool tiles. It was already too much, one baby and another on the way. Lauren Rose did not think she could cope. Had she made a mistake? She knew Jack was out there somewhere, banging around, working himself up. It would only be minutes before he would pound on the bathroom door, blaming her for something else. He would tell her that she would never live up to his expectations, that his mother had been right all along. He would tell her again, not how beautiful her dress was when she came down the aisle on that bright autumnal day, but how that was the first time, the very instant, he realised she was all wrong for him. But how could he have embarrassed his mother by saying so in front of all those people at the wedding M had so lovingly planned?

"I don't love you," he would tell his wife, "I never did. I just didn't know what else to do."

That was what he'd said this very morning as she juggled the baby on one hip, made eggs, toast, coffee, and at the same time had a premonition that the second baby would come early. Of course, she knew her husband did not mean it. He was tired, overworked and had so many more important things to think about. In the shower she turned the faucets from hot to cool, and then back again. Then, her waters broke; contractions began.

Lauren Rose almost slipped getting out of the shower. "*Hail Mary*," she began praying. "*Hail Mary, Hail Mary, Hail Mary, full of grace...* please, please, please, help me get to the hospital in time." She wrapped herself in a towel, swooped up Mags in her other arm and looked out the window. Jack had taken the car.

She dialled the number slowly, carefully. Mags had lain so still in the womb, even her birth had been a quiet one. This baby kicked, jerked, recoiled and flexed. The taxi arrived, and Lauren Rose left a large, poster board-sized note for Jack by the kitchen sink, just in case she couldn't reach him by phone, which was often the case.

Mags is with Philippa next door. Please come quickly. I've taken the bag. Taxi to hospital. I think this is it.

The driver took one look and said, "Gee, lady, you shoulda called an ambulance. You look sick."

"No, no," she said, "I'm just having a baby. The base hospital, please, emergency!"

"Okay, be still, I know a thing or two. Just breathe."

Lauren Rose rolled down the window and kept Mags tucked into her side until her neighbour took her gently out of her arms and promised that all would be okay. She would continue checking with the hospital and be on the lookout for Jack. Before Lauren knew what hit her, she was in the delivery room. How, she did not know, but Jack arrived and sat in the waiting room.

He anticipated the news he would shortly be hearing, imagining it over and over again: *Lieutenant Preston, you have a son, a boy.* Job done. He rehearsed his bashful reaction. He had cigars ready in his pocket. His buddies were waiting over at the officers' club.

"Lickety-split!" That's what the doctor kept saying. "This one is in a hurry all right... oh my, oh my, what a beauty! Mrs Preston, you have a gorgeous baby girl."

The nurse cut the cord, and while people say you cannot really feel anything as a baby, I am sure at that moment I did. Right after Mr Lickety-Split said 'baby girl', my mother fainted. I checked in and she checked out. She kept falling, sinking further down, down into the mattress. I knew in some odd way, from that moment on, I was basically on my own.

As a premature baby, I was automatically placed in an incubator. Not only was I early, my lungs not quite ready to breathe of their own accord, the instant they cut the cord I had a seismic, in infant terms, heart murmur. I went into intensive care. My father did not take the news of my arrival very well.

"Are you sure," he asked in disbelief, "a girl?"

"Absolutely correct. Gorgeous," the doctor said, slapping him on the back. "Congratulations, sir."

They wheeled me right past him.

He stood there until the special care nurse came up behind him, ordering, "Hurry up. Follow me." In that moment she was his commanding officer. By now Jack Preston had been in the service almost as long as he had been in civilian life. He had a wife and two daughters dependent on him. What kind of a troop was that? Little women.

The nurse was massive, and she manhandled him into what he thought was a pastel nursing gown, strapped a mask around his neck, then up and over his mouth and nose. "Now look at her," she commanded. "Count her fingers. Count her toes." Jack slipped his big hands into the blue gloves built into the side of the plastic box. I had tubes down my nose, electrodes on my chest. An EKG sputtered off to the right. Frightened, and way out of his territory, Jack turned to the nurse.

"Put your hand under her," the nurse ordered. "You've got to do it if your wife can't. Your wife's had a severe progesterone drop."

"Do I cradle her head?"

"Yes." The nurse smiled.

Jack watched the small heart pulsate under the bony ribs. It seemed the beating itself would kill the little one. He had seen this before. The struggle before death. He found himself galvanised by the sight, repeating aloud: "Beat, beat, beat. Fight, fight, fight. That's it, that's it!" He wanted his daughter to live.

Abruptly, without warning, Jack removed his hands from the blue gloves and ripped the mask from his face. Where was his wife? Wasn't this her job? He could not strip off what he considered to be women's paraphernalia fast enough. He patted his chest quickly, relieved he still had his uniform on after all. He fled down the hall, far from the special care nurse and the emergency room.

"Lieutenant Preston," she called after him, "aren't you concerned?"

"No," he shouted over his shoulder as he ran down the hall, pulling cigarettes from his left-hand pocket. His voice echoed behind him. "No, I'm not. She's a goddamned fighter."

He wanted to get to the club where his buddies waited, already toasting him and his newborn daughter.

"Lieutenant," the nurse cried out, "you could at least name her."

But Jack Preston was already gone.

Lauren Rose sank deeper and deeper into the mattress until she practically disappeared. Of course, there were beautiful bed jackets for her to put on at visiting times, and she'd nod her head up and down or shake it from side to side. She smiled sometimes and all the nurses remarked how beautiful it made her look. She honestly tried to breastfeed, but couldn't seem to wake up. It was as if night had quickly turned into day, or maybe the other way around. She just wanted to sink through the bed and emerge on the other side of the world. Or any world. She wanted to keep her eyes closed, pretend she had slipped back into the past.

She would be on her way to school, rolling her skirt up or down. She would be buying a lipstick with all the money she had.

She would be graduating with the other girls or fooling around, riding on the bumper of a truck, dressed in short shorts for the Macy's Thanksgiving Day Parade. And later, graduating as an airline stewardess, receiving her wings. She recalled when they were pinned to her chest. Anna had been so proud of her. Michael stayed sober for the ceremony. Sean and Danny had picked her up and twirled her around. She was on her way. Lauren Rose was their beacon. Someday, they knew, she was really going to be somebody.

Lauren Rose wanted to go back to that time. Sometimes she would think of the boy from the neighbourhood who'd told her: "Hundreds and hundreds of kids, forever." It was too late now, she knew, but in this moment, she knew for certain that he had meant it. That boy would have loved this baby girl. He would have loved two girls or however many she had. But now all she felt was that everything, another baby, was a terrible mistake. Jack had wanted a boy, and that was going to make all the difference in the world. She was a mistake and this baby would be, too.

Divorce? Might as well contemplate suicide, which was unthinkable… "Baby girl," she heard them say as they pushed a glass-sided box on wheels in and out of her room. "Beautiful baby girl."

Lauren did not want to be alert anymore. Everything was racing away from her. She wanted to give up. She was so safe here, away from Jack and all the big mistakes he found in her. Sinking, sinking, she could go anywhere in the world. Away from here.

"No excuses now, you come here, Lieutenant Preston, and name this baby girl. It's been a fortnight, and I'm afraid your wife is still weak. You have to do it. Didn't you have a few in mind?" the same bold nurse cajoled my father.

Jack didn't answer, but he was thinking. His mother was on her way to visit, and clearly naming his second child was long overdue. But what was he going to do with Lauren Rose? She seemed to be losing her grip, turning her back on her responsibilities. He did not especially care if she never woke up, maybe he would even be better off if she didn't, but this baby girl held his attention. He was impressed to see she was out of the incubator, wriggling and thrashing about on her own.

"You made her better," the nurse said, "the minute you took her in your arms. The heart's okay now. No more murmur. Time to name her."

"I don't know." Arthur Gabriel kept coming to mind. Emma, Penny, Lauren, Anna, Anne, Rose… no, he did not want any of those.

"You don't leave here without naming her. It's two weeks. Enough already!" the tough special care nurse persisted.

"Let me go to the cafeteria and think about it."

"No, you stay right here. Smoke a cigarette in the waiting room. I'll get the coffee. Black?"

"Yes," he said, and then smiled because he recognised this was a war nurse. She knew only non-coms took sugar and cream.

He racked his soldier's brain. He was not trained for this. He could name an aeroplane, knew exactly the decal he would paint outside the cockpit or the tip of the nose, but a baby girl? This was beyond him.

"Well?" the nurse asked, putting the coffee down beside him.

"Nothing."

She couldn't help herself. She curled one fist and pressed it against her waist. With her free hand she pinched his ear between her finger and thumb. "Come with me."

They hovered over the bassinet together. "Name her," ordered the nurse.

Jack stood, looking the baby over. She had his blue eyes, he saw. Was one of them maybe still kind of unfocused? Must be a baby thing, he decided. Same sort of hair as him, blonde and lots of it. The nurse said that was rare for her age. Her cheek looked kind of flushed too, just one of them. Maybe she'd been lying on it. Then it came back to him, first in a light refrain, and afterwards loud and clear, an old soldier's song. He knew all the words by heart. How many times had it gotten him through a long night on sentry duty? *My God*, he thought, *I learned it when, scared to death, sitting in a wet, dark trench, none of us imagined getting home.* Everyone knew 'Lili Marlene'. He sang the words softly to himself, remembered the song about the soldier imagining his girlfriend waiting for him in the lamplight.

Yes, he thought to himself, *that's it*. He continued humming, letting the little girl curl her fingers around his thumb.

"Could I hold her?" Jack asked the nurse.

"Certainly, sir, she's yours."

What would M think? He didn't care.

"Lily," he told the nurse. "That's her name."

"Good. Now I need a second one. You're on a roll, let's go. Two names."

Jack thought hard. He was a war strategist. That was what they trained him to do. Who was the most significant person to him? He ruminated, thought back through all the books, the training. Who did he admire most? It came to him in a flash.

"Lee," he said as if he had won a prize.

"Lee?"

"Yes, General Robert E Lee," Jack said, as if she should know. "The most famous general in all the world. Why? He won the Civil War by surrendering."

A lecture on tactics was more than the nurse had bargained for. She frowned.

"Don't you get it? When he saw that one more battle would cost not only him, but the other side too, more men than it was worth, he surrendered."

"So?"

"It was the mark of a great leader. For him the men came first. To surrender. To know he got it wrong."

The nurse's bulldog features softened slightly.

"Yes, I see."

"Okay, Lily Lee Preston. That's it."

"I've heard worse," the nurse said under her breath, but now at least she could fill out the birth certificate.

Jack strode out of the hospital, proud of himself, thinking repeatedly that Lily Lee could just be the first female general.

Back home at last, Lauren Rose perked up considerably. She had Margaret by her side again, and Sean had come down to visit. *Now this*, she thought, *is what I really need and want: my family.* They laughed and talked a great deal, and took turns feeding, bathing and rocking the little ones.

I screamed a lot. In fact, for hours and hours, and days on end, I never slept. No one was quite sure when the wailing turned to chatter.

"What's that?" people would ask.

"Oh, that?" my parents would respond, looking at each other. "That's Lily. She talks to herself, all day long."

I had my head up before they knew it, and at eight months managed to scale the side of the hand-me-down crib passed on from my sister. They labelled me dangerous and pulled out the old playpen, with wooden railings, deep sides and a metal safety latch. This I liked. I could roll in it, I could kick, I could really let my vocal cords rip. I could throw fits. I could finally get what I wanted: a warm, wet kiss.

No one was really surprised when the chatter became clearly formed words, but what did surprise them was what I said first. I did not say the melodic-sounding, pleasant humming M-word, Mommy, or the harsher D-word, Daddy, or even a lighter sounding Da-da-da. I would roll on my back and look up at the most lovely pair of eyes in the whole world. They were gold, with tiny flecks of soft brown. Her hair was mostly ginger. She had the most mesmerising nose. Her ears meant hours of distraction for me. She never left my side, and I clung to her shiny collar. She was my guardian and protector. She loved to tickle me, make me laugh and babble. My constant mediator with the world, she would ply me with endless affection. Who could have had it any better?

She never grew tired, and I could say her name forever. In fact, I called it out non-stop to the rest of the world, to whoever would listen.

"Mayday, Mayday, Mayday," I shouted, and the Brittany spaniel, named after the international call for distressed ships, came at once.

"Mayday, Mayday, Mayday!"

Ironic, really, that my first baby words should have been a madly repeated call for help.

SIX

The long-awaited Arthur Gabriel finally appeared on a sunny day in late May, with no complications, exactly fifteen months after I was born. Placed nose to nose we could have been twins. 'Two peas in a pod', we would be called from then on. At first sight people might have thought Arthur had erupted fully grown from our father's head, with blond hair, blue eyes and massive limbs; he certainly resembled a Greek god. However, in temperament, he was wholly and totally Lauren Rose's child.

His arrival gave her a sort of reprieve. It was as if she had scaled a mountain, and Arthur Gabriel was the trophy, her own tiny soldier. Jack was satisfied. Like Mayday, my devoted friend and mentor from whom I was inseparable, I learned to fetch. Baby bottles, diapers, hairpins, lipstick... you name it, I could roar into the next room, or the next, or the one after that, and get it, whatever it might be. Every possible new skill was acquired in my newfound quest *to help*.

While many people find it difficult to discern the exact moment they decided they loved a sibling, I do not. It was a Sunday morning, fifteen months after Arthur Gabriel was born. I was two and a half. I was on a *getting* mission, locating, if I remember correctly, a washcloth. *"Quickly, quickly,"* my mother would say, and placing the baby boy down on the dining-room table, she removed her hat with the fine mesh veil, setting it upside down and beside Arthur. "Are you wet?" She sighed. *Not another change.* This would have to be fast because Jack was in the car, warming it up. The horn had already honked twice.

My mother carefully took off the diaper and set it aside. Arthur gurgled as she lightly touched between his legs, and I, standing by with washcloth in hand, looked up, and in that instant saw that my baby brother could pee straight up and then into a perfect arc, right into my mother's hat. Lauren Rose laughed long and hard, and so did Artie and I. That was a happy moment.

I barely had time to appreciate the artistry with which my sharpshooter brother could pee, however, because the next day there was something wrong. I knew it by the way in which my mother dressed herself and me. She breathed heavily and didn't natter as she tucked me rapidly into my blue dress, the one with the ribbons and lace around the waist. The one that required me to walk with my arms stretched out at a forty-five-degree angle so as not to crush the skirt too much.

Even I knew what *eye* meant, and frequently said it along with everything else.

"My eye, your eye, Mayday's eye, two eyes, Mommy's eyes, Daddy's eyes. Peek, peek, peek."

Apparently there was something wrong with one of my eyes.

"Lazy eye, roaming eye, weak eye… call it what you like, it's a hereditary thing," the surgeon explained.

My mother kept smoothing the curls on the side of my head, very gently, using her hand and not the hairbrush. I could tell that she was afraid, so I held very still, sensing the danger. There was something she didn't want to do.

"Let nature take its course," she said to my father and his

mother. "Didn't one doctor suggest that she might outgrow both of these conditions?"

"Eyes don't automatically uncross."

There had been no further discussion. I would have surgery on my lazy eye. Jack and M had every faith in their ability to improve on nature.

The station wagon grew hot, and my mother did not talk much while we drove, except to say that I would be staying in the *hospital*.

"Lily, you are going to stay overnight in the hospital. You are going to have an operation. You are going to have a lot of fun and meet some new friends. I will see you in the morning and then you will come home with us."

I instantly knew it was not going to be fun, and seeing her in the morning meant that I would not see her at night. I knew only one thing: I did not under any circumstance or for any reason want to be separated from my mother. She was to me everything that was warm and safe. I knew that she would protect me and I could always tuck myself into her lovely arms. That was where I wanted to be. What was separation? It seemed an impossibility.

Contrary to my usual behaviour, I refused to imitate her. I did not repeat the word 'hospital'. I would not say 'operation'. I did look down at the blue dress and my arms, which even while I was sitting had to be held akimbo, and I knew I was under some special obligation to behave myself. I already sensed that I was odd man out in our family. Mags was first; she got to stay. My mother loved her. Artie was a boy, so naturally he got to stay. My mother loved him. But I had no value unless I could fetch things, help, remember words that had more than three syllables. I had to do tricks constantly so that somebody would notice me.

"Eye operation," she repeated, fumbling with the knobs on the radio dial, "and that little mark on your face? They're going to take that right off too."

"My kiss from God?"

"It's a birthmark."

What she had always called a kiss from God was now something called a birthmark that someone was going to take off. I knew instinctively it was my grandmother who'd started the ball rolling to get us where we were now, riding in the car to the operation. I clearly recalled M peering into my face one day, turning my head from side to side and lifting my chin while she frowned down at me.

This operation and the enforced separation from my mother was the result.

The Army hospital loomed before us, slab-like and pristine white. My mother had difficulty finding the parking lot, then a space. All the while I was calculating. No other child in the car, no dog, no Dad to order us what to do. I no longer pressed into my mother's side but started clinging to her shoulder and arm. The smell of antiseptic permeated the entrance hall. In the elevator, my mother lifted me from the crush of adults, and the endless prattle that happened whenever I wore the blue dress. She balanced me on her forearm and against her chest as she tugged the hem of the dress smartly down. She watched me and the numbers on the floor indicator while the other passengers spoke.

"What a cute little girl!"

"Beautiful face, apart from…"

"Yeah, it's a shame."

"Pretty dress, girlie."

"Cat got your tongue?"

I panicked. *The blue dress. Hospital. Operation. A cat that will take my tongue.* I sucked it hard against the roof of my mouth.

"Thank you, thank you," my mother said.

I was lifted out of her arms, stripped of my dress and put in a crib. I knew something was wrong. This was not my bed and my mother was terrified.

"Be a good girl," she said, leaning in to kiss the top of my head. "I'll see you in the morning."

The race was on. I did not want to be left alone. Before she reached the door, I was out of bed. Before she reached the elevator, I was beside her. Two nurses trailed and caught me. My mother returned with us to the crib, where she said goodbye again. *This is it. Artie is not dispensable, Mags is not, but I am. This will be the last time I ever see my mother.*

I grew still, feigned sleep until my mother disappeared once again. Then I was up, over the side and out, beating her to the elevator this time. I am not sure how it happened, but suddenly I was trapped inside with her, going down.

Chaos ensued. My mother vanished, and I vomited down the front of someone else's pyjamas. Two strangers picked me up, and I started raging.

"I want my mommy!"

"You will see her again," they said, as they cleaned me up. "You will."

"All right," another person said, "all right."

"Lay down, sweetheart, night-night."

Someone patted me on the head. I surveyed the door, the crib, the room. I tried to recall which way my mother went. *Where's the car parked? Can she get the radio on without me? I can help her. I don't want to be abandoned like this. I can do tricks.*

"Little monkey," a man in white said, "it's time for you to be in bed."

He tied my feet. I screamed non-stop.

"Mayday, Mayday!" I called for my dog.

Two women tied a sheet across my chest and my wrists to the rails. I could not move, and yet my whole body fought to rear up. The same man patted my head again and pulled from behind his back what I imagined was a spark plug, something my father put in the car. "Never, never touch," my father had warned.

"It won't hurt," the man said as he leant over me and gave me the shot.

Still I struggled while he stood and watched.

"I can't give her anything else," he protested.

"She's going to break her legs."

"Okay, wrap her up."

"No," said a voice from across the room. A male nurse pushed the two women out of the way and picked me up. "There, there, baby," he said as he loosened the sheets and held me to his chest. "We're going to go for a little walk, you and me."

I listened to the low hum in his chest, and I fell asleep, but not before receiving a great and unexpected gift: the kindness of a complete stranger.

Shortly after I arrived home from the hospital, the family focus changed to France. Moving seemed to energise Jack, who was soon towing the entire family along in his wake. 'France', 'C-12s', 'the Congo' and 'classified' played on my mind, mystery words until, the following year, when we actually took a twelve-hour flight to mysterious France. I had new glasses and a smooth-sided hole in my cheek. Although my mother promised me again and again the angels had kissed me there, this time I knew better.

SEVEN

"France," my dad would say, "I am being posted to France and this is going to be one helluv-an adventure."

And we would say, "Yippee!"

"Yeah!"

"Yeah!"

"Yeah!"

All three of us, Mags, Artie and I, harmonised without knowing what on earth we were talking about.

Then Jack would lead us in a chorus of 'The Air Force Song', with even Arthur smiling along, kicking his heels against the back of the black plastic car seat. And then, if Dad was really feeling good and our mother was not with us, which allowed him to drive at very high speed with his three children in the station wagon, he would sing what he called 'The Army Song'.

We would shout at the top of our lungs with all the windows down, "Then it's high high he, In the Field Artillery... that those caissons go rolling along."

These were the moments when it was great to have a dad like

mine. In fact sometimes, even then, I thought he was just a great big kid himself. We also knew the Navy song 'Anchors Aweigh' and could sing it at the drop of a hat. We could have been heading into the most natural of disasters, but it was like chanting, as we often did, "I scream, you scream, we all scream for ice cream," which we completely understood. Dad screamed for France, and we most certainly did, too.

We each had our marching orders. Mine was the diaper bag, hauling it up the metal ramp to the plane together with the added responsibility of my brother in his bow tie and plaid jacket. I never figured out why those big white shoes of his could not make it from one step to the next. I just let him crawl while pushing, tugging, begging, "C'mon, Artie."

"Yes, sir," I said, at three and a half, taking my father's orders, making sure I pulled my own fair share of the weight; and often, Arthur's too.

"You sit together," my father would say. "Your mother and I will sit here, in front." He pointed out the seat, and then added the phrase I learned to love and dread above all others: "You, Lily, are in charge."

This directive made Mags furious because she was the oldest, but as I saw it, she had a hard time getting into the swing of things, even if she was already five years old. Dad had the same problem with her that I did: she acted like a girl. All she had to do was to learn a few extra choruses of those songs he loved to sing, and of course she should also learn to march: throw all her weight onto her right foot, while throwing out her left arm and shouting, "Right," then step on the left, saying nothing, with the right arm tossed out. It was easy: "Right, right, right."

Once Mags got that part down, with her arms alternately swinging, she had to chant with the perfect intonation, very deep, then slowly rising straight back up: "I don't know, but I been told, a soldier's heart is hard to hold. Right, right, right." If she didn't want to say, "Right, right, right," she could just as easily have said,

"Hup, hup, hup." It was as simple as that. Oh, and she should also learn to salute, correctly.

"Such a sissy," my dad would say to her.

Even Artie could get it, and he was just over two years old; or, at least, he had a good time trying. I figured Mags was just being stubborn. She did not want to learn. She seemed preoccupied with her handbag, which matched her shoes. Artie grinned when Dad said I was in charge. We had a sort of secret, unspoken language. When I was *boss* it meant, relatively speaking, we could do whatever we wanted, assuming we didn't get caught, which we never did.

While we didn't particularly want to dismiss Mags because, after all, she was part of our squad, we did anyway because she always seemed angry and never actually did anything interesting when she was boss. In some big way we had interrupted her party, the eternal legacy of being the firstborn. I was the primary culprit: where did I come from? Then Artie, born in quick succession to me: where did he come from? Mags could be kind but would never forgive us. This was apparent in her often-withering glances and her vice grip, a perfected, paralysing hold that she used indiscriminately when no adult was around. With her thumb and forefinger squeezing evermore tightly around the back of our necks, the jugular vein to be specific, she would have us beg for mercy, which we quickly did.

"Enough?" she'd ask. "Had enough?"

"Yes, yes!" we'd cry.

"Uncle? Say Uncle."

"Uncle."

"Say it again."

"Uncle, Uncle!"

She lived on another planet, and we mostly left it that way.

The five of us sat near the front of the plane cabin. "Look at that, Artie," Dad said, turning around once we were airborne, with everyone settling in for the long flight. "That's the cockpit. That's where the pilots play."

"Cockpit," Artie repeated after him, "cockpit."

"C140," I said, not looking up as I played with my Betsy Wetsy and her steamer trunk, "a cargo plane, which is not a B52, which is a bomber. This one is for the Congo and for classified missions." I had no idea what I was talking about. I just liked identifying B and C-words, repeating things I'd overheard. I repeated everything I ever heard anyone say. I didn't like to sit still for long, or to have nothing to do.

"Lily," my father said under his breath, "shush. No place to run here."

"Yes, sir," I said, really wanting to race up and down the aisle.

"Maybe Lily would like to see the cockpit," Lauren Rose suggested.

"Lily, would you like that?" Dad said without really asking, just assuming it would focus my energy on something better than waking up the other passengers.

With me in his arms, we greeted both pilots. I felt sure that they would let Dad fly, and then we would all sing 'Off We Go', but they didn't. Instead, my father pointed to the skies ahead. "Cumulus clouds," he said, directing my attention to what appeared to be two large scoops of vanilla ice cream bathed in butterscotch, "but the ones to watch out for – right, guys? – are the thunderheads."

"Yes, Captain," they answered him, as I drummed with two fingers against the side of his neck where the aftershave still smelled good.

"Cumulus," I said, adding another C-word to my vocabulary, vital information, better than thunderheads, on my way to France.

My mother, on the other hand, never said any of it was going to be an adventure. In fact, even to me, it was clear, from the moment she stepped inside the C140 and took her seat, that she was a fish out of water, waiting for the worst to happen, eyes wide open, gasping for breath.

EIGHT

Unlike his wife, Jack Preston did not want to live on the Air Force base. He wanted to live on a farm, in a farmhouse made of fieldstone. He wanted his family to experience the real thing: France. He thought it would be great for the children to find one of those places hundreds of years old, where there were pastures with sheep and a couple of goats. *Nothing like growing up on a farm. Till a garden, cut back the grapes. Lauren Rose could even plant a few of those stinkin' geraniums she's always on about in some of those oversized terracotta pots of hers.* The smell, he thought, green like upturned earth. He tried to envision her nonsense about geraniums being a society 'must-have' to overpower unpleasant smells. What did she know about society? The children could learn to speak French.

"Yak like the natives," my father said, "what an opportunity!" He had learned a smattering of Japanese, even Korean. "The world," he liked to say, "needs more of this, especially from Americans. We have a responsibility to mingle – to learn about each other. If we know each other, we won't kill each other."

"Don't touch my moustache," he taught us, which is Japanese

for 'you're welcome', and comes after 'thank you very much', which he never taught us. Learning someone else's language, he told us, was the biggest compliment you could pay them. "Now repeat after me: *parlez-vous français?*"

Before long I beat Dad at his own game, learning to speak almost as soon as we had touched down, the way children do, by osmosis. While he managed *les au revoir, les bonjours* and an *enchanté* or two, I, by the age of four, ordered the gasoline, the groceries and, on occasion, two glasses *of le vin blanc* or *le vin très rouge*. Or *une bouteille de vin pour ma mère*.

Language, I found, brought with it power, control, even if my only real ability was to repeat everything I heard like a trick parrot. I could always get a laugh, often the cigarettes or a couple of extra glasses of *vin ordinaire* on the house, and these people, 'the natives', as my father called the French, did seem to like it, while I, maybe more importantly, for the most part, learned to like them.

Jack claimed to have never really known his father. We learned that M had gotten herself pregnant and they had eloped, despite her father's threatening objection. After that, M lost everything, except for a small trust fund. All ties had been cut, which was why, Lauren Rose reminded us, we needed to be kind to M no matter what; we had to remember that we were part of the only family she had left. Dad did let one thing slip, despite there being an unspoken rule never to speak about his father, or certainly not when M was around: Grandfather Preston had wanted to have a farm, keep dairy cattle. That I assume is why in France, first chance he had, Jack Preston made that dream his own. He would get as close to it as he could for the time being; we would have to go along with it, like it or not.

Surprised, Jack wondered why Lauren Rose hadn't put up a fight; farming wasn't really her thing. Perhaps she was losing her spark. When was the last time she had laughed? *God*, he thought, *I've given her so much. This is a long way from Lower Darby, isn't it?* He could hardly remember that megawatt smile he first saw on the most beautiful woman in the world, the airline stewardess on his flight home from Korea in '51 who had happily offered him a piece of Juicy Fruit gum. *Seven years ago? How time flies,* he thought. *Lauren Rose,* he thought, *should take the kids to the officers' club; use the pool when the weather gets hot. Socialise with the other wives. What more could she want? That'll make her smile again. That, and shopping at the Post Exchange and the commissary.*

The farmhouse, made of stone, with cold slab floors and no central heating, proved difficult for Lauren Rose to manage, with three small children scrambling around amidst space heaters and lanterns. I loved the farm, the house, the garden, the yards. I could run, race and double back with no one shouting, "Stop! Stop… slow down, watch out for that." I even liked the danger of open lanterns and the oily smell of kerosene. Dad demonstrated how to pump the gas, and light wicks – carefully. However, one or other of us children was constantly burning ourselves, and the house stood too close to the road, so near that the walls shook when a diesel truck brushed past the sixteenth-century masonry, showering the basement windows with loose gravel and bullet-sized pebbles. The washing machine and dryer proved temperamental. Jack explained the ancient, rural electrical grid, and Lauren Rose listened, depressed; France was not the USA.

As for her husband's whereabouts, half the time she had to guess. She knew better than to ask but he was out there, somewhere, doing his job, on a classified mission. Was it to the Congo? She should be prepared, he told her, any time, day or night, to go home to America. He could die in the line of duty. She would get a phone call.

"If anything happens," he said, "don't worry about it. Just call M."

One of those times, when he had been gone for over two weeks, and when the odd glass of apple or pear brandy in the evening didn't seem to pick up her spirits, Mom decided she would go to the base. She needed company. She would find the officers' club; it should be an easy drive in from the village to the base, then one of the guards on sentry would help us. It was hot. The children, she thought, deserved a break, a swim, to be around other Americans, and maybe, just maybe, Lauren Rose could find a friend, have a chat, among the other officers' wives. Her children spoke French; why was she still only speaking English?

Lauren Rose dressed in her summer clothes, the things she would normally wear at Sandy Cove or to Atlantic City. She wore her silky red Hermès scarf with the blue and green birds, tied under her chin and around behind her neck – just so. My mother, an authentic American beauty, looked as if she'd just stepped out of a magazine, off a billboard or out of the TV. After rolling down the windows, she allowed us to sing. She clutched the steering wheel, manoeuvring out of the difficult driveway. As she hesitated, with no view of oncoming vehicles, Mags piped up and guided her like Dad did: "Look both ways, then floor it. They'll get out of your way."

Mom laughed. "Thank you, Mags." Then she let off the brakes and pressed the gas, and we were off. Feeling happy, I smelled Mom's perfume, Chanel No. 5, as it wafted over the back seat. Mags, Artie and I clip-clopped our flip-flops against the soles of our feet, while pounding the tin buckets decorated with red, white and blue seagulls given to us by Granddad, Mom's dad. He'd said when we saw him last at the going-away party that he was sure France had a beach, a summer shore where we could all relax. "In fact," Granddad had said, "it may not be as good as Sandy Cove, but it's called Normandy." When he'd said that the whole party grew quiet, and I guessed it was a special place.

"Bring my Lauren Rose back," Granddad had said, which sounded more like *don't take her away*, or *I will die without her*.

"Yes, sir," my father had said, and then Granddad started crying, which seemed to me the strangest thing a grown man could do. My mother wiped his tears away, just like she did mine on a bad day; Dad didn't say anything. He pretended not to see. He hated crybabies.

Ecstatic to be going for a swim, I was even more thrilled Mom was up and out, and in her red scarf. I felt we were on our way to Sandy Cove to see Granddad and Nana, Uncles Sean and Danny. We found Dad's base. The soldiers were friendly; they seemed to recognise her, treated her like a queen. They couldn't take their eyes off of her. They couldn't do enough for her or us. Mom looked relieved when they offered to take us directly to the officers' club. She laughed and smiled with them. They even found a table for us with its own striped umbrella right by the deep end of the pool. The lifeguards picked up right where the soldiers left off. My mom was a hit. She made people happy, the same way she did me, Artie and Mags. I appreciated that. After Coca-Colas and hot dogs, Mom smoked a cigarette and sipped a beer. She enjoyed herself, and we were pleased.

On the way home we stopped at the garden centre, next to the commissary, and Lauren Rose bought so many red, white and pink geraniums that I could not count them.

"Do you think Nana would like these?" she asked me. "I will plant these inside and out. I love them."

We sat in silence in the back seat.

"In those big terracotta pots," she said to no one in particular.

Lauren Rose acted like her old self again. I guessed it was the fresh air, seeing other women at the club or even buying a car full of flowers. That night she rubbed us down with Johnson's baby cream, especially our shoulders and the tips of our sunburned noses. All tired and happy, we ate dinner in our 'jammies'. "When you all three are in school," she told us as we ate, "I may get a job." This was the first time my mother mentioned work. She liked to work.

This didn't mean anything to us, but apparently it made her feel good. She said she might find a job on the base. She said she might grow to like France, that she just needed a little help and

40

a few friends. Lauren Rose was certain Jack would support this, especially as he found her fearfulness repugnant. "You can smell fear," my father always said, "and it stinks."

Lauren Rose danced around the kitchen that night telling us that she might even learn a little French, and after dinner we watched our old French TV, ate popcorn and read books in bed. I thought it was a good time to ask Mom why Dad's mom M acted like a wicked witch. She chuckled and ruffled my hair the way only she did, and said, "No one is a wicked witch, young lady."

"Oh, yes, she is," Mags chimed in without looking up from her book.

"You two young women need to understand your grandmother."

"She doesn't grow anything. Why doesn't she like flowers?" I asked.

"Not everyone likes growing things," Lauren Rose answered, pulling me closer and patting the coverlet for Mags to lean in. "Your grandmother had a rocky beginning, a nasty accident, they tell me, but more importantly, she lost her mother when she was only six."

"How, Mommy?" we asked in one quick burst.

"A fire, my darlings. A house fire."

I imagined M's mother disappearing into thin smoke, and someone bundling up the little girl, cupping her cold feet in dry hands. I could never imagine losing my mommy.

"Is that why she is so mean?" Mags asked.

"Imagine this little girl losing her mother, and then she had a stepmother – a new mother – and was sent away to school when she was your age. Then her terrible accident."

"What sort of accident?" Mags asked. "Is that why she looks all humped over like a witch?"

"I don't know, darling. Dancing. Skating. Whatever it was, we need to look out for Grandmother M. She needs lots of love, like I do and you do, too. Now, *bonne nuit*."

41

Tucking us both in, pulling the fresh, crisp sheets taut, my mother kissed us. I for one couldn't have been happier.

"*Bonne nuit, Maman.*"

"Night-night."

When I was sure the door was safely closed, I rolled towards Mags. "I still think M's a witch."

"Me, too." Mags yawned.

My mother felt a sense of adventure awakening within her. She counted her geraniums, one hundred and fifty seedlings, and decided she was grateful for the Michael Ryan smile she had inherited. It had gotten her flowers into the car and out of the commissary, while she'd commandeered three kids. She was proud of herself, and she guessed that Jack, even if he never mentioned it, must be, too. She hung out the beach towels from the pool. What was the name of that nice gentleman, the officer who also flew in Jack's squadron, the one with two kids? She would mention it to Jack. His fellow officer had been so helpful with that unwieldy cart.

Dad showed up as he often did in the wee hours of the morning, banging on the thick, front door, dropping his flight bag that often contained gifts. Once there was a brass bowl, bought at a bazaar in Turkey, which rang with seven different tones when he flicked the rim with the side of his finger; another time there was a soapstone statuette of Athena, goddess of the arts and war, bought at the Acropolis. This early morning he had nothing. He was angry. We, like Mom, had learned to sense it. He stormed into the bedroom, where Lauren Rose had closed her new American edition of *Vogue* and gone to sleep.

"What was the problem?" he shouted, waking us all up.

"What?" she asked.

"Did you go there alone?"

"Where?"

"The officers' club."

"No, I took the children."

"Did you drink?"

"I had a beer."

"Did you flirt with any of the pool guys?"

"What? Are you crazy? Jack, there were no pool guys. It was a hot day. I took the kids. They went for a swim. We had a really good time."

"I bet you did."

"Jack, what's wrong?"

"Nothing."

"Look, let's not wake the children."

Then there was a pause like the one that sometimes precedes a thunderstorm when the rain is still a way off. It was short and sweet, and I climbed into bed with Mags. Our listening became synchronised. Certain Artie in his own room was doing the same thing, I moved closer to my sister. She pulled the covers up and over me, tucking them around my chin the way Mom did. She held me to her. It was just one loose-sounding thud against the ancient rock walls. It reverberated through our bones. I went to get Artie, to check on Mom, but Mags held me back.

"Don't!" she whispered. "Stay here."

"Don't ever tell me what to do," Dad shouted, "and the next time I'm out of town, try to keep your clothes on."

He paused, and we hoped he was through. Mom hadn't even worn her bathing suit, the pretty one with the roses; she'd worn shorts and her new French jacket, and the red scarf was left in the car.

"Tell me, Lauren Rose. Why is it that whenever anyone meets my wife they have to tell me what a real looker she is?"

The whimpering continued for a long time after that. In an old French farmhouse, sound carries. Like a mild rain, my mother cried, softly and for a long time. Dad had gone into the garden, where we had stacked the wooden crates of flowers. One by one he kicked them over, but the most frightening of all was the sound of the terracotta planters that he smashed to pieces, leaving blood-red dust all around.

We cleaned up the mess the very next day after he had gone to the base. Mom rescued the seedlings and planted each one out, wearing her blue silk scarf with patterns of the Eiffel Tower on it, pulled low to shield her bruised eye. I helped a lot. So did Artie. We mostly didn't talk, but my brother sang like Granddad as he shovelled dirt. He hummed 'You Are My Sunshine'.

"You know," my mother said, her fingers rich with the black Norman earth, "a white geranium will keep a snake away."

We planted one in each flowerbed and one in the flowerboxes to either side of the front door. Artie tried to make Mom laugh. She returned smiles; he gave her so much joy. She carefully hid her tears from everyone, and repeatedly told herself as she dug into the earth that it had been an accident, her husband punching her in the eye, a freak mishap. She planted flowers for Anna. Maybe Nana and Granddad might come for a visit, she said. Wouldn't Nana be surprised – geraniums like hers in France, Normandy even. *Jack had not meant to do it. He just had so many things on his mind.*

Mags, of course, kept her feelings inside.

When Mom went to take a nap, Artie twirled his silver toy pistol in and out of the leather holster he wore around his hips. He aimed at the horizon, the door, and then the photograph of Dad on the shelf.

"Shoot 'em," he said as clear as day, out loud and to no one in particular, afterwards blowing on the end of his gun.

My father built a go-cart that same afternoon, and painted it green. With a black-and-white goat from up the road harnessed to it, we took turns riding round and round the circular, gravel drive, but we never again went to the swimming pool at the officers' club, and it would be a long time before I saw Lauren Rose wear her red Hermès scarf again. It was put away in her special drawer, with her stewardess's wings and the Chanel No. 5, only coming out once when she let Mags wear it for a school play. The sand pails Granddad gave us grew rusty from catching the drips that trickled

44

through the old slate roof, and sometimes when it rained it really poured, and then, of course, we could hardly stop the water from coming in.

NINE

Not every child got a real duckling for Easter. We did, each one of us. Two brown, speckled ones for Mags and Artie, and a white one for me. My bird was the snowy colour of swans, of mythical creatures with wings that could carry a child far away on a fairy night. Automatically I became a princess, and of course my duck was every feather royalty, too. I christened her Angel.

I could cup Angel in the hollow of my hand, stroke her, feed her – morsel by morsel – all day long. That was the sort of dad I had. He gave his kids real chicks, ducks and an old nanny goat that could pull a go-cart round and round. In the stone farmhouse, I found nook after nook, perfect places for a princess and her magic duck to hide.

With Lauren Rose's bruise healed and never mentioned again, life went on. I had things to do, and places to go. The outbuildings, full of hay and firewood, left over from when this place had been a real farm, called out to me, Artie and Mags. Days and days passed, lost in adventuring in and out of the farm buildings, the fields, the house. I hardly missed my father. I merely smiled as an aeroplane flew overhead. That would be my dad, handsome, smelling of Old

Spice and wearing his metal dog tags on their ball chain around his neck.

Ducks grow fast and fat on a diet of bread, water and corn, freely bestowed by the hands of a four-year-old girl. In a very short time, it seemed, the ducks, mine in particular, were as high as our knees, then practically level with my chest. I would fly away on Angel's back, I promised myself, just as soon as her wingspan stretched wide enough. She followed me everywhere, and made a tremendous amount of noise, especially if I had food. We played endless games of chase around the garden with all three of our web-footed beauties.

Angel proved to be special. A forever friend, she knew my secrets and understood my plans. While my mother nursed her plants, and my father flew off somewhere in the skies, I found comfort especially at nighttime knowing Angel was out there, somewhere, sleeping with her bill tucked behind her wing when I, too, was sleeping with my knees folded up, tight against my chest, with a cotton nightie pulled snugly down over freshly bathed and powdered feet.

"We're going to have duck," my father said one day, triumphantly, robustly and straight to the point. Mom and Mags both shrieked in the same instance.

"You can't," my mother said.

Excited that he was eager, but not really knowing what he had meant, I trailed after him, his first lieutenant. Mom suggested to Dad that I stay behind with her and the other kids, but he would not have any of it. Neither would I: we would have duck. Mallards aren't hard to find. Angel came whenever she was called. All three domesticated birds clamoured at my father's feet in the building he sometimes called the garage and we called Fairy Hall. Those ducks squabbled, each wanting more grain than the next. I waited patiently for my father to shovel corn from the feed sack. *We would have duck.* I could still hear Mom calling after me in the distance, from the front door, punctuated by cries of, "Jack!" Mags shouted, as Mom held her back. Artie had picked up his pistol and holster, as he stood behind Mom.

"Jack!" she cried out again.

In Fairy Hall, suddenly, from somewhere high and out of sight, Jack Preston reached down and grabbed Artie's speckled duck by the neck. I heard a snap, then saw the black eyes cloud over as the head fell backwards, limp against the wood-chopping block. With the axe whistling down so fast, I missed everything except seeing the duck stand up, wobble for a few, short steps, then collapse, without her head.

Before I could think, my father had a second bird. My heart raced. This was Mags's duck. Angel flew off, landing high up on a bale of hay by the rafters, keeping perfectly still.

"That's enough," my mother said, now standing at the door to Fairy Hall. "Lily, you come with me."

"Alright," my father said as he took the headless bodies trailing blood away, and I took my mother's hand.

Motionless on her perch, Angel stayed still with her heart beating visibly in her chest. "Stay there," I whispered, "I'll come back."

Walking back to the house with Mom, I could hear my father humming. His humming grew into song as he strung up the ducks. I didn't feel like singing, not the Army, Navy or Air Force Song, now or maybe ever again.

"The farming life," he kept saying, "that's for me."

While I couldn't make sense of things, I knew that Angel needed help, maybe even to escape. My heart beat as heavily as hers. I needed to make a plan. My duck would not lose her head. So that night, I pulled my nightgown down over my toes, without any intention of actually falling asleep. Angel would be waiting for me. I delayed, listening until I heard my father's familiar snore.

Cold stone under my feet, I crossed the farmhouse floor, creeping out of my bedroom, down the hall and past all the shoes and boots, coats hanging by the doorway. Pushing at the heavy door, I slipped through the narrow gap I'd made. I imagined the axe descending, my own head on the chopping block. I would take Angel out past the stone pillars that marked the very end of my world and let her go.

"Sweetheart, never, never go past the gate." I heard this many times, every single day.

Angel would go free, then someday when her wings were wide and strong enough, I fantasised, she could come back and get me. If she stayed she'd lose her head. This I knew. My father liked farming; he even sang about it. He'd find Angel, and off would come her head. I knew it. Past the mound of geraniums, stirring ever so lightly in the night, I found Angel in the Fairy Hall, far back and up in the rafters atop four square hay bales, which I scaled ever so carefully. Sitting up on the hay, I petted and stroked her.

"I'm very sorry," I told her, "you will have to go away."

From where I sat, the pillars seemed to hold up the vast, dark sky on either side of the gate. I would run fast, carry Angel and not be afraid. Scooping her in my arms and against my chest, we made our way down the hay and into the yard. I did not want to let her go, but I now knew clearly what 'having duck' meant – a revolting stew served in silence that no one ate, not even Dad.

The grass and the gravel left imprints on my cold feet. Angel's heart beat against mine. At the gateposts, I froze. A neighbour's dog bayed, and a light went on, then off, in my parents' bedroom. I crossed the line quickly and ran as far as I could. Standing on tiptoe, I used both arms to throw Angel into the night sky.

And she flew.

She totally disappeared. I watched, alone beneath a deep vaulted sky, on a road that seemed to run on forever. It felt good, standing there; I didn't want to leave. As I took it all in, the neighbour's dog barked again. A breeze lifted the hem of my gown as I raced back across the lawn, past the flowerbeds and slipped inside the house. In bed, with my knees to my chest, I imagined Angel's pale wings against the sky. Mags turned in her sleep, then opened her eyes.

"Where'd you go? How far did you run?"

"Outside, not too far."

"Did you let Angel go?"

"Yes."

"That's good," she said, and then started crying.

I jumped in bed beside my sister and pulled her to me while she whimpered. Her duck was dead. While she cried her eyes out, I prepared, just in case.

"Where'd she go?" my father might ask, next time he wanted duck.

"I don't know," I could honestly say.

I reasoned, if he could take off a duck's head, what else could he do?

The day that Emma Preston came to visit our farmhouse in faraway France, shortly after the ducks disappeared, I began to understand my dad better.

Before her arrival, I had no real memory of my grandmother. I dimly recalled a bony sort of woman, who was as small as a child, and that her right shoulder rose higher than the left. I recalled that she did not like my face. Recoiling from her was not allowed, unpardonable in fact, even if that was the way I truly felt. My grandmother knew that, of course, because she was a witch.

"Give M a kiss," my father commanded, even if he and my mother were not really excited about her arrival. It all seemed very pretend to me.

I did kiss her, though reluctant to touch her. Her skin was paper-thin, almost transparent. I could see blue veins snaking this way and that. She smelled fresh, like new laundry, but she did not smell kind or loving. The minute she set foot in the house, heels clicking busily across the stone floor with Dad bringing in her Samsonite bag behind, Artie shouted out.

"Fire in the hole!" he hollered. "Fire in the hole!" He kept shouting until Mom told him firmly to be quiet and Dad told him to shut up and put away his pistol.

I didn't like the way my grandmother broke my father's name into two sharp syllables. "Ja-ack," she would say, "now where is it exactly I am staying?"

I recognised a witch when I saw one. Only witches came in this size and shape. I didn't need a fairy tale to tell me this. She was the Wicked Queen, my mother Snow White. Poison hung in the air. I envisioned her talking to herself in the old mirror in the hallway late at night.

"Who's the fairest of them all?"

"Certainly not you," the mirror would reply brusquely. "Has to be Lauren Rose."

That's why, and I am certain of it, my grandmother never saw our freshly sprayed hair, Artie's new bow tie or tricky ball kicking. She never saw the hot-from-the-oven fig squares Mom made especially for her visit.

"Two saccharin," she requested briskly for her coffee.

"Sorry, M," my mother said, eyes cast down, "I forgot."

"No saccharin?"

"No. I forgot."

"Never mind," my grandmother sighed.

Mom smiled. We brightened. But somehow it had been made plain to us we had all made a big mistake. No, perhaps *we were* the big mistake. Despite the highest, most bobbing ponytails, clean teeth and fingernails, and the newly baked, still-warm fig bars, which were really tough to get in France, we'd failed. Emma Preston sighed and brought her own clear plastic, compartmentalised, travelling box of saccharin out from her new suitcase into our own warm kitchen.

"Never mind," she said again, wearily.

"Your Aunt Penny," my grandmother told us proudly, "has the cleanest trash cans on her block. The garbage men tell her that it's a pleasure to pick her stuff up."

What about our trash cans? Were they good enough? Were

we? I didn't know. My grandmother liked to leave us guessing. We had a report card with no grade, which meant, unlike Penny and of course her twin daughters, whom I imagined could also make a trash can shine, we weren't good enough even to fail. My mother would never pass, I guessed that already, and while I did not want to admit it, by default, neither would I.

My grandmother was not impressed with the goat cart Dad had made for us.

"Let her have a turn," I kept saying.

I pictured her going around and around the grassy mound in the middle of the driveway. I saw her falling out like Humpty Dumpty. *Even witches must get it in the end*, I thought. Those were the rules. I could just smack the goat and let her run off, up the road. She could take this grandmother away forever. I didn't like her. She was very mean to my mother, and often to me.

When I was at the point of actually shoving my grandmother into the cart, my father caught my arm.

"Lily," he said, "calm down."

"Sorry," I said, instead of: "Let's get rid of her before it is too late."

My father wasn't smart. He couldn't see that his own mother was up to no good. He couldn't see that she was a bully and a sneak. Couldn't he sense that there was malice in the air? Why couldn't he stand up for his own wife? Maybe even for himself? And what about me? Was he sure that Aunt Penny's daughters, like her garbage cans, were really as perfect as we were told? Did he not see from the photos that her kids were *not* perfect? Didn't it bother him that his own mother failed to call any of his children pretty or handsome? Even I knew this was intentional.

My father was not smart.

I didn't say this out loud. I said it under my breath instead and in French, except for the word 'shit', which I did say aloud.

"*Merde.*"

I learned it from our garbage man who drove the old truck

that wheezed and hacked. "*Merde*," he said when an empty box of commissary-bought Cheerios had blown out the back and across the rows of newly cut hay.

We took photographs of the three of us in the clothes my grandmother brought all the way from the USA. She was in Europe for work, she claimed. I imagined it was the same sort of special thing Dad had to do when he went away. She told us with great bravado that her work colleagues called her Little Lenin. She seemed to like that. Dad laughed and told us who Lenin was, but I couldn't understand it. Why would a woman want to be named after a man?

Finally, she left. I hoped for good, but I felt sorry for Dad. I didn't know how these stories were supposed to end if your own mother was not a fairy princess. What happened to you if all the time you were growing up, she was really the wicked witch? Could you kill her off? Or would you just continue to smack your wife? At almost six, I had no answer for this. I just knew both Mom and I needed a very long sleep. I knew Angel wasn't coming back, and I knew a single white geranium would not keep a snake from coming right in your own front door.

TEN

Mags went to the American school in a yellow school bus because she was old enough. I went to French school, and took my brother with me because Dad said even if Artie was only three, he looked five and so he should just pretend to be old enough. This was unfair because it put a lot of pressure on me to protect him. Artie was like Mom. He laughed a lot, but the other boys, especially the five-and six-year-olds, liked to pick on him for obvious reasons: he was American, he was new to the school and he was only three. All the kids could smell the fact that he was barely past babyhood.

"It will be good for him," Dad said.

"No," I explained, "that's not how it works," but I lost. Dad seemed to have forgotten the schoolyard rules, or he certainly did not seem to know the first thing about French schoolyards and French boys. I had to endure the pain, the taunts, the times they followed us around the schoolyard shouting, "*Américains, Américains, Américains,*" as if it were some sort of plague while they batted the rabbit-fur pom-poms that swung off the back of my cap.

I dragged Artie around with me, until one day, while I stood ready to pop anyone who dared lay a finger on him, something unexpected happened. Arthur broke free. He rolled up the most enormous, hard-packed snowball I had ever seen. With one World Series pitch, he knocked tall, skinny, leader-of-the-pack Emmanuel right in what my father called 'the kisser'. Smack! The blood gushed, and all our French schoolmates fled.

Artie smiled up at me and said, "Lily. Was that a nice shot?"

I gave him a great big thank-you kiss, just before the nun with the foggy glasses swooped down on us, yanking my brother up by his throwing arm. "*Non, non, non,*" she said, smacking him on the bottom, something even Mom didn't do, and I prayed, "Please, please, please, God, do not let them use the switch." I had heard that sound once before as I came down the hall, past the frosted glass of the mother superior's office: a French kid was shrieking his head off, interspersed with the stiff swish of a willow whip.

I saw Artie later in the day, after lunch, standing in the corner of the schoolyard where the bad boys were sent. He was pinched with cold, his nose running and his eyes all red. 'Idiot', I knew how to say that in French, or 'stupid', I could say that, but how far would that get us? How could I explain to the old cross-eyed witch of a nun that my brother was only three? His behaviour was not bad, just typical for his age. I couldn't say much because they were always after me to sit down, to stop running and to please just be quiet.

I slipped Artie a couple of M&Ms I had found stuck in the bottom of my smock pocket. He winked, and I winked, which was our private language for: *Hold on, it can't last all day, and I am sorry anyway.*

At first I wanted to kill the French kids, ambush them, have my dad bomb them, but I kept these thoughts to myself. I was learning that the new kids were always pestered, at least for a while. After the boys saw that they had got Artie in trouble, they calmed down, and it freed me for a while from acting as my brother's watchdog.

I enjoyed the nuns' soft-centred chocolates. I excelled at French, colouring and spelling bees. I could do anything ten times as fast as the others. This actually was not very difficult because these kids, unlike me, were not programmed to win. They were not even competitive. They probably didn't salute their dad.

I don't know if Artie was a lot smarter or dumber than he looked, but he managed to lull everybody, including me, into a false sense of security. If only he had warned me first. Was he seeking belated revenge? Then again, maybe it was just an accident, but the day Mom let him bring a can of Coca-Cola to school in his lunch bag, he was back in the bad-boy box and I think he did get the willow switch this time. Did he deliberately shake the can before giving it to the nun with the cloudy glasses, the one who had, for the love of God, started to overlook his previous bad behaviour? On this particular day she had tousled his hair, called him '*mon petit garçon*', and then it happened.

First she looked at the red can with delighted curiosity, like all the children in the lunchroom. She didn't know what to make of this strange thing and as she pondered the grandchildren of her one-time liberators, the Americans, she popped open the top of the can with some ancient rusted instrument. Foam instantly sprayed up her nose, over her glasses, across her white coif and white bib, splashing sacrilegiously over her rosary beads with their dangling carved wooden crucifix.

No one moved. The lunchroom had been held in thrall – the American kids were having a Coke – and only Artie knew it would become something even more spectacular. He doubled over with laughter.

"Kaboom!" he shouted, gleefully.

I immediately tried to explain, "He's only three. This is funny to a three-year-old," but it was useless; my behaviour would also bring second glances. Soeur Agathe shook off her rimless glasses, jerking Artie's arm savagely to force him to follow her. I wanted to punch her. Didn't she know she could pull a small child's arm out of its socket? – or at least that is what my mother always told me – *be careful, he is only three.* Artie kept on laughing.

The nun looked back at me, and I quickly assumed a serious expression. I must remember I was guilty until proven innocent like the rest of the kids, but as soon as she turned her back, leading Artie away, I laughed out loud. Could life get any more complicated? How was I supposed to handle a couple of natives who could not open a can of Coke properly, not to mention beating my baby brother who liked to think of a soda can as a hand grenade? How could I explain that his 'badness' wasn't premeditated? He just loved it when things went 'pop'. Why couldn't they speak English – just a little bit?

"Artie," I said on the way home, "don't tell anyone anything. It was an accident."

"Okay."

Who would we tell anyway? Mom wouldn't understand and Dad would automatically blame Artie. Dad viewed his son as a private first class rather than a small giant who looked five instead of three. It seemed so unfair on him to be such a big boy at his tender age. Mom and I were the only ones to let him be a baby.

I don't know if Soeur Agathe was unpopular with her fellow nuns but the next day half the nuns were running their fingers through Artie's hair and calling him '*mon petit garçon*' and '*bon enfant*'. He became the class favourite, a regular hero. Everyone seemed to think he was innocent. Well, maybe. You would have thought he coined the word 'kaboom'. Everyone was repeating it, even the priest in the school's small chapel as he prepared for the Eucharist. Those Americans, weren't they funny after all?

"Kaboom."

"Red alert," I told my brother one morning some months later. It was a code Artie knew very well, meaning 'be quiet'. I'd thought about this all the previous night. I'd also pondered something else. Mom was strangely quiet. She had grown more and more that way since we'd started school. While she happily bought our smocks, satchels, pens and pencils, she tried to make us think school was the next best thing to heaven. She even told us she would have liked to have done more of it herself.

Once Mags left on the school bus, my responsibility was to take Artie and myself across the street to the French school. I was to look both ways and 'hotfoot it' across the difficult street where we could not see the oncoming traffic, but this morning something told me to stay home. Maybe I just wanted to play hooky, but I preferred to think of it as a premonition. I kind of felt Mom asking me to stay. In any case, I did look both ways, and took Artie not to the school but to the shed where the wood was chopped and stored. We hid, setting the bag lunches that the maid gave us up on a dusty shelf by the coffee cans filled with corn for the rooster and six white hens.

"Funny thing," I said to Artie, "did you see that Mommy didn't get up?"

"Yeah," he said, but I could have said anything and he would have agreed. He stood beside me, imitating, straining to see the front door like me. I pressed him flat against the wall with my forearm bracing his chest. We mustn't be seen. We might have to do hand-to-hand combat, unexpectedly. I kicked open the shed door with the side of my foot. We were not going to school. That was that. Over and out.

We climbed around the twin barns, carefully, so as not to disturb the geese or the neighbour's black Labrador. Then we heard the siren, coming from a long way off. It died as it turned into our driveway, but the red light continued to flash.

"Red alert," I hissed.

"Red alert," Artie repeated after me.

We scrambled into position, a place from which we could observe the front door. There was the maid, with her kinky red hair pulled back in braids and her striped, long-sleeved shirt, and there was Mom being carried out on a gurney. Two men slid her into the back of the white station wagon with the light on top, still going around and around. They were Americans because in clear block letters through the frame of my binoculars I could read 'USAF Ambulance'.

"Mommy," Artie pointed.

"Red alert."

I was not sure what to do. I didn't want the maid to see us, so I just told my brother to pick up his lunch, and we left out the back of the barn through a gap in the siding. Wandering into the pasture, we visited the sheep. We especially liked the younger ones, and they liked us, sucking on our fingertips. The morning light was bright, growing warmer towards lunchtime when we shared our sandwiches, sitting on a fallen log along with a handful of geese. Arthur took a nap, resting on my lap. I thought hard. I wanted to run away. I had no desire to go back ever, to school or home, but I wanted to follow Mom. Angel flew off, why couldn't we? I would take Artie with me, I decided, somewhere safe, but instead it was the farmer's garden next door that caught my eye, and we drifted that way. Following Mom seemed like an equation too advanced for me.

Some of the sprawling leaves were perfect for us to crawl underneath and hide in the golden-green light, especially the squash and the grapevines. We plucked old fruit, pressed our cheeks against a cold pumpkin. Looking at Artie in that instant I knew somehow, and for always, that he was truly my brother. Eventually, we made our way home, stroking a large dark cat and two orange kittens.

We pressed flat alongside the wall by the shed door. Surprisingly – what was he doing home? – Dad stood with the maid at the front door, shouting, "Lily, Lily, where are you? Arthur, Arthur! Come home."

I half expected him to shout, "Ollie, Ollie, in come free," as if it were a game of hide and seek, but he didn't. Instead, he went around the house, calling and calling. I felt sorry for him. I assessed the situation. He wasn't crying for Mom, so I guessed he knew where she'd gone. Mags came up the drive, carrying her oversized satchel and her plaid lunch box. The yellow school bus backfired, and we halted in our tracks.

"Enemy," I said, "at nine o'clock," looking at Artie very closely. He was filthy. I brushed some of the loose dirt from his cheeks and told him to blow his nose hard into the underside of my smock. I smoothed his hair with some spit, then yanked my ponytail apart, which pushed the rubber band up and closer to my scalp. I had lost the grosgrain ribbon and the two blue barrettes. We – I – could get in real trouble for all of this, and I knew it. We had been AWOL all day.

They went inside, and I repeated, "Red alert," adding, "Artie, you must really listen to me because this is top secret."

"Red alert," he repeated carefully.

Creeping inside, we stood quietly in the hall outside the kitchen.

Dad spoke excitedly into the telephone. "I don't know where they are, they were last seen at eight o'clock this morning... Both blond... I don't know... maybe five or six years old." He was smoking a cigarette and waving his arms about. "No, no, my wife had an emergency. I got called—" Apparently, he was being cut off. "Yes, okay, I'll be waiting... the base MPs. Okay. Thanks. I appreciate it. I don't speak French, not really."

Where is Mom?

The maid, who was trying unsuccessfully to speak English, rattled on. Mags ate an Oreo with a very large glass of milk. She looked at me through the kitchen doorway with her dark Mom eyes, and I couldn't get a read: was I in trouble, double trouble? She would not let on.

My father turned when the maid gasped on seeing us. Mags kept scraping off the white cream from her cookie against her bottom two front teeth.

"Where have you been?" Dad asked, and for the first time in my life I felt the sting before the slap.

Artie didn't say anything, just pointed outside.

"Have you had anything to eat?" the maid intervened.

"Eat," said Dad, imitating the maid, not knowing what else to say, afraid of what he might do in his anger. I had never seen my father so afraid. He was right; you could smell it, fear.

"Go to bed," he hissed. "Get out of my sight."

We were off the hook. Artie and I had a quiet bath, just listening to the maid rambling in French, knocking us every once in a while in the side of the head. She was furious, she said. She would be blamed for this, and tomorrow she would walk us, march us, straight over to school; she would have the nun with the foggy glasses call her if we ever, ever failed to show up again. Did we understand?

"*Oui*," Artie said, shooting her with the clear plastic water gun with which he had concealed his penis.

"Don't," I said, taking the toy out of his hand.

He went to his room, and I went to mine, where Mags was already propped up on her bed, arms folded behind her head.

"Where'd you go?" she asked.

"Nowhere," I said, not trusting her a hundred per cent.

"Nowhere? You didn't see anything?"

"Nope."

I missed the smell of the Johnson & Johnson's baby powder. Mom would have dusted me after my bath. Turning to the wall, I recalled the golden-green leaves, the russet vines, the pumpkin, the sheep, the squash, the dark rich red earth – the sun that journeyed across the sky. For no reason in particular, I thought of Angel. I liked running free, even if the maid or no one else liked it. I liked speed.

"Mags," I said eventually, "do *you* know where Mommy is?"

"Nope," she answered me, as we listened to our father pouring a drink and mumbling to himself downstairs.

Dad's silver lighter snapped open and shut all night long, cigarette after cigarette. I thought I heard him say, "Yes, that was the moment I knew it. Damn it. That split second." He, of course, was speaking about his wedding day, when Mom beamed at him from the vestibule, leaning on my grandfather's arm.

"Dad?" I asked after tiptoeing up to his chair.

"Sorry," he said, inhaling deeply. "I didn't mean to wake you."

"I was awake," I said as I watched the blue smoke travel in a thin line, over our heads, then up and out the old Norman chimney. "Tell me about when you met Mom, when she was a stewardess for American Airlines."

"She wasn't a stewardess for American Airlines," he said as if he had an eraser that could expunge everything good that was my mom.

"She was," I said as he escorted me back upstairs and helped me climb back under the sheets. After he left, I imagined myself curling up in the rich soil of the flowerbed, next to Mom's lemony, peppery-smelling geraniums.

The red rooster crowed early, at the crack of dawn as usual, but I was amazed how different he sounded, how sharp and empty, now that Mom was gone.

ELEVEN

"It is not forever," Madame Belfond told me the day after the ambulance came to take Mom away, "your *maman* will only be gone for a short time, *pour un petit dodo.*"

The Belfonds were friends of the family. They were helping Dad out by taking me to live with them for a while. He'd met Monsieur Belfond one Saturday afternoon while pumping gas.

No one had to tell me that Mom needed a little nap, a short sleep. I thought she really needed quite a long one, and I especially knew that the best thing for her, despite missing her with all my heart, was to get her away from Dad.

If you met my dad doing something ordinary, like running errands on a Saturday or pumping gas, he could seem like a nice, regular guy. He wasn't. In particular he was not nice to his wife. It was hard to understand why he could never just leave her alone, or why he could not say to her simple things like 'hello', 'I love you' or 'thank you'. He did not seem to have any joy in him or love of little things the way that she did, and that we did, too.

He never once combed my hair – something Mom did with precision every day, sometimes twice, for all three of her children. She would start with Mags, combing the hair straight back, then swiftly up, knotting the ponytail, straightening the bangs and placing two pink barrettes on either side of my sister's head before shooting her with a quick, please-cover-your-eyes shot of Aquanet. Then she would tie a neatly pressed pink ribbon snugly around the ponytail. I would be next. My mother would deftly execute the same swift, smooth ponytail. Mine would be tied with a bright blue ribbon. Artie had the same treatment, only with a dab of Brylcreem to hold the natural cowlick in place. As my mother's child, I knew what it felt like to literally have every hair in place.

What exactly was my father's problem? I tried to figure it out for as long as I could recall. He never laughed easily, and he was prone to violence. Sweetness, I could see, was missing from his nature, but at that time men did not do that – sweetness. Perhaps it was something just for women. Or maybe because Dad's mom used saccharin, which she said was an artificial sugar, his family had no sweetness at all.

"*Petit dodo*," Madame Belfond said again, as she pulled the top of my head into her chest and wrapped her free arm around my shoulders. I waved to Dad and the other kids in the Rambler, as it pulled away from the town house. Artie and Mags were on their way to stay with the Browns, an American family, while my mother was having her long nap. I worried about Artie, but because Mags would get to be boss I knew she would be all right. I imagined them singing 'The Air Force Song'. Maybe not. Not without me. I envisioned Mom resting, taking *un petit dodo* in a USAF ambulance.

I'd never had my own room before. I had never even considered it, but here I was at the Belfonds' with a room of my own. It seemed like the most amazing gift. The room had tall ceilings, a deep, dark bed with silk coverings. I wasn't afraid. On the contrary, I loved it – both the room and being separated from my family, even if it was only temporarily. I supposed it was because I knew my mother was safe, in a hospital, resting, sleeping, after the strain of living with my dad and hosting a visit from Lenin.

With the rich quilting tucked under my chin, before falling asleep I pictured each of the Belfonds in their beds. They would be as happy as I was in mine. There were the girls, aged eleven and twelve, the two boys, aged sixteen and seventeen. Then, of course, there were Madame and Monsieur, Véronique and Nicolas.

Tomorrow I was promised a *crêpe Suzette*, or even, the cook told me slyly, a *crêpe Lily*. The wind rattled the latches on the floor-to-ceiling shutters over the big bay window, letting in pinpricks of light from the streetlights below. I imagined the walled-in demesne and the tidy, sizeable vegetable garden. Streetlamps ran the full length of the road outside and then on over the footbridge. They lit up the green river that snaked through the village and turned into a small cascade by the triangular churchyard, where, beside a weeping willow, I discovered a shortcut to the local school. Funnily enough, at the Belfonds', I never had the desire to run, never felt like a plane revving up for takeoff.

The black lacquered *armoire* in my room was wide and deep. In it, Madame Belfond kept extra blankets and pillows. She gave me the key in case I should need it. I drifted into sleep with it in my hand, feeling as if I had become the daughter of royalty. Mom was somewhere safe taking a much-needed rest. Madame Belfond agreed that my mother deserved one.

"How can a young woman with three little children, with little help and a husband who is not at home, survive in a strange country?" she asked.

I don't know.

"*Non, non, non,*" she said to no one in particular, as I helped her separate wet iris stems from their blade-like leaves on the wooden table in the orangery.

"*Non,*" I responded, as I watched her place the flowers in three separate vases.

"Your mother is clever," Madame Belfond said, "and beautiful."

Clever? Beautiful?

I carried a wicker basket with a selection of miniature peach blossoms. I'd never heard anyone actually say this.

"*Oui,*" she added, "*c'est une grande tragédie.*"

"*Oui, une tragédie,*" I repeated.

I never heard anyone defend my mother before, much less say she was clever or beautiful. These were things I observed but never quite got to grips with, like the forgotten saccharin or watching my father arrive home from who knew where and fail to say hello or even hi to my mother. I never once saw a nice-to-see-you kiss, and it was embarrassing when he brought home gifts for us children, but never one for Mom, even when she baked for days before he arrived and dressed carefully in a new sweater and black pants with stirrups that tucked neatly under the arches of her feet.

Did Madame Belfond know what it was like to wait for a father who could not tell you where he had been or when he might be back? Or that if anything should happen, your mother should just call M, the wicked witch?

"*Et toi aussi.*"

I am the same. Beautiful. Clever.

"*Oui.*"

Madame Belfond walked me up the stairs to my new room. She placed a posy of peach blossom in a porcelain vase beside my bed and turned it around slowly. *Did I like them? Did I like the taller ones in the centre, the shorter ones around the edge? Did we need more green? More water?*

"*Non,*" she finally said proudly, "*ceci est parfait.*"

She kissed me on the top of the head.

Long after she left the room, I sat on the edge of the bed. I studied the posy, then the view of the river outside my window. Light bounced off the tree in the garden and over the narrow canal boats below. I spied cumulus clouds: good for flying, but I wanted to keep my feet right on the ground. I memorised Madame's kindness. *Your mother is good, clever, intelligent, and so are you. Parfait.*

Time stood still.

I did have *crêpes Suzette* most mornings, and I had *petit pain* with butter and jam. I had *café au lait* and *chocolat.* Because there was so much talk around the table, I easily stole extra sugar.

"Deux Sucre Lily," the maid would call me as she turned red-faced from the stove or the open oven. Most days, I could watch her dress a chicken, or go with Madame to the vegetable garden, into which I was never permitted alone, to pick fresh vegetables for the day – big heads of lettuce, a few potatoes, carrots, maybe cauliflower, sometimes spinach, onions and dark green leeks. In town we would pick up milk, cheese, and go to the *pâtisserie* for bread, *pains au chocolat* or an *éclair* for the afternoon. Véronique always chose fresh, red meat, and allowed me to linger in the stationery shop, where I loved to stand and breathe in the smell of paper, pencils and stamps.

After teatime, I had the full run of what Véronique called the dollhouse. Made of solid stone, centuries old, it mirrored the big house in every detail. With furniture and antique dolls of all ages in four separate rooms, this was a perfect hideaway. My imposing dollhouse was tucked away in the back of the garden, shaded by a massive tree, and everyone had to knock twice before entry. As with my palatial bedroom with its silk quilt and sweet-smelling posy, I was amazed to find myself here. I had a place, a name, a face.

School was easy. I let myself disappear into French. On the way there, I took the short route. One day I lost my balance and slipped on the grassy spot overlooking the cascade by the weeping willow. Usually, I brought bread in my smock, left over from breakfast, or crumbs saved from lunch. Most of the ducks were mallards, but more than once I'd seen my own, or so I thought. I was sure it was Angel. We both had escaped.

She paddled by herself, and even came up to me once, sitting on the soft lawn and eating from my hand. She was okay, I thought, like me. I'd done the right thing. I was sure she went to sleep among roses and experienced comfort similar to a pat from Madame Belfond's soft hand. I envisioned Mom also, flown away, safe, drinking a *café* with two or three *sucres*. It was only then when I was not at the Belfonds' or the new school that I thought about Artie and Mags.

How could I want a life of my own?

I worried about my mother. Was it my job to protect her? Where was she, exactly? But in this delicious moment, Mom wasn't my responsibility. Neither was Artie, or even Mags or Dad. No one was, except lucky me. I was my only duty, and even then I had Véronique to help me. I'd flown down the road, soared into space and been taken in. I felt permanently on holiday. I never wanted to go home. I wanted to stay here for the rest of my life, with Véronique. I wanted to watch her sons slapping on Brut cologne and combing their hair just so while they stood there with their bare chests and tight blue jeans. I wanted to watch her daughters comb each other's hair, trade dresses and match pearls.

I could, I would, if they would only let me, stay forever, but I knew the day of reckoning was coming. I could sense it, no matter how many hiding places I scouted for up in the attic, including its highest reaches, the extra room above the chandelier. There was nowhere I could hide, they knew the house better than I did, and so finally one day it came.

"Tomorrow at noon. Your mother is well. It is good news?"

I burrowed into the dark, oak-framed bed. The double posy beside it gave away Madame Belfond's true feelings, along with the fact that she climbed into bed beside me and put her arms around me.

"*Ma petite fille.*"

I was beginning to get a terrific headache.

Goodbye, goodbye. Goodbye.

The blue Rambler arrived early. Mom and Dad had not

brought Mags and Artie. She wore a white blazer, black pants and a silk scarf. Dad had on his uniform. Mom had her blank, tense stare and I felt my headache return, and I knew with or without my mother, without Lauren Rose, nothing felt quite right.

Did I really think it could last forever?

I walked down the stairs from the room above the chandelier. I studied from my lofty vantage point. I could hear Véronique calling me. Now I wanted to sprint.

"*Vite, vite!*" She clapped her hands.

My parents were holding hands. I ran down the last few steps. I was no longer a French girl. I was back to being American.

"Lily!" they called out, and we embraced.

How bad could it get?

I held their hands.

I thought about Véronique. *Clever, beautiful. Intelligent.* I held on to every word that she had said to me. I tried to hold on to every memory of this welcoming house, every nook and cranny, the ducks, the school, the *sucre*, the small waterfall.

We sat down to eat.

"*Rôti de porc* with new potatoes, *haricots verts* and *une salade*," Véronique said, as I watched her toss the fresh leaves we had picked together that morning.

I studied her. I studied the leaves. I studied normality as if my life depended on it.

TWELVE

"Guess what, Lil'?"

"What?" I asked.

"We're living on the base now."

Dad drove the car as he always did, with precision, as if it were a fighter plane. While not quite dark, it wasn't light either. My headache dulled a little, but I was still dizzy from the long lunch and all the going-away gifts, especially the silver hand mirror, inlaid with mother-of-pearl, with a matching comb finely etched with my initials. This was a present for a grown-up girl. Twirling it first in my right hand, then my left, I contemplated the Belfonds' final invitation: they'd said they would prepare lunch for me on the day of my upcoming First Holy Communion.

After placing the mirror back in its case and snapping it shut, I stood up and threw my arms over the front seat, clasping my hands tight around my mother's neck and shoulders. She let out a sigh of relief, and I guessed that this meant the base was going to be a good thing. I sat back down. I was the protector again. Holiday over.

"Great," I said.

"You're going to go to the American school."

"Kindergarten," my mother added.

American, I thought. *All things English. Not my favourite*. But instantaneously I let go of all things French, if not by choice. The Belfonds and their dream house just slipped away behind us as we rolled down the road, Dad chain-smoking as he piloted us. Their rock-solid home, poplar trees and freshly baked bread were simply jettisoned right out of my head. I think I realised it was the safest way.

"Okay," I said to the two people in the front seat, who if nothing else looked nice, smelled good and drove a lot faster than the Belfonds, who hardly drove at all. These were my parents, I reminded myself. They were like something in a movie or late-night TV. "Mommy," I said, "*tu es* beautiful, clever and *très intelligente*."

"Thank you, Lily," she said. "Now try to speak only in English."

It turned a blue sort of dark as if in the distance there was still light, somewhere out there, over the edge of the world, racing away from us. I thought about the base, of which my only memory was the pool at the officers' club. When it turned pitch black, my father pointed out the white lines on the highway and asked me if I wanted to drive, to which I answered – of course I did – by saying, "Yes, sir," and clambering in that same instant over the back of his seat and into his lap.

Driving the car was akin to sitting on top of the world, being queen for the day, or as close as I could get to flying – the strange and mysterious thing my father did. *How did he get off the ground?* Pushing back the seat, he wrapped his warm hands over mine, and in the green glow of what he reverentially called 'the instruments', I drove on and on. I felt him think.

"See those," he said, "out there, those white lines, Lil'? At the side. Keep your eye on them and you won't go off the road, even if something comes at you. Even for a moment, if you are temporarily blinded by oncoming light."

Mom fell asleep, and I stared at the broken white lines, then the solid ones, coming towards us, going away. Sadly, despite waiting for the moment in which I would find myself unable to see, I was disappointed not to be tested. I would not have the opportunity this time to hang carefully on to the centreline, or the stark rim of the road, which seemed to hold out some rare and peculiar promise, but I still liked driving – the heat of my father's concentration, the hope that at any second the car might actually take off. For that was the state in which we perpetually lived – liftoff.

Dad took over the wheel. Smoothly pulling into a driveway, he said, "Here we are," shifted gears and popped the brake. We'd landed. It could have been anybody's house because as far as I could see all the homes looked alike, evenly spaced and uniformly lit. I immediately learned our number. Seven. I did not want to get lost, go to the wrong house; get mixed up with someone else's kids, another family. Again.

It was a little like my idea of holding to the centreline, or watching the edges, of not being blown off course by the unexpected. After all, Mom had vanished, even if she was currently back, the old farmhouse was nowhere to be seen and now the Belfonds simply did not exist. It was tough to know what was what, what to hold on to and what to forget. In that instant, I learned to memorise. Burn everything good into my heart. For dear life. Twice.

Dad rang the doorbell.

"Surprise!" he said. "Guess who's home."

Mom gave everyone a kiss. My brother and sister wore their pyjamas and were freshly bathed. I could tell by the red faces and the hairdos, cowlicks in place. They were eating popcorn, which meant they were watching TV, waiting for me. Artie jumped off the sofa. He was so big. Mags stayed seated.

"You're going to share my room," she said.

"Okay," I answered, handing over the box of chocolates Madame Belfond had given me.

"We have a new maid," Artie said, as if she were his own.

"*Oui?*" I asked, then corrected my language. "That's great."

"Yes," Dad said. "This is Marie."

A dark-eyed French girl smiled at me.

Mom took my suitcase and the gifts to the room at the end of the hall. Then she helped me bathe and shampooed my hair, wrapping me tightly in a snow-white towel. "I love you," she said. "I missed you."

"Me, too," I answered.

Mags interrupted, "Follow me."

"Okay," I said as Mom helped me button my pyjamas in record time. I raced down the hall to my new bedroom. I did miss Véronique, but the truth was that she was not Mom. Only Mom was Mom, smelt like Mom, hummed like Mom and said I love you like Mom. I was surprisingly happy to be home.

"Over there," my sister said, "your stuff goes over there. That's your bed. I get the window."

"Okay," I said. My bed was by the door. It would have to do. From there I could see down the hall, into the living room and all the doors leading to the bedrooms. But better than that, I could tap messages straight through the wall to Artie, and from the foot of my bed, sleeping feet to head, I could see – what a stroke of luck – the television set.

"I just want to say one thing," Mags interrupted my reconnaissance, "I will help you on your first day at school."

"Okay."

Before I could get back to the living room, the chocolates were gone and so was my father. He'd left to take the maid home, and my mother, in her best imitation of him, said, "Okay, kids, lights out. School tomorrow."

When there wasn't another sound, I crept into Artie's room with the big surprise I'd saved for him.

"Red alert," I said softly.

"Red alert," he replied.

We snuggled together in his bed, pulling out the lemon drops in the oval container I'd hidden in the zipper compartment of my new suitcase. We ate until we were almost sick, and my brother caught me up on the latest news: two blue robin's eggs – he could get them for me, he was going to pre-kindergarten, and how he figured out, if you pumped hard enough, backward and forward, you could tip the new swing set straight over. Then we fell asleep.

I awoke in my room, my lips still sticky and sweet. Under my arm was a surprise. Bound in dark leather, embossed with a gaggle of long-necked geese, was a book, the pages edged in gold. I had just the vaguest recollection of my father picking me up, tucking me in, pulling the clean, crisp, military-tight sheets up and around my chin. He'd slipped the book carefully in beside me, and afterwards he had just for a moment lightly touched his fingers to the side of my head.

"Welcome home, Lil'," he whispered. "This is for you. *Fairy Tales from Around the World.*"

It sounded magnificent, and I wanted to read each and every one of them.

THIRTEEN

"Thorazine."

"For what?" my mother asked.

"Hyperactivity."

I put the 'Th' word into the magical category, like 'Alakazam'. I heard it only once. My mother's reaction to it was also a first and last. She rose up to her full height. I had never seen her angry, really angry, before. If she had been a goose, she would have had her wings fully stretched. She would be flailing them and emitting the odd honk, and she would frighten anything in her path, the way a goose does when its goslings are endangered.

A dog, however, or any raptor, always had the advantage. They understood that a goose will never leave its offspring. They could, and eventually would, attack her long, exposed white neck. A mother goose with three goslings could not possibly fly away. She was stuck.

"Thorazine," my father said, "might slow Lily down. It's what she needs."

"No!" my mother screeched, loud enough to startle me. It was the only time I heard my father abandon an idea. My mother said no to Thorazine and no to allowing me to skip grades, even one, which was the other suggestion made by the American school counsellor. Mom thought it was a bad idea. What would happen when it was eventually time for me to go to the prom? Who would I date? I would be younger than all my classmates. It would be unfair. Who would I play with? My mother won the argument, but afterwards turned quietly to me. I only wondered what a prom was or a date.

"Lily, you cannot dash to school, outrun the other children. You must slow down."

"It's the sneakers," I told her. "Mom, they fly like the wind."

"I know, but you mustn't fly."

"But you said that's how you can spot me."

"I know, but now I will spot you in other ways."

How could she? If I wasn't flying, how could she spot me from the kitchen door? I had to be out in front, line leader, bouncing, jumping off the road. I had to be Flash, faster than the wind. I had to be first.

"There are lots of ways for me to spot you. Your blonde hair, your blue eyes. Just promise me that you will not run, that you will let some of the other children win occasionally. Don't blurt things out or read all the books on the advanced shelf. I will have some here for you at home. You can pick them out yourself."

"*The Dragon Who Liked to Spit Fire*?"

"*The Dragon Who Liked to Spit Fire*," she agreed. "And something else. You can wear my charm bracelet."

"Your charm bracelet? From your honeymoon?"

"Yes, for nap time. To help you keep still. You can count the letters and make up words... just do not ask Miss Barton for a book or to go to the bathroom more than once. Put your head down and keep it down. This will be our secret. No more running and racing. No more making things up. Understood?"

"Understood."

Dad was thrilled. Mom was scared. Miss Barton wanted to speak to them again, about school and about me. I had a hard time keeping my feet on the floor. We talked about my teacher for a week.

"Is it true? Is she coming after school to eat dinner here?"

"Yes," my mother told me right up until the very night my favourite teacher actually appeared at our front door.

"It's a special book," she explained to my parents over the meal, "about gifted children."

"Good," my father said, forcing a look of enthusiasm.

"Lily's not gifted," my mother said. "She's just had the advantage of a few extra years in French schools."

"It's about creativity in primary school," Miss Barton went on, "and I just want permission to publish her story."

"Sure," Dad said as I wanted to run, but forced myself to walk, around the dinner table, finishing my spaghetti between slow laps while laughing with Artie. We wanted to take Miss Barton, whose real name I now knew was Emily, to the playroom. We wanted to show her the Easy Bake Oven and the Erector Set.

I didn't care about stupid old *Mother and Her Kittens* by Lily Preston. It was a vocabulary assignment. A week ago Miss Emily Barton had handed out eight-by-ten-inch photographs. Mine was of three kittens on a stairwell, their paws draped over a banister. I simply had to write a story based on our word list. That week's word was 'crazy'.

I had willed my shoes to stay on the floor, fingered the capital A on my mother's charm bracelet and thought about all the cat stories I knew: *Le Chat Botté*, 'The Three Little Kittens'. Then I thought about Artie. I thought about my sister and myself. We could have a great time. We could have fun, run like the wind, lose our mittens and drive without our seatbelts on. I would be called Flash. Artie would be Dash. Mags would be called Match. Their father would be on a classified mission. Their mother would be so unhappy with it all that she would just go – *voilà* – crazy. *Fini.*

After I handed it in my teacher had waved the story around like the American flag.

"Come up here, Lily," she said. "Read this to the whole class."

All I could think was: *Alakazam, alakazam!* Keep your feet on the floor. Do not bounce. Do not jump. What was that other warning? Do not draw attention to yourself. This was dangerous. I was going against my mother's rules.

Emily Barton had me read the story aloud to every class in the school. By the sixth grade, with the principal sitting in and his secretary looking on, I almost fainted. A wall of knees towered over me. My mother had been right. *What would have happened if I had skipped a grade? I'd be the class midget.*

Back in my own classroom, I lay down for rest period. For the first time I took a nap and did not have to play with my mother's bracelet, ask for a book or go to the bathroom twice. All sorts of pictures ran through my head, story after story. I could run at wind speed, and no one would notice me. I could do all sorts of things, and not only would everyone let me, but if I used the right vocabulary word they didn't call it running, jumping or interrupting; they called it creative writing.

Peace at last.

Over dinner with my parents my teacher asked if they'd read my story.

"No," they both said, "we haven't seen a thing."

Emily Barton gave them one copy of the story each. She also gave them the photograph. Dad said he didn't have time at that moment but would read it as soon as he could. He had slipped it into the side pocket of his flight suit when he left that night. Mom waited until our lights were out, after we were all tucked in bed and the dishes were done. She didn't watch television or turn on the hi-fi.

Instead, she curled up in her silk pyjamas and robe on the corner of the sofa, under our brightest lamp. I heard the pages' sharp flip.

Crazy. It was just a vocabulary word. Something Dad said when he referred to Mom, but I did not mean it. She would have to know that. It was just 'writing'.

I don't think she did. For the first time, after a very long silence, I heard my mother get up and make herself a drink.

FOURTEEN

The headlights crossed the wall. The flight bag hit the floor, and Mom's bedside lamp went on.

"Hi, hon," she called out.

"Don't *hi, hon* me," he said. "What do you have on?"

Silence pervaded the house.

"I didn't get promoted," he said.

"I'm sorry."

"Take that thing off," he added, "you look like a whore."

A whore. What was that? Sounded like an H-word. She had on the long blue nightgown covered with tiny seed pearls all the way, she'd said, from Hong Kong. It was her waiting-for-Dad gown.

"Have you been drinking?" he growled.

"No," she said.

"Any repairmen in?"

"What are you talking about?"

"You are so stupid. People talk, you know."

A gasping sound then my mother's voice again. "Nobody is talking about anything!"

The ashtray, meant to hit him, crashed to the floor. My father shouted out for me to come and clean up the spill. I lit out of the bottom bunk, where I had been listening with Artie. I took two steps and slipped face first on the rug by the bedroom door. My new front tooth broke off at the crown. I screamed, and both of my parents came running. They stood in the doorway. The officer and the princess. They picked me up and gradually prised away my hands until they uncovered my mouth – only to discover that I would have to go to the emergency room.

"Small tooth," the paediatrician said. "Shame it's a permanent one."

"You know children," my father told him, "always running."

But who cleaned up the ashtray?

"Silver cap, 'til we get a porcelain one," the surgeon said.

My mother stayed throughout the drilling, the needles, the Novocain, the tubes down my nose and the awful stench of a tooth being filed off and the root nerve being removed. I felt the water jet at the back of my throat and squeezed my mother's hand. I didn't want her to faint, or to feel any more pain.

"One last trip," my father said, "before we go home."

"After your First Communion," my mother added.

My father said 'home' as if it had a capital H. Home. USA. United States of America. It was clearly a place he loved. He would die for her, he said. I was not sure. I had no idea what it was. I thought France was home. I was happy because he was happy, though. My mother was happy too, and I busied myself learning to smile with my mouth shut. I was not sure if a silver cap on a front tooth was something to smile about.

FIFTEEN

I most liked our new house in America because we had a flag. 'The Stars and Stripes', my dad called out as he ran it up the flagpole. Stateside is where we now were. Home.

It wasn't that I didn't want to go to the elementary school in Rhode Island, USA; it was just that I feared what might happen whilst I was there. The inside of the doorjamb was white, and I clung to it. They couldn't budge me. *I am not going to school.* Artie pushed, my mother shoved and, eventually, they won. I walked to the bus with my head lowered, and Artie continued to shout, "Come on, Lil'." At the front of the house, Mom's nightgown billowed just inches outside the door.

Something is going to happen to her. I pulled the satchel into my lap and gripped it, watching the house disappear. *What will I do without her? Who will comb my hair?* I still could not make a ponytail. Artie sat beside me, and Mags got lost in the back of the bus with the other kids, who chanted, "'Fraidy cat, 'fraidy cat, who's afraid of school?"

What do they know? At school I found the nearest girls' lavatory and locked myself in one of the stalls. Then, with all the force I could muster, I slugged myself in the nose. The bleed was instantaneous, and so was the help I received. I could lie down in the nurse's office. We became friends. She told me why she wore pink ("It's fresher") and said I could go to the library whenever I felt better. There I read all the mysteries. Mysteries with detectives. Nancy Drew.

"Some kids are like that," she said, "they bleed easily, and for no reason at all. Just tilt your head back and let me know when you're ready for class."

In time, when it looked as though Mom would still be there when we returned from school, I got straight off the bus and went right to Mrs Diamond's second-grade class in the modern elementary in Rhode Island. My father was at school too, attending the Naval War College. These were important words, I understood, filing them away with other names, dates, phone numbers and the all-important zip codes. Rhode Island. War College. Just-in-case words. Just in case of what? *Just in case*, I thought, *I ever get lost.*

Mrs Diamond was not interested in a class pet, but she warmed to me because I could do the memory tray, covered with all sorts of knick-knacks from thimbles to plastic dinosaurs, day after day, and no matter how many times she changed the items or the configuration, I was one of the few who could recall where each item stood, even after she had covered it back up with her black silk scarf. I recognised the pattern of the roses on the tray itself too. It was identical to the one we had at home, used by my mother to serve drinks, popcorn balls and apples coated in caramel for Halloween.

I studied the spines of the books on the white shelves by the clock, over my desk, on the wall, memorising them all.

"Okay," Mrs Diamond said, "let me see your phonics."

I handed her the printed words, with the accent going in the opposite direction from the way it had in France. It was guesswork, a mystery to me: which syllable got the major and/or minor emphasis.

"Perfect," she said, and I relaxed.

It was an afternoon like any other, and when we got home we expected the same Kool-Aid, milk, Oreos or Fig Newtons, but the house was quiet and Mom was in bed. Mags did her homework with the TV on; Artie broke open a fresh pack of Crayolas; and I noticed the sky go from blue to pink to gold. No one made dinner; Mom remained curled up. She needed sleep, but I wished she'd get up before Dad came home.

I tried to wake her up, but Dad got there first. I watched as he jerked the covers off my mother's body, leaving her blue nightie hiked up. She raised her hand to stop him, but it didn't work. He poured the stream of lukewarm beer he'd found in the Tupperware pitcher hidden in the linen closet over her face and hair. It caught and beaded there. Her body was so small. I thought, *Even I could pick her up.* Then: *Maybe this is what you learn in war school. Beat someone hard enough, and long enough, and eventually, they will buck up.*

"Come in here," Dad called to Mags and Artie, but they were already there, standing in the doorway, powerless and pretending to be men. He splashed the last of the alcohol over the constellation of freckles I knew so well across my mother's chest and tossed the plastic jug against the headboard, where it ricocheted, nicking her in the side of the head.

"Take a good look," he said, "*this* is your mother," and left the room. We looked at each other. Artie picked up the pitcher. Mom pulled her nightie down, stood up and drew all of us into the side of her hip, covering our eyes in her waist for a split second (we knew she didn't want us to see her like this). She went into the shower. I went after her, put my hand on the bathroom door, but before I could turn the knob, it locked.

Mags finished her homework with the TV off; Artie stripped all the paper off his fifty new Crayolas before breaking each one in two. In the kitchen, I made a Raggedy Anne Salad from the *Betty Crocker Kids' Cookbook* as my father spoke to M, who lived all the way in Columbus, Ohio – zip code 43222. He said, "You're right. It's what I gotta do," then put his hand over the receiver and motioned for me to bring him a beer. "You're right," he said again, "it's something I gotta do."

That night Mags let me sleep in her bed.

"Lily," she asked, "do you know what happened today?"

"No," I answered.

"President Kennedy got shot."

SIXTEEN

The picnic hamper held two thermos flasks – one for Tang and one for lemonade. There was enough room for nine sandwiches, cut on the diagonal – two peanut butter and jelly, two liverwurst and mayonnaise, two with tomato and three with American cheese. There were cookies, an apple, some Fritos and maybe, if we were lucky – if Dad did the shopping with me at the commissary – some Twinkies, Hostess Cupcakes and a package of pink Snowballs. Sometimes, for Mags, we bought chocolate chips.

My job, of course, was to pack it, watch it and distribute it at high noon, which Dad said was exactly when both hands would be pointing straight up. In that same instant I was to look straight up, count ten floors and wave to the place where Mom (and Dad) stood. Holding my fingers around the pink strap, I was glued to my Cinderella watch, counting like a nurse.

The windows were tall, covered with thick screens and grey bars. They were arranged in straight rows, six across and twelve down. A siren sounded one short blast off in the distance, which coincided with the sceptre-shaped minute hand on my watch twitching finally into place. I shouted, "That's it. Look up. There's Mom."

My brother stopped racing around the picnic table and came to an abrupt halt. Together we spied the high tower, the centre window, the brick under the arch.

"Wave," I said. And we did.

"Now," Artie asked, "may I have lunch?"

"Tang?"

"Okay."

After I poured the drink of astronauts into the thermos lid that doubled as a cup, I looked back up at the window. *Was that it?* Did I see her, the black hair, the red lips? I could not be certain. I knew I saw a massive brick building and a lot of bars.

My father came out at precisely three o'clock, glanced at his watch and signalled for us to load up. It was time to go home. He drove, and we rode, in silence. Everyone focused on the white lines in the centre or at either side of the highway. Dad made spaghetti that night the way he said it was done in Italy – rinsed with cold water, very quickly, after cooking. *But how is Mom?* Nobody asked.

"Next week," he announced, "it's Family Day, and then we're all moving to Virginia."

"Yippee!"

"Now, Lily," he added, "you clean up."

"Yes, sir."

I did.

In the living room, they turned on the TV and read the Sunday comics. Mags promised she'd come back to dry the dishes, which she did. A window over the sink was something my mother always demanded. As I looked out from it, night crept in like a slow hand moving first over the sprinkler, then the jungle gym next door. With my hands in the soapy water, I made a secret pledge. *Dear God, if you will, please just make Mom okay. I will help in every single way.*

Although she would deny it, and certainly my grandmother

would never admit it, my mother tended to be the prettiest woman in any room. It made her shy, uncomfortable, as well as making me timid too. People looked at us, no matter what we did, for even the simplest thing – pulling a loose thread from a hem or brushing a stray hair into place. They hung on every word, even if it was only: "Okay, Lily, quick, quick, into the hanky, give me a quiet blow."

For Family Day she wore her oyster white dress with the splashy blue roses and the collar that stood up, almost coming off each shoulder. She looked like Mrs JFK long before the Eternal Flame. She showed us her room. A single bed wedged between one wall and the window looked cosy, adorned with two stuffed dogs and an embroidered pillow that read 'I love you'. Two closets held her crisp trousers, her blouses and white linen jacket. Hooks behind the door held her nightgown and the blue robe. The vanity for her make-up, lotion and perfume had a little wooden stool. Daisies on the windowsill bobbed in the breeze, and the picnic table, ten floors below, seemed miles away. I wanted to stay. It seemed like such a small win – Mom having her own room.

Standing in a semi-circle, halfway across the room, my mother's friends introduced themselves and their children. My mother stood up when she presented us, including Dad, too. But I wished he hadn't worn his uniform. He gave that friendly little salute he used to disarm people – two fingers to the side of the head – and sat back down.

"Lauren Rose," her doctor said as we finally stood outside in the driveway, "I want you to call me if you should ever find yourself in a bad way."

"Yes," she said.

"Lauren Rose." He shook her hand, and then held both of them tenderly.

He loved her. I could see that. In his presence, my mother lit up. My father smiled, shook his hand like a soldier and the doctor gave him a packet of papers. "Major Preston," he said, "you left these. Take them home, read them. Lauren Rose needs you, and you need us. Eventually, you might find that you need her, too."

This doctor did not understand. My father did not need anybody except, on occasion, M. And sometimes now he called on me when he needed a sort of first lieutenant, someone to be in charge when he was away. He was a *soldier boy*. Didn't the doctor know? In uniform my father was practically Superman. Everyone expected him to be invincible, and that extended to his family too. *His wife, my mother, can't drink again, even socially?* Was the doctor out of his mind? Lauren Rose was a Preston. Illness? Weakness? "Balderdash and poppycock," M had said, "it is, my dear, all in the head." My father's job was not to be afraid.

In the car we waved until the doctor and the hospital receded into the distance. My father loosened his tie, and said he needed a drink. "Lauren Rose," he asked, "how about it?"

She smiled, still full of sunshine. *Is he joking?*

"No," she said, clutching the papers he'd thrown on the dash of the new car that we'd be driving all the way south to Virginia.

"Well," he said, "we have a long drive ahead. God, I am glad to be out of there. I hate you mixing with those loonies. I hate mingling with them. Did you see that beatnik, the loser with the goatee and sandals? Julian – was that his name? What a failure. Psycho. All a guy like that needs is a stint in the army."

"Jack?" My mother hesitated.

"I'm going back to the Pentagon," he told her proudly.

"We're not going home?"

"No. And I bought a dog – a German Shepherd. Named him Scout."

"But I…"

She looked over the front seat, directly at me, while Artie raced Tonka toys in the far back of the car, up and over the wheel wells. Mags arranged and rearranged items in her purse. My mother gasped. I still can't recall whether or not she actually said, "*Help*," but her eyes rolled back in her head as she fell against the front seat. My father swerved to a halt, wedged a stiff eyeglass case between her teeth and shouted for Mags to run to the nearest house and have them call an ambulance.

"Tell them your mother is having a seizure," he shouted after Mags.

I thought Mom was dead, like those ducks. Her eyes froze in that plea that was so easy to read. I reached out to touch her forehead, but my father barked.

"Stop that. She'll take your hand off."

"No, she won't," I said, and sunk into the back seat. *She just doesn't want to be trapped. You take all the sunshine away.* I hoped, I prayed, that the ambulance would take my mother straight back to that doctor who loved her, who tenderly held her hands.

All I could think about to take my mind off the commotion all around me was that Artie could teach our new dog Scout to stay, to come, to sit and to speak. He was good with animals. He always claimed they could talk and they could keep fear at bay. These are the things I wanted to say to him but he just pressed himself against the car window with tears frozen into place.

We did move to Virginia. My mother joined us much later. I put the small things where she would like them, especially the Hummel figurines; children that looked just like us. I was the one spilling cherries out of a large paper cone, held behind my back. Mags was the girl with the goose. Artie knelt, peering into a half-open box. He wore orange clogs. The Waterford crystal, all the way from Ireland, I put on a top shelf in the dining room. The porcelain tree trunk with the three-leafed clover sat square in the centre of the reception-room table. Roses I placed in the yellow vase with the two blue sparrows.

Lauren Rose stood in the doorway and took it all in, as if she remembered, which is what Dad had been asking us ever since we moved back to Virginia.

"Don't you remember?"

"Well, sort of," we told him, but tried to remind him, it was hard to recall what you last saw when you were only one, two or three. "France," we added, just to cheer him up, "we remember that." Mags lied. She said she recalled Virginia exactly – the house and everything.

I took Mom's hand, and Artie grappled with her suitcase, banging it up the stairs one step at a time. Mom bent down and pulled Mags to her chest, saying repeatedly, "Darling, let me look at you," as I waited for my turn. Mags emptied her purse.

"Yes, yes, yes and yes," my mother said. "Kleenex, comb, cologne and Chapstick. But you forgot—"

"The Juicy Fruit," we all chimed in.

She opened her purse and handed Mags the package of chewing gum to distribute.

"Mommy," Artie said from behind my back, as if he were just testing.

"Yes," she answered, licking her thumb, taking a single smudge from his cheek. "I understand you have a well-trained dog named Scout."

"I do," he said, beaming from ear to ear.

Lauren Rose moved from room to room, touching the surface of things. Remembering. No dust. *She ought*, I thought, *to recognise who did this*, and I waited for my turn.

Suddenly, she spun around. "Who did all of this?"

"I did," I answered.

The blood drained from her face. I didn't understand. Was she going to hit me? She didn't say a word. She just looked from place to place, for a spot to put down the hat she was lifting off her head. It was the same hat Artie had peed in years ago. She didn't know where to put it. Her eyes flitted from side to side. Two small birds on the side of a vase. She gave me the look she had given me from over the back of the car seat on Family Day – the day she'd fallen dumb, and Dad said she'd take off my hand.

"Quickly," I said, "give the hat to me, Mom, I know exactly where it goes."

91

"Thank you," she said, I think.

We sat down for dinner. Dad made spaghetti and I made a big surprise: fig bars the way Mom did. I followed the directions right off the box. Sitting directly across from Dad, I could get in and out of the kitchen just as fast as anyone. I would make good on my secret pledge – help in any way I could. Mom sat to his left in my old chair.

"So, tell us," Jack asked Lauren Rose, clearing his throat first the way he did when one of us brought home anything less than an A– or a B+, "what was it like?"

He cut his pasta with the side of his fork.

"What was what like?" my mother asked.

"The loony bin," he said. "Shock therapy."

Dad gave Mom a big fat red Magic Marker F–. Even at my age, I knew that this was not something you said when someone had 'been away', especially not a man to his wife.

"I could use a drink," he added.

SEVENTEEN

It was a birthday present. My father spent a considerable amount of time thinking: *What to get for Lauren Rose?* She already had everything. A house, three bedrooms, two and a half baths, two cars and one garage. A coppertone dishwasher, refrigerator, washer-dryer and a freezer. She could even have had them all, if she had wanted, avocado-coloured. The patio he laid out himself, flagstone by flagstone, with the aid of a few buddies, a pack or two of beers and a barbecue. She also had a snow-white trellis on which she grew the Dublin Bay roses from which everyone wanted a cutting. And of course geraniums in terracotta pots all the way from Italy.

She didn't need to work. My father did that. He conferred with M on the gift because M knew, more than most, what women wanted, what they needed, and besides, she would be putting in a bit of the cash to pay for it. Jack Preston agreed with his mother: a mangle was a good idea. He had seen it in a magazine. A woman, a model, looking not unlike Lauren Rose, with a great big smile, sat in front of a machine that was advertised as being able to iron anything. He asked his children, and they agreed.

"Sure, Dad. Sounds great. A mangle."

Except for me. I asked, "A mangle... what's that?"

My father threw open his arms as if he'd been waiting all his life to explain. "A machine," he said, "a professional iron. Sheets, linens, tablecloths, drapes – you name it, you don't have to iron them by hand any longer. Pillowcases," he snapped his fingers, "just like that."

He might have been describing an aeroplane. Supersonic. Anything to make my mother happier. We were to keep it a secret. Truth was that we forgot until the weekend before Mom's birthday when the two men who helped Dad lay the flagstones, drink the beer and grill the steaks, arrived again.

This time they unpacked the machine, hoisted it on their naked shoulders and carried it down the narrow stairs to the basement. Mom stood in her khaki shorts, striped shirt and little black slippers, and watched the three men wedge and shimmy the great white square down the steps.

"A professional machine," my father announced as they placed the appliance in the corner, under the small window that looked up and out to the rainspout near the patio. Through the stray brushstrokes across the small windowpane, a thick vine hung off the trellis and one full-blown Dublin Bay red rose bounced backward and forward in the wind.

"The laundry room," he said, "and look, you're not far from the toilet." He held open the door. My mother, he imagined, could happily stay in the basement all day long now that she had a special corner in which to sort, wash, dry, fold and mend.

"Thanks," she said, as she held my right hand in both of hers.

"Strip off the beds," my father said to Mags, and, turning to my mother, he patted the seat of the new piece of equipment. "Sit down, honey, let's see how it works."

My mother sat down at the machine that was bigger than a piano, and we trailed dirty linen down the stairs. "Naturally," Dad said, "wash 'em first, but this is just to see how it works." He almost pushed my mother off the stool that swung out from under the massive rollers. Some levers she would work with her knees. "Like brakes," he said, "stop and go." Others she would work with her hands.

"Off limits," he warned us.

On the patio Jack grilled burgers and hot dogs, Lauren Rose mixed potato salad and we sat in the laps of the men who helped deliver the birthday present. Mom seemed pleased, drinking ginger ale and 7 Up.

"Maybe," Dad said, "you could use some more light down there," and he made a mental note to add another bulb.

Jack loved this house because he'd bought it when he was a young lieutenant and now it was really worth something. Every single thing he did just added value. In fact, it had gone up by almost thirty per cent, he liked to say.

"How about that?"

We jumped off the school bus one day, ran to the back door, but no one was there. Mom didn't meet us, and she wasn't in the garden with the roses, or on the patio sunbathing with the radio playing beside the geranium pots. There were no snacks ready. The house felt empty.

Mags and Artie changed out of their school clothes, had Cheez Doodles and turned on the television set. I started the *clean sweep*, as Dad would say, beginning upstairs. I checked the closets, the bathrooms, the side porch, the bedrooms, the living room, the dining room, the kitchen – twice – the patio, the garage, even behind it, and then the place I least liked to go: the basement.

The stairs creaked. The glazed door we never opened cast a dull light over the racks of winter clothes. The hot water heater and the fuse box stood sentinel in the corner. The door to the toilet stood ajar. A Dublin Bay rose vine scratched the windowpane. Upstairs I heard cartoons. Laughter fanned out. A cat hit a mouse, or maybe a long-legged bird ran into the side of a mountain and a coyote fell into a gorge, but it never failed, the sound of it, to hurt my ears.

Past the cartons of soda and seltzer, where I once built a fort and Artie overdosed on root beer, I found her. She held very still.

"Mom," I said once.

I waited a few minutes and tried again. "Mom."

She didn't answer. The mangle was warm.

I pulled up a little bench. Starched pillowcases, sheets, tablecloths and the pink and beige drapes from the living room lined the counter between the sink and the wall beside her. Dad's shirts swung ever so slightly from a rod that partially blocked the doorway. The new light bulb, under which she looked so pretty, was switched on. Her hair was washed, a shiny black-blue, brushed away from her face, her make-up well done, her nails perfect half-moons, her blouse white and starched, her denims creased down the front. She looked like someone out of a magazine. Her suede moccasins barely touched the floor.

We sat there for a long time.

"Mom," I said again.

Finally she answered me. "Look. Look at this."

She sprayed a lace-edged handkerchief with starch. Or maybe it was water. I noticed her hands. Such delicate things. The linen square was fed through the machine. She held it up. Perfect. Then she held still again. The car pulled in the driveway. The back door slammed.

"We don't know!" Artie shouted in anticipation.

"Lauren Rose!" my father bellowed.

We didn't answer. He pounded through the house. My mother turned towards me and started to speak. She fought to keep her composure, to hold off her terror, and I fought with her. *It's Dad, isn't it?* Tears pooled in the corners of her eyes. *No, no, don't do that. Not here. Not now.*

He came down the stairs two at a time. "Lauren Rose!" he roared.

"Over here," I said, jumping up.

"What's going on?" Dad asked.

"Nothing," I said, pulling the lace hanky from my mother's limp hand, "we're ironing."

"Yes." She smiled. "Ironing."

Then he went upstairs.

It wasn't until midnight, long after I'd gone to bed, that she finally got out the words she'd been trying to say all day – for all I knew, maybe all month, all year, all her life. My father egged her on, the same way he did almost every night, no doubt sitting with one arm cocked behind his head, leaning against the giant bedhead, smoking cigarettes. He used the voice that signalled we should pull our pillows over our heads, our ears, because this could go on all night, well into daybreak. It would start with something simple, something Mom was trying to say, and then erupt into a litany we all three knew by heart.

Who did she think she was? Nothing without him. Nobody. Lower Darby. Her father was a drunk. What would she do? Call somebody? Yeah, who? Go ahead. His mother had been right. A safety pin. And salmon-coloured geraniums – common, cheap. He should have known. Schizo. He might have the phone removed. What did she think about that? The bill was two hundred dollars last month. Did she know that? Yeah, even her own family didn't want her. Why didn't she ever say she had a crazy aunt? Kept that a secret before the wedding, didn't she?

"She's not crazy," my mother insisted. He always pressed her on that. "Just simple… handicapped." She spoke of the aunt whom she knew as *special*, the one who made knitted things and soft toys for small children. The one who was happily caught in a net of nieces and nephews and siblings, who never thought of her as crazy, just different. She was always out in the open. Didn't he see her at the wedding?

"Yeah, right," Dad said, "go take a tranquiliser." And turned over in bed.

97

Instead, my mother walked to the window. *Why did she try to explain?*

She stood there for a very long time, silent. Maybe she was counting the stars, beads on a rosary flung far into space, or else talking to God, but then she opened up like a jackknife in the middle of a street fight.

"I want out," she screeched, and put her fist through the windowpane.

The wrist fountained blood. My father shot out of bed, telephoned the police and called the ambulance. Mags, Artie and I ran into the bedroom.

Witnesses.

It seemed just an instant before they buckled her into the jacket and tied her arms around her while she was still trying to speak, going a long way back. She mentioned the house in France. I knew what she was talking about.

"She wants out," I said, my voice just as cool as the night rushing through the star-shaped hole in the broken glass. "She wants out," I said again, "because..." And then I stopped. Everyone cocked their heads towards me the way some people do when they are listening to children. I thought they would let her arms loose, but they didn't. No further words came out. I saw my mother's hands again, running the hanky back through the machine in reverse – restoring it to its priceless, irreplaceable, wrinkled natural state.

"Lily," my father said, "go back to bed, take the other children."

"Lil'," she whispered as they bundled her down the stairs and out into the night. I'd gotten it right, but what good had it done? Because now we were just waiting for *the last time*. Being the daughter of a fighter, I knew, a fighter fights until he wins. Which meant somebody always had to lose.

My mother went down.

Scout barked on and off throughout the night, and I could hear Artie's voice comforting him.

"Come on, Scout. Quiet now. Thank you for warning me. Now that's enough. Enough."

I could see the flat of his hand rise and fall in my mind, telling his beloved dog to lie down. Back in our bedroom, with the pillow over my head and Mags in her bed across the room, I pretended I was that puppy and Artie motioned me to be still and to rest.

EIGHTEEN

With Mom gone, I became M's bull's eye. With her, it was always, "Who's next?" I was it, both by ill luck and by design. I could call her off the scent of the others by agreeing to be her target.

"This house is a disaster," she said. "First things first, get rid of these flowers. None in the house! Salmon pink, so cheap. Common."

"They get rid of cooking smells," I offered.

"We spray air freshener for that. And strong bleach," M took great pains to tell us as she removed the dust from every crevice in the woodwork between the top landing and the bottom stair.

"Here," she said, handing me the cloth, "wrap it around your finger like this, and dig, all the way into the corner."

With a can of Pledge she demonstrated, and then knelt back.

"There," she said. "Properly cleaned."

I discovered nooks and crannies I'd never known existed. *Right under my nose. How could so many things have been left undone?* According to my grandmother not only were they left unfinished, incomplete, dirty, but they were also a clear indication that my mother was out of her mind. *Out of her mind? What does that mean? Did she live on the ceiling, which is where I imagined you went if you chose to go out of your mind? Right to the top. You would just float up.*

"You must do better," my grandmother said, "you are a Preston."

She would show me, and I let her. I would stay in my body. I would clean. *Who wanted to be out of her head? Look where that could lead.*

Even M was impressed. Not only had I buffed the oak steps to a high shine, but I also had lifted up the long-forgotten black mat outside the basement door and hosed down the concrete steps. I was a girl on a mission, a girl who would not go mad. By anyone's estimation, especially M's, I could clean.

"You are a Preston," she went on. "Remember always to hold your head high, your shoulders back. Your stomach in, your *derrière* under."

Derrière, of course, was the only proper word for 'bottom'. We should never use the words 'butt', 'fanny', 'ass' or 'backside', and we should certainly not associate with anyone who did. I managed this proud contortion, while I continued to polish. Artie did the same. He scoured the garbage cans with Tide in the gravel driveway in front of the garage because, again we were privileged to hear, Aunt Penny could eat out of hers, or maybe it was the garbage men who did that, or maybe both. I forgot. My grandmother talked so much. It was paramount to her what the men who jumped off the back of the moving garbage truck thought because, she said, they knew all about everyone's business, especially ours.

Mags cleaned the bathrooms. Each bit of caulking was scrubbed with Clorox. She did this job because she was the oldest. My grandmother believed in this sort of order – top to bottom, smallest to largest, one cup inside the other, shoes side by side, books even on the shelf, one after the other. Mags got to watch the wonder of what we called grout, and my grandmother called black, turn white while the bleach disinfected it.

I envied my sister. She watched the magic all on her own, without my grandmother talking on and on. She was able to look out the window sporadically and catch sight of a bird hopping from leaf to leaf. She was able to think about Mom. My brother could play on his own, spraying everything in sight while he was meant to be cleaning the garbage cans. They ignored 'head up and shoulders back'. They played between the rounds M would make to check up on whether or not their jobs were getting done. They were spared the one-way conversation that always began *Your mother…* They were spared the awful impulse I had on occasion to get a word in edgewise, that always ran the risk of being received as *back talk*, whose definition like its penalty was left solely to M's mood and discretion. This could result in practically anything, from sitting alone or, much, much worse, spending an interminable amount of time with M while she thumbed one page at a time through a very thick, pictureless book, listening to the clock tick.

"You sound like a broken record, M," Artie had said that very morning at breakfast, at which, amazingly, my grandmother laughed.

M liked Artie. It was as if he had chucked her under her chin, amusing her the way Dad did. I, on the other hand, wanting to make things really clear, perhaps even win a small smile myself, thought I would speak up.

"No, it's not a broken record, Artie, it's a stuck needle." I could see the turntable, the gramophone needle repeatedly catching in a groove on a record.

"A stuck needle?" my grandmother asked, without smiling.

"Exactly," I said, wanting to be precise.

"You think I sound like a stuck needle?"

"Yes, I do."

No one laughed.

"Do you know to whom you are speaking?"

"Yes, M, I do."

"I don't think so."

"But I do."

"Don't…" she began, and I already knew the end of the sentence. *Back talk.*

M strapped on the kneepads she'd brought all the way from Ohio, and we started at the top of the stairs. I would clean with her. *My punishment.* She spoke non-stop all day while we prepared the floors, the stairs, the cupboards and the beds for someone, anyone, perhaps Aunt Penny, to eat their dinner from.

Your mother, she said to me, over and over again. Sometimes this was a sentence. Sometimes it was a sentence that she could not finish. I kept waiting.

"It's a crime," she said, "a shame. A real crime. Criminal."

"Yes, M," I answered carefully, not fully understanding what she meant, except for the night the policemen swept my mother up in a big blanket and carried her down these very stairs. *So who was the criminal? My father? My mother? Me? What was the crime? Murder… robbery?* My mind raced. What would my favourite heroine, Nancy Drew, do?

In the distance I heard Artie shriek, splashing under the hose. "Dad's home!"

"Lily," my grandmother said, "you are excused."

Nancy Drew would look for clues.

"What would you all do without me?" M asked daily. "Something has got to be done. These children are in the wrong school. They must go to a Catholic one."

With no more warning than that, we were transferred from Burlington Elementary to St Patrick's Catholic School. This meant not only a different bus, but also new uniforms, which M showed us how to starch and iron. The correct order over which we were constantly quizzed was cuffs, collar, sleeves, down the front, in and around the buttons, then the back and the yoke. The iron's steel tip with the addition of steam was the topic of endless discussion. The mangle wasn't used, wasn't even mentioned.

"I don't have much time," she would say, "you know I have a job. I am using up my valuable vacation days. I am a line manager, you know. For the US government. I made it on my own. Raised two children on my own – your father and Aunt Penelope. Your mother…" She would trail off, and we all knew what that meant: Mom couldn't hold a candle to her or Aunt Penny and her trash cans. I imagined M as a fierce line manager, keeping aberrant lines in order.

M inspected everything, inside and out. Everything should match. The new uniform was a Black Watch tartan – blue, black and green. M described how this took away decision-making. We needed five white, long-sleeved blouses, five pairs of navy knee socks and two uniform tartan pinafore dresses to be alternated. We needed white cotton panties and two slips. Mags got a bra because M said she should stop making a spectacle of herself. We also wore a loose black tie and plain, polished loafers.

"Military academy," my father added to all the talk about schools. "That would be good for Artie."

"Divorce her," M told Jack.

"What?" my father asked, and I listened hard.

"You can't go on like this. I can't continue to rescue you. You have the children to think of, and your career."

My father fell silent.

"It would be legal for you to have her committed."

My father still did not say anything. I was hoping he would hit M.

"Have you kept a diary?"

I thought this would be it, but it wasn't.

"Yes," he said. "Last time I even called the police. They'll have filed a report."

Mags sat beside me on the bus. We weren't sad to see the back of M, but when she left, having used up on us all her vacation days,

I had a sense of foreboding. M had set something in motion, but I did not know what. I remember Mom saying we had to love our grandmother because of that curvature in her back and because her family had kicked her out, but I couldn't. For me, she was then and was now the Wicked Witch of the West, flying in and out on a broomstick. Lauren Rose was wrong: all the love in the world can't make a crooked spine straight.

Mags did not chant: "'Fraidy cat, 'fraidy cat, who's afraid of school?" She was scared, too. Not about school. But about Mom, just as I was.

My sister sat stoically, without a word of reproof, while I simply bent forward and vomited all of my breakfast onto the bus floor. *Now*, I thought, *she knows why I was anxious.* It had never been about school. We held still. I studied the half-dissolved One-a-Day vitamin under my foot, while she looked ahead as if she were driving the bus herself. She was sorting out a plan, even if it was only to save herself. Sometimes she took my hand, especially if one of the other kids said anything like, "Pee-ew," or, "What's wrong with her?"

"Nothing," Mags would say. "Shut up."

"Something wrong with *you*?" Artie would add. I think he wanted to punch someone in the face.

I would wait for the bus to stop at school, and I would try not to think about Mom or Dad or what might happen next: like divorce. I knew at school they would take me once again to the office. St Patrick's did not have a nurse or an infirmary. I would have to speak with Mother Superior.

"So what is it that causes your sickness, Miss Preston?"

"I don't know, Mother."

"This must be stopped. It can't go on. Not at a school like this."

"Yes," I said. "It will be stopped."

I wanted to say: *My parents are getting a divorce. They fight every night. My grandmother goes up and down the stairs on her knees with a damp cloth. I am terrified my mother is going to*

disappear, die, never come back and I don't know how to save her. I
want to say the word divorce, but I can't. Even I know it is a mortal
sin.

The word 'divorce' stuck in my throat. It made we want to
throw up again. I knew something about divorce. I'd learned in
CCD, the Confraternity of Christian Doctrine, that whole families
could be dammed for all eternity after a mortal sin like divorce.
Could I be kicked out of school? What about Mags and Artie?
Would I bring the whole family down if I told Mother Superior the
truth? What if the garbage men caught wind of it? Would it stink?

"Yes," I said again. "It will stop."

"Now go to class," she said, handing me the pink pass, "take
this to Sister Catherine and be well, Lily. Remember, whatever it
is that is disturbing you will pass. Nothing lasts forever. Do you
understand that?"

"Yes," I answered, remaining still, unspeakably petrified.

The tests were distributed. Sister Catherine motioned me to sit
down. I looked at the quiz. Long division. It was not the way I had
learned it at Burlington. In neat block letters at the top of the page,
and in a clear voice, the nun reminded us that we were dividing
down the right side and not across the top of the equation.

"Anyone who fails to follow these instructions will find their
paper thrown out. Is that understood?"

She said this with the same power, precision and certainty
with which she'd told us in Catechism class that divorce, murder
and suicide went hand in hand with something worse than death:
excommunication. Excommunication meant being forever cut off
from God's grace.

"Don't do it any other way," she intoned.

I didn't know what to do. This was the New Math. I looked
down at the page, around the room and at the clock. I tried to
figure it out, but I couldn't. Then I thought about the divorce,
things breaking and excommunication. I couldn't write.

"Miss Preston," Sister Catherine said impatiently, "please come outside."

I stood up. I followed her out, and I started to cry. I could not stop. My stomach rose up. *Do not vomit*, I told myself. *Not every day.*

"Miss Preston," she said, "if you think crying will get you anywhere in my class, you are sadly mistaken."

This is not the real me. I normally make As, one hundred per cent, but I haven't been here long enough. I don't understand.

I couldn't say anything. I felt I didn't have permission to ask. I didn't have the right to not know something. My nose started to run. I imagined Mom under a very big thumb – Dad's. I would be the girl who failed to get into the corners, to clean really well. I would be out of my mind like Mom. I wanted that suddenly. Right then and there. I felt myself fly straight up to the ceiling.

"Miss Preston," Sister Catherine barked, and brought me back down, "are you listening to me?"

"Yes, Sister, I am."

"This is because you don't do your homework, isn't it?"

"No."

"Then what is the matter with you?" she asked.

How could I explain? Division and divorce seemed to go together. I wanted to tell her what I had overheard, but she was bearing down on me, her thick, rimless glasses and the band of her white headdress cutting deeply into her pink flesh. She pulled at the rosary hanging from her waist and ran her hand under the starched white bib. Would she hit me? *Division. Divorce.* My family, I wanted to tell her, I was afraid they would all be damned.

"Go to the lavatory," she ordered me, "and come back when you've cleaned yourself up."

I wanted to walk straight out the double glass doors and into the street, back to Burlington where I was reading *We Were There with George Washington on the Potomac*. I could see the book right on the shelf, where I had left it. Teachers there did not flap down the halls like giant crows. The lights at Burlington were not dimmed to save money, and no one had to eat fish on Friday. No one seemed to be on some ancient mission.

However, things changed for the better the day Sister Catherine marched me back down to Mother Superior's office and left us alone.

"So you're Irish?" the headmistress asked me, and that let the light in. "I am, too."

"How do you know that?"

"Files," she said, patting a stack. "I know everything," she laughed.

"Yes. Well, my mother is. Her grandfather was from Tipperary."

Our being Irish, even in part, was the reason the nuns began to show us Prestons respect, and my mother by extension. I was certain that was why, when my mother showed up one day unexpectedly at mid-morning, they treated her with open affection. They flocked around her, even kissed her on the cheek. They let me, Mags and Artie leave without the prerequisite double signature, one from Mom and one from Dad. They just let us go. They waved us off as if it was a benediction.

"Quickly, children," my mother ordered. She shoved the automatic into reverse. "We're leaving."

"Where are we going, Mom?" I asked.

"Home," she answered. "I am going home."

NINETEEN

I'm not sure how we did it, but there we were – Mags, me and Mom – huddled close together by the aeroplane's emergency door and the stainless-steel galley kitchen where the stewardesses entered and exited like clockwork toys. We had gone from airline counter to airline counter trying to buy tickets that would take us from Dulles Airport to Philadelphia. My mother had only one hundred dollars, and we had no idea how she got it because Dad always said, "What do you have? Nothing. And even that I can take away from you."

We were being chased. Not yet, but I could sense it coming even if we had gotten a head start. My mother was finally doing it: running away. And we were going, too, except for Artie. He would not get in the car again. Once we'd gotten home from school, while Mom ran inside to pick up the oversized Samsonite bag, Artie ran into the garage and up into the loft. I called, Mags begged, but Artie refused to come down.

"Do you know how mad Dad will get?" he repeatedly said. "He will murder us."

"Yes," I cajoled, "but we'll be gone. Please, Mom says let's go, so come on."

"But who will take care of Scout? If I don't stay he will starve. Who will take him for a walk?"

"Artie, Dad will feed Scout. You must come with us. Now. Be brave, please. This is red alert. Seriously. Remember? We've got to go. This might be Mom's only chance."

"No, I can't," he answered, thinking that to go would be worse than staying. "He will kill us. He will kill her."

"Artie. Please. I will help you. Please, Artie. If we don't hurry, when will Mom be able to do this again? Mom needs us. Now. Artie. Please."

"No," he answered, crawling further back into the eaves.

"Artie, I will give you every piece of candy I have for the rest of my entire life, forever. Please come down now."

Artie, in his own way, was trying to save us. He felt he was a bit like a lightning rod that took the heat.

Mom pushed me out of the way and pleaded with him herself. "Artie, listen, we are just going to visit Nana and Granddad. We will go to the beach. Daddy can visit us there. We can come back. I promise. I promise with my whole heart."

Silence spread its thick and impenetrable darkness. Artie would not budge. I'd never heard my mother lie before, and it was as if a clock mechanism unwound. She would never come back. I knew that.

"Artie, I love you," my mother said. "The car is running and we must go. Won't you please come help me with the suitcase? I need you to come down now. Please, we must leave all together.

No answer.

"Artie, I love you," Mom said again, turning away from the ladder to the loft and finally the garage. She knew and we knew she couldn't carry him down. "Artie, I understand," she called out. "You stay and help your father. He will need a big, strong boy like you. Will you remember that I love you and I will come back for you as soon as I can?"

It nearly killed her to leave him there. She hovered between going and staying. Mags sat impatiently in the car. Every second counted. Mom was racing against the clock. I became angry. *What is Artie trying to prove? Can't he see Mom is about to give up? Isn't this the thing we have always hoped for?* But he remained lodged up in the far reaches of the garage. It was Mags who finally honked the car horn, and shouted, "Come on, Mom, let's go."

I agreed with that. I didn't say, "Dad will catch you sooner or later," though I wanted to warn her.

Onboard the plane we were served extra Coca-Colas and the uniformed women Mom called *the girls* gave us even more packets of peanuts. Mom rested her chin on the top of Mags's head as she pulled us close. The man behind the ticket counter had said that was the best deal he could offer, three adult seats, stand-by, for eighty-five dollars. Mom looked the young women in their uniforms up and down. She was looking at her past self, she told them.

"You don't say?" one stewardess replied, shaking her head from side to side.

"Wow!" the other one added. "Guess what?" she called out to yet another. "She flew for American, too. Back in… when was it?" She turned back to Lauren Rose.

"Late '40s, early '50s," my mother said, "before I got married." And then she paused, took a deep breath and kissed Mags on the forehead, then squeezed us both.

Respect. That's what they showed Lauren Rose, and, by association, us too. Mags grinned, came out from under her personal shadow, where she always seemed to be waiting for the sun to come out. I beamed also. This is what my mother deserved. This is what Dad and the Wicked Witch should show her. Why they didn't, I never understood. Well, the sun did shine in that late afternoon on an aeroplane bound for Philadelphia, and we bathed in its glory.

"They let me go stand-by," my mother explained to the 'girls'.

"Anytime," the stewardess told her.

"You deserve it."

"Those were the days."

They leaned back against the wall, talking to my mother as if she were the queen of it all. She laughed. She was one of them. Now, I liked landing as much as I liked taking off, but in that moment I wanted to keep on flying forever. I wanted those women and my mother to keep smiling. I didn't want to ever touch down because, up here, my father could not reach her, or us. We were running away. We were winning, and this was the mother I secretly cherished. People liked Lauren Rose, and we liked them for liking her. When I thought about it, I realised this was probably the woman my father married. Before he set out to destroy her.

I relaxed, had a second Coke. It was nice to have a stranger smile at me just because they thought my mother was good. I envisioned the future: no more Dad, no more bullying, no more fighting. No more harassment, day after day. Goodbye to all that. We could help Mom stand up, just the way we were now with Mags braced against her on one side and me on the other. Together, we made a sort of pyramid; solid as a rock.

Somewhere after landing in Philadelphia my mother found a big hotel. It was late, and I was sleepy. She paid the taxicab and brushed peanut salt off my lapels. We washed our hands, brushed our teeth, said our prayers and hopped into bed. In the morning, it seemed like a miracle to be so far from home. I had dreamed about this, waking up without Dad. No one bad here. Lauren was not incompetent. Hadn't she gotten us here?

But I couldn't stop thinking about Artie. Did he come out? Did Dad go home? Oh, Artie was correct: Dad would blow a gasket, be beside himself, want to kill us, not because he missed us or was afraid for us, but because Mom had gotten one up. She didn't feel that way, but he did. He was such a kid, a bullying kid.

I tried not to think about it and did just as Mom said to do: "Take a bath, and freshen up."

The world looked fine.

In the dining room we sat down for breakfast. With white tablecloths, pink roses, heavy silver, the room looked as elegant as the photographs in one of Mom's magazines. Mom set the table like this when she felt good. And this morning, we felt great. It was more than a new day. It was something else. Lauren Rose read the menu and then went cold. As she looked around, I sensed a problem. Mom looked nervously through her wallet, flicking through her last few coins. She looked up and appeared lost. *We can't very well beg for food.* I'd already had a sip of my orange juice, and Mags bit into a piece of buttered toast. Mom had already poured cream in her coffee. *We can't very well eat stand-by.*

"Mom," Mags said, folding her napkin and replacing it under the heavy silver, "let's just go. Let's call Nana."

"Yes," my mother said. "That's a good idea." And I felt all the glory and the high-flying of yesterday start to slip away.

Somebody, I guessed, would feed us.

"The menu," Mom whispered, "is too expensive."

Out we sailed, past the waiters in their white coats. They didn't seem to notice. Back in our room, where we had slept all together, three in a bed, we packed everything back into the oversized bag. In the elevator, no one said a word, and out in the sunlight, Mags quietly said to me, "Mom's one hundred dollars has run out."

On a grassy bank overlooking the hotel, we sat together. This didn't feel as good as sitting on the aeroplane. Running away had now gotten a little more difficult.

"Stay here, together. I'll be back soon," my mom said before she went back into the hotel to find a phone booth.

The sun baked my patent leather shoes, while Mags snapped and unsnapped her small purse. I grew sick watching cars race by. A couple of times I thought I spied a station wagon with Dad inside and momentarily looked for a place to hide, but no wagons stopped. Hunger and sadness, sitting on the side of the road, were much better, I concluded, than watching Mom get beat up.

"Guess what?" Mom asked as she made her way up the grassy embankment.

"What?" we echoed back.

"Uncle Danny and Uncle Sean are coming to pick us up!"

"Hooray," we sang out.

I said I was hungry, and my mother held her hand to her mouth. *What next?* Mags leaned in to hold her up and pulled out an extra bag of peanuts she'd stashed in her little white purse. In the middle of a tangle of highways that ran around us, north and south, like a four-leaf clover, we laughed and shared peanuts. I guessed where I might be on the school's geography map: the East Coast of the greatest nation in the world. "Freedom," my teacher had said. "Democracy. That's what we are all about." As my tummy rumbled and I imagined my father in hot pursuit of us, I attempted to square those facts, but then I heard the double toot of an irresistible horn and forgot all about it. To my outright amazement, there stood two of what seemed like the most handsome men on earth, two angels, my mother's brothers – Danny and Sean.

"Which way to Kalamazoo?" the one with the muscled-up arms said, while he leaned back into the convertible and honked the horn again twice. His infectious grin sent us all tittering. "How is the most beautiful sister in the entire solar system?"

"I'm good, Danny," Mom said.

I felt resplendent. Someone loved my mother as much as I did and was not afraid to say it, shout it, and right out loud – right there, in the middle of the entire world.

As we piled into the red Mustang, Uncle Sean picked up our luggage as if it weighed nothing at all. "What did you pack in here?" he asked.

"Everything," Mom laughed.

Snuggled next to Uncle Danny as he drove, I grinned. We were rescued, and astonishingly, like the women on the aeroplane in those neat uniforms, these good-looking men thought Lauren Rose beautiful. And I did, too. We were off to a new life. Eating, I could do later. And Mags had her peanuts, so she, too, could wait.

Mags held Mom's hand, Uncle Danny fiddled with the radio and we all sang along – something I never heard a real man do – in tune even. He crooned, like off *The Ed Sullivan Show*. We belted out 'Downtown', 'Stop! In the Name of Love' and then 'Ticket to Ride'. Sean chimed in, and even Mags lightened up, tickling Mom.

We made music all the way to Lower Darby, which the Wicked Witch had convinced me was a war zone or at least a garbage dump, but it wasn't. It was a neat little neighbourhood, where the houses all lined up in single file without a front lawn in sight. Steps, stairs, porches and trellises with red roses repeated themselves from one house to the next. My mother put an arm around Mags and blinked back the fact that she wanted to cry. Nana appeared in her apron on the front steps, while Uncle Danny beeped at two girls in checked school uniforms. They waved back, which caused Uncle Sean to blow kisses.

"Mom," I said that night as she tucked me in, "let's never go back."

"Okay," she said, "I'll do the very best I can."

She turned out the light and stood as she usually did, just for a few seconds, in the doorway, lit by the glow beyond, with the murmur of voices coming from downstairs. She was one of the gang here, not a sad woman, and I liked that.

"Night, night," she said, "don't let the bed bugs bite."

And for that night, not a one did.

TWENTY

"Well, what are you going to do?" Anna Ryan asked her daughter, as she stood by her, pouring coffee from the pot she held in one hand while at the same time tucking a stray curl behind my mother's ear with the other.

"I'll get a job," my mother said.

"That's good. You and your girls can live in this house for as long as you want. I'm happy you're here. Let's get Artie too as fast as we can. I can make room. Might be a squash and a squeeze, but we can make do." My grandmother wiped marmalade from the vinyl tablecloth, and under my cup. "I will help you – all of you."

"Thank you."

"No need. That's what family is for."

My mother didn't say a word as Nana kissed the top of her head.

"It is not her fault," I said. "Dad beats her up, tells her to stop drinking, then sets her up. Gives her a drink," but before I could finish, my mother's hand flew up and over my mouth.

"Lil'," she said, "did anyone ever tell you, you talk too much?"

She kissed me on the side of the head, and Nana took a deep breath.

"Okay," Nana said again, "we will make this work. Might have to pinch and crowd, but together we can all work this out."

That evening my mother bought, with what I don't know, two geraniums for Nana, one pink and one white, in twin clay pots. Nana, of course, was moved to tears.

"They're just small ones," my mother said to hers, "I love you."

As my mother presented the flowers, she told everyone the good news. A friend she'd met in Rhode Island (*Did we remember Julian Hervey, whom we met at the hospital on Family Day?*) had practically an empty mansion in Stone Harbor, New Jersey. We could use it. He would give us the maid's quarters, an apartment below the main house, which included two bedrooms and a large bathroom. Lauren Rose told Nana and Granddad that the apartment would be good enough, would allow us a fresh start while she got some money together.

I remembered Julian, the man with the long hair and goatee. Dad thought he was a loser.

In exchange for the apartment, Lauren Rose reported she would help Julian Hervey out. She would be a secretary, an administrative assistant, which I assumed was as good as an American Airlines stewardess any old day.

Our new place, she reported, was just a short walk from the beach, and yes, we could go there every day. She even semi-promised a small dog to replace Scout, whom I imagined was still in Virginia barking his head off like the day we left. Artie, I was certain on second thought, whatever else, would be taking care of Scout, running him through his drills – sit, stay, down, speak, follow me – giving him fresh water every day. But the truth was we still had no idea because Granddad said Dad put out an all-points alert, a missing persons bulletin, on us, which meant the police knew we'd run away, even though Granddad called Dad to say we were okay and gave him our new address. My father wouldn't give us any information about Artie, where he was or whether or not he was okay, because he said there was a danger of Lauren Rose kidnapping him.

Mags told me to face facts. Dad was gathering evidence.

"Of what?" I asked, watching my sister brush her jet-black hair. Meticulously, it parted and she snapped in the tortoiseshell barrette. Her beauty shone when she smiled and said nice things, which wasn't often because she felt she had to think for all of us, because to her everyone else was a moron.

"Lily," she said, brushing my hair back from my face and into a ponytail, "sometimes you are too stupid. Don't you know who this new boss is? The guy who owns the mansion, Mr Hervey?"

"That friend of Mom's we met at Family Day?"

"Exactly, the guy whose arms came down to his knees. The one who didn't really say anything, except: *Yep, yep, yep sir, yep siree.* The nutcase. Beatnik. No wife, no kids. A guy with arms like that is born sick. Deranged. Cuckoo. Dad said he was going to give Mom enough rope to hang herself. Well, little sister, she just did."

"Shut up!"

Mags didn't like the new start, but I did.

Uncle Sean and Uncle Danny moved us in this time, and afterwards we grilled hot dogs and marshmallows on the beach. We sang songs around the fire and didn't go to bed until long after the stars came out. I loved our new home, even if I wasn't speaking to Mags. I blamed what she'd said on that cloud she always walked under, the burden of being the firstborn, all her thinking, of not always getting her own way, or maybe of just not being pretty enough. Wasn't it a relief to her that somebody, anybody, was helping us out? *Enough rope…* why did she always have to look at things that defeatist way?

While the flames scorched my marshmallow, I loved studying my mother by firelight. I liked the sound of the sea and the night wind, the stars in the sky. They were lovely. Nana had asked Lauren

Rose if she would be getting a divorce, which, for Catholics, was really bad news. Hell would beckon as a result.

"Maybe," Mom said, "or just get a separation, perhaps." She had smiled hopefully. "Jack will come to his senses one day."

This rocked Nana and Granddad, but they both took their daughter in their arms, and merely said, "We want, as we always have, only the best for you. The best for all of you."

"I know," Lauren Rose said as we all stood on the front porch of that house in Lower Darby. We left with hope, high singing hope, which is where I took after my mother: I always had hope.

My optimism wobbled when I met Julian. Mags was right. Those arms – how could I have forgotten? Whether he was standing up or sitting down, they almost dragged on the ground. Upstairs, in the weatherworn summerhouse, we said hello to him. The house seemed to groan with furniture from another time and place, when the boardwalk was busy and ladies used parasols to protect themselves from the sun. Glass chandeliers sparkled, and the scent of furniture polish masked the perfume of the sea. A table was set and cleared by a woman in a pink uniform. Eyeing us with suspicion, Julian waved her out as if he were God himself. He directed us, too, motioning us to follow. His eyes seemed permanently popped out of his head, and he spoke in a long, languorous way. A strong smell of paint both excited and concerned me, and fear took me by surprise as we rounded the top of the stairs and found his art studio. Lauren Rose took my hand.

"Beautiful," she said, "Julian, they're lovely."

"But they're all black," I cried, before my mother slid a hand over my mouth.

"Death and dying," Julian rattled on, "the depth of black... Brushes are for fools." He waved his hand. "I prefer aerosol. Pure, modern magic."

Mags and I couldn't get downstairs and out of the house fast enough.

119

"Cuckoo bird!" Mags whistled. "Worse than Dad."

I didn't know what to think. I just worried who would protect my mother when I went to school.

Just a few blocks from Julian's mansion, where we lived in the basement, stood my new school, a smart little red schoolhouse. My new class was mixed, third and fourth grade, which I loved, and just when I thought things couldn't get any better – I didn't have to see Julian or his work, and Mom was a real secretary, typing letters and speaking with galleries, food was in the fridge and on the table, stories were shared at night and seashells decorated the windowsill – Lauren Rose said I could bring three friends home from school for fig bars, hot cocoa and macramé. This was an absolute first, or at least something we hadn't done since who knows when.

I skipped for joy on the afternoon I brought my new friends home. *No running, keep my head down and don't go to the bathroom too much.* I took it all in – the gulls, the ocean, the blue-grey sand, my sister Mags, who still would not smile, and of course my new, three, best friends. Our little summer town, Stone Harbor, in the off-season. *Lovely.* Our mailbox, at the end of the drive, Mom painted with a heart so we wouldn't get lost. *This is our house.* She typed upstairs and got home at three o'clock sharp when she served us, piping hot, a mug of Campbell's tomato soup or New England clam chowder just to warm us up.

The only thing missing was Artie. But Mom said she would work that out. Sooner or later we would all be back together.

Even before I turned the corner that afternoon, I sensed danger. I wanted to throw my arm out, stop my friends, run the scene in reverse, but they were in a dead run now for Mom's pastries. *Why did I talk so much?* I instantly knew what Mags meant – that short rope, the guy with the long arms, false hope. I got it. I was unable to halt my friends. They sailed past the wonderful red heart on the mailbox at the end of the drive. *What was I thinking?* They giggled and jiggled each other, racing to the basement door and inside, the way I did at their homes, leaving the bell tinkling.

"Children," said a gruesome-looking woman, forcing a smile at them. (*Is this my mother?*) "I apologise but you must go home. We can do this another day."

They didn't have to be told twice. As they quickly left, Mags walked in. "Mom," she practically shouted, "what happened to you?"

Her eyes were bloodshot, and her face blackened. "I jammed the nozzle," she said, "on a can of spray paint."

We didn't believe her.

"Julian painted on you," I said, and our eyes met.

"Yes," she said, "that is correct."

Mags helped me off with my backpack and jacket, and then in the tiny bathroom, off the kitchen, we went to work helping our mother dissolve the thick layer of paint that covered her face from hairline to chin and ear to ear. Using nail polish remover, then turpentine, we delicately worked across her face. Then I made macaroni and cheese from directions straight off the box. *What is it that a secretary actually does?*

"Mom," Mags cautioned as she scrubbed the last bit of paint from Mom's face, "I think we need our own home."

Mom found a new place right away, not far from school. Even more surprising, a letter from Dad arrived saying he would pay the rent and send our things. Relieved, we compiled a wish list of the things we wanted most – my Barbie & Ken Dream House, Nancy Drew books, everything really, but first and foremost Artie and Scout.

We stayed in Julian Hervey's old house until the day the moving van arrived. Mr Hervey, Mom said, would no longer be around. "On holiday in Spain," she said, which was okay by me because I knew that was way across the Atlantic, out of reach, and frankly of no consequence because it was not included in the

USA book of zip codes. Dad, I decided, had turned over a new leaf.

Moving day arrived early and bright, with a hint of dew still left on the ground. I imagined our furniture like pieces in a dollhouse. One thing here, another there. I could see it all with a bird's-eye view in our new house, which Mom called the jewel box. I lifted the roof off and even saw the garage with the tiny new car, which Mom promised to buy when the support money arrived.

"Money?" Mags looked at me incredulously. "From where?"

"Dad," I said. "Support money. Because we are his kids and that is the way it works. He loves us."

"Lily – support money? Think again. Did Dad give Mom money when she was virtually his personal slave?"

"What?"

"Where have you *been*?"

"I'm here, and you are not going to ruin everything. He is going to help us."

"Yes, Lily, that's right. He's going to help us alright."

As we waved goodbye to the creaky, old, salt-washed place and said good riddance to Mr Hervey, Mom swore she'd paint a new mailbox – this time with four hearts, one for each of us, including herself and Artie, whom we guessed might now come to visit us because we were *stabilising*.

The moving men arrived, heaving and hoisting all the cartons inside. Just for a minute, I wished I had my old bed, and that things were different, that they'd never changed, with the exception of Dad getting a grip. We yakked about our things, anything, everything – the electric can-opener, the spatula, the cake tins, the television, maybe the hi-fi and, of course, the transistor radio. I would show my friends. One by one we opened each box. Practically like Christmas morning, Mom sliced through masking tape, popping open lids and unwrapping. We plunged right in. Her old petticoat, the red one, the silly one she'd made one year for the can-can she danced with the other wives at the officers' club, came out first.

As I put it on, Mags laughed. Mom drummed on a hatbox and whistled. We hoisted our non-existent skirts, kicked up our heels and in quick succession did three even splits.

"Listen, girls," Mom said, the way she once spoke to those stewardesses on the aeroplane from Virginia to Pennsylvania, "we better stop foolin' around. There's a second truck."

"There's no second truck," Mags said, her face darkening.

"Of course there is," Mom said.

"Wait," I called out to the driver and the two men who were stacking blankets in the back of the van.

"The second load?" my mother asked them.

"There isn't one, ma'am. This is it."

As they double-checked the paper-thin inventory list, Mom continued to ask, "The furniture, the washing machine, the dryer... what about all that?"

"No, ma'am, just clothes. That's it."

Mom gave them a small tip, which at this point even I knew was extravagant of her. "Thank you." They smiled, embarrassed, and left.

We hardly knew what to say. The party was over. Mom pounded her fist on the yellow countertop in the new kitchen, the place where we had already planned our next Thanksgiving dinner – one Butterball turkey, three yams and chocolate, chocolate, chocolate. She shouted, "Damn, damn, damn!"

"Let's go for a walk," my sister said, as she dragged me out the door.

A cold spray misted the sand. Mags didn't want to walk; she wanted to talk. "Listen to me," she said, "Dad's lied about everything, support, our things. Everything. Mom doesn't get it. He's never coming round. And something else..."

"What?"

"There's someone following us."

"What?"

"Look."

At the far end of the beach a man stood smoking a cigarette. He took a slow inhale, then flipped the butt.

"You're nuts," I said.

"He's been trailing us for two weeks. Mom saw him first, then I saw him outside of school, and around the corner from the Quick Shop."

"So what?" I asked.

"So we don't have any furniture, and we don't—"

"We can use boxes," I stopped her. "We can sleep on the floor."

"No, Lil'. We can't." My sister tried to hug me, but I slipped from her embrace.

"I won't go back to him."

"You will," she said, placing her hands firmly on her hips. "And I will."

"No."

"We can't go on like this, Lil'. Mom can't. Granddad and Nana have to know. I'm calling them."

"No, Mags. Please don't," I begged her, "please give us a chance. We can earn money… we can babysit."

"Listen, Nitwit. We can't." She tried to cuddle me again.

"Don't," I said, "I hate you. I absolutely, positively hate you."

Racing down the beach as fast as I could, away from the man with the cigarette, who stepped into his car, I refused to cry. The sting of the salt spray and the crack of the surf gave me hope. With each crash I knew there must be some fresh possibility, some alternative, an option, an idea, anything rather than give up.

"The Atlantic is one of the world's seven great oceans," I shouted out, as Mags disappeared towards the new house, where we would, I guessed, sleep on the floor.

I wished Artie were with me. Where was he? We would win against Mags and her give-up attitude. How could Mom be strong if we weren't? Artie would say, "I love you," just about now, and I would say, "And me, you, too."

Sea foam scalloped in neat rows, and I recalled one summer at the shore when I let Artie's hand slip. No one ever knew. Out too far, too deep, in the grey-green water, I lost my footing with a wave bashing overhead. Sucked under, just for a second, I lost my baby brother's hand. In that moment, terrified, I knew he was gone into the bottomless, churning pit forever. Clawing through surf and rolling sand, I miraculously found him, caught him and brought him to the surface gulping and straining for breath. He coughed, laughed and smiled at me.

That was something.

That's how I felt now, except it was me going under with Mom, with no help, and then just as I was about to agree with Mags, it dawned on me: I could collect soda bottles off the beach. I could return them and make money to help us survive. I vowed then and there that I would never, ever lose my mother. No one I loved would ever be taken away from me.

Back by dark, I marvelled at my bounty. I counted twelve empty Coca-Cola bottles and four 7 Up cans, but it was too late. Uncle Danny and Uncle Sean heaved the same boxes we'd just unpacked into the back of a moving van. Mom met me, taking each bottle and can from me, lovingly wiping off the sand.

"Thank you, Lily," she said, "this will help out a lot."

She was lying. I knew that.

"We're going to Granddad and Nana's," she said, "and we will work this out. I promise."

My uncles did not sing this time. We drove in silence until one or other of them said, "Bastard."

"Careful," my mother said, putting one arm each around Mags and myself, "these are his children."

"They should know who he really is," Uncle Danny said as he hit the steering wheel and flipped the turn signal sharply.

"And who is that?" Mom said with a hint of steel.

Yes, I thought. *Push back. Fight, Mom, fight. But why are you fighting for Dad?*

"It's written all over your face," Uncle Sean added, thumping the dashboard.

"No, it's not." Mom loosened her scarf and opened her purse to find a tissue.

"You made a mistake," Sean said. "I'm sad that I can't turn this around or change anything for you. I am your brother and I love you. You and your kids deserve better." He held back his tears, but I could see he wanted to punch Dad.

"We will work this out," my mother said. "You don't understand."

"No, *you* don't understand," her brother said. "It's killing everyone, the whole family, to see you like this. And your kids."

"Jack's a soldier."

"A real officer and a gentleman," Uncle Danny sneered.

"It's complicated... he only understands combat."

"No, Lauren Rose, it's simple," Uncle Danny told her, and I believed him.

Everyone sat in silence. The rope had run out. Even when he wasn't there, my father was there, beating us all up. As for Mags, I felt I would never forgive her. I would hold her directly responsible for whatever happened next because she was a coward, a chicken, incapable of making a red petticoat into a tablecloth or a bed out of a box. It was incomprehensible to me how my sister could do nothing, how she could literally just give up. I would not give up, I vowed, not on anything – Mom, love or a cardboard box.

TWENTY-ONE

I counted to the rhythm of my mother's ragged breaths. The three of us slept in one room: Mags and I in one bed, Mom in the other. Nana put a lot of effort into accommodating us and we were grateful.

Lauren Rose ached. Her wrist and elbow hurt from the constant lifting, switching and dialling. As a temporary telephone operator on-call, she travelled into Philadelphia on the train, sometimes early before we awoke, and often she stayed late, long after we'd gone to sleep, but she never brought enough money home. I knew because Nana counted the money out then hushed her daughter, always saying, "We will work this out."

"One more mouth, two more mouths," she'd say, "what's that?"

Mags once tallied the folk around the table, and answered, "Nana, it's five. Can we feed five mouths, and one more if Artie gets here?"

"Yes," my grandmother said, "of course we can do that."

I learned to be careful and not to grab the last potato or butter more than one piece of toast. For jam, I negotiated. At Granddad and Nana's, we did not have Froot Loops, Coco Puffs or Sugar Frosted Flakes. We did not have all we could eat. However, quietly and with a bit of a twinkle in her eye, on rare occasions Nana gave us a nickel, or the odd dime, to go to the corner store, where the best deal for that price was a small carton of waxed, look-alike Coca-Cola bottles the size of my thumb, filled with red, yellow and blue sugar water. I'd bite off the top and spit it out. If we pooled our money, we could get a bit more: a Fudgsicle, an ice-cream sandwich or an orange vanilla ice-cream cone. Mags usually bought the candy necklace, which she stashed until it eventually turned to rock. However, no matter what, *cross our hearts and hope to die*, we would never tell Nana or Mom that we did not have enough.

The rail tracks on the viaduct not far from the row of small houses shook throughout the night. Most mornings, if I was up early enough, I could spy the carpet of geranium petals that had fallen like an early snow over the small back garden.

Like a second blanket, my mother's fatigue lay over me, heavy and warm. No one saw it in the daytime, just as they never saw the bit of her that I saw float up to the ceiling when her breathing came in and out in those ragged short bursts. Maybe this was what M had meant when she said Lauren Rose was *out of her head*. With each exhalation, I imagined her floating up, and with each inhalation, she would drift down. Then, momentarily, I felt relieved. *But what if, one day, she just breathed out and never came back down?* I worried and often I could not fall asleep.

Drained and hurting after her long days on the switchboard, Mom also couldn't always sleep. She'd creep out of her bed to make some of the strong Irish tea Nana sometimes made. Stealing out after her, we'd sit on the springy old couch in the front room. That's when I'd ask her a million and one questions, especially about Dad and M and Aunt Penny. They seemed set apart from other people, to be living on a separate little island lost in space. I imagined M as the Evil Queen in *Snow White*.

Lauren Rose tried to explain it to me in so many ways, saying that M had just been dealt a bad hand and like all of us was doing the best she could. She said my grandmother, for whatever reason, had a hard time saying sorry, or ever admitting to making a mistake.

Despite Mom describing M's tough start, having no mother and having to raise Dad and Aunt Penny alone, I still did not understand how a person could turn into a wicked witch. I shivered and threw my arms around my mother, making her a solemn promise.

"Mommy, I will never, ever let you go."

"Me neither," she said. "I love you."

Our new school, Sacred Heart, was Mom's old one. The nuns warned her, "Lauren Rose, you pull them out once, and that's it. They don't come back to Sacred Heart." Those were the rules. It was almost comforting.

Mom got her high-school diploma at Sacred Heart, and on the front steps before the great double doors of this old school was where her graduation photograph was taken. That portrait now stood on Nana's wooden sideboard beside the mirror where Lauren Rose set her hair each night before the next day's work. We were proud of her, Nana, Granddad and I; we loved that photograph.

On one particular night Mom didn't set her hair. Her breathing faltered. I heard it. Sometime after Mags fell asleep, Mom got up, but didn't go to make tea. On alert, I wondered if I should join her. But that night I didn't want to hear tales of love or sadness. I wanted, just like Mags, to go to sleep.

An hour later, just after the cuckoo clock in the kitchen struck eleven, Nana shook me. "Lily, Mags, please get up. I need your help. Your mother is not well."

Tiptoeing after her, over the floorboards that creaked, I cupped the banister, running the full length of the landing right into the bedroom Nana and Granddad now shared. Lauren Rose lay in one of the two twin beds under the illuminated Sacred Heart of Jesus. Granddad sat on the other bed, leaning in, cooing to his daughter, the way he once sang to me when I'd fallen and bruised my arm on a swing. It was the tone he used when he sang 'You Are My Sunshine'. Nana sat back down in her black, high-backed rocker, the one in which her three children had been nursed, rolling rosary beads between her fingers and watching over her daughter.

"Your mother said you would know what to do," Granddad said.

"I do," said Mags, putting one arm on my shoulder. "Tuck her arms in tightly with the sheets," she said, which they had already done. "And go get a spoon – not a wooden one."

A what? They looked at each other but didn't say a word.

"Press her tongue down with the spoon, but watch out because you don't want her to bite your fingers off or to swallow her own tongue, which would make her suffocate. She's going to have a fit."

Granddad went straight to the kitchen, and Nana hovered close.

"Thank you, girls," Nana said, just before my mother's eyes rolled upwards and she lost consciousness.

"Michael," my grandmother called out, "telephone the doctor! Immediately." Clearly, Nana had never seen anything like this.

They got the spoon, a large tin one. My mother thrashed and moaned. When the doctor came he asked urgent questions, then left quietly.

"Go back to bed now," Nana directed us.

Stillness fell over the house, except for the rattle of the milk train on its early-morning run. I dreamt of one white petal drifting down. Waking as the first rays of light broke against the slightly frosted glass, I climbed out of bed to make sure Mom was all right.

Nana pitched slowly forward and backward in her chair, guarding her dark-haired daughter. Granddad sat and stared at the wall. He wanted a drink and struggled against it. Lauren Rose lay quiet, her thick hair piled against the pillow. Was she dead or just asleep? Creeping toward the edge of the bed, I thought she looked like an angel.

Suddenly, Nana leaned forward, and I crept onto her lap. "Who did this to her?" she asked.

She wasn't talking to me; she knew the answer – my father, his mother, their whole family. *The criminals.* Nana sent a perfectly fine daughter out into the world, and now look, look what they'd sent back. The brokenness of Lauren Rose… Nana didn't think she could mend it and it was too much for her.

"Who did this?"

I climbed off Nana's lap, backed away from the bed. I knew who did this. I did. I did it. Looking after Mom was my responsibility, and I'd failed to do the right thing.

"That woman did this," Granddad said, "with her high and mighty ways. Jack did it, too. I wish Lauren Rose had never laid eyes on him. Between the two of them, they've crushed her. And you too, you kids, all of you Prestons."

I backed away.

Nana said, "Be still, Michael. Lily's just a child. She's not responsible for this."

Granddad's anger grew. This was more serious than divorce. He shouted obscenities about M and Dad. Would Mags and I be thrown out? We were Prestons, too. But I thought Granddad was right. I wanted to shout those same nasty things about my father and his mother. *Who was responsible for this?* Jesus held two fingers to his sternum, right over his Sacred Heart. *The way and the light.* I looked up, seeking direction. A nod, a wink, a bob of the head. Mom looked to be dead to me, her skin pale and wet. "Granddad, Nana," I wanted to say, "you are right. I'm Jack's daughter and I couldn't stop any of this."

My fault.

TWENTY-TWO

Nana served oatmeal with cinnamon, Granddad drank his coffee black and Mom slept. She wasn't going into Philadelphia today. Mags didn't know what was going on, and I didn't have the words to explain.

We walked under the viaduct to our new school. Our blue uniforms cost Mom a small fortune, but Nana helped out. My teacher, Sister Adrienne, was pretty, even when she slapped her pointer against the blackboard demanding answers to questions.

"Lily Preston," she would call out, "your turn." Then she would smile as if her show of authority was all a bit of a game anyway. This morning I wanted to arrive early. I hoped to carry Sister Adrienne's satchel from the ornate door at the back of the convent, across the playground and into the classroom. Heavy with books as it was, I jockeyed for the honour. Sister Adrienne stuck to one simple rule: whoever caught her eye first was chosen.

Mags had dawdled, brushed her teeth, combed her hair and rearranged her book bag this morning, but I couldn't go without her. Mom routinely warned us to stick together. "Do not be separated, no matter what. Go everywhere together, never alone. Come straight back home."

Something waited out there, large, looming and menacing. I knew what threatened: Dad.

"Hurry up," I called out to Mags. "I don't want to be late."

"Why?" she whined. "Want to hold Sister Adrienne's book bag?"

"I do."

"Why?" Mags asked as we approached the first of three intersections before the viaduct. "You guys look like puppies squirming at the teat."

"I just want to carry her bag," I answered.

"No, you want to be her favourite."

"What's wrong with that?"

Just as we passed under the bridge, I froze. Mags stopped dead in her tracks.

"No," she said for the both of us.

Dad appeared like a ghost. With grey skin, dark circles under his eyes and that right clenched fist, he give the impression he might kill somebody, anybody, one of us.

Where's Artie?

"Hi, Mags," he said. "How about a kiss?"

Don't separate. Nowhere alone. Straight home.

Ambushed. Who would have expected him to appear on a boring, anyday morning, while we were walking to school, thinking about nothing more than carrying Sister Adrienne's satchel? Had the detective given him our timetable, the morning route to school?

My father stood before us like a phantom in full uniform. He didn't look real, and I told myself he wasn't. He looked rough, like when he'd driven the car far too long. He looked like himself and then not quite at all. His uniform hung from his shoulders more like a coat on a rack. He coughed.

Isn't Philadelphia far enough away? Will any place be far enough away?

133

Mags didn't move an inch, but I could sense her calculating. *Will she give up, give in?* Exhaust billowed in a long plume from the back of the station wagon.

Run, Mags, run.

Behind my father, horns began to honk. The idling Rambler created a roadblock. *How can I escape? Will Mags come too? Can she keep up?*

Dad's hands scared me. They opened and closed, just waiting to catch us. We were out of his reach, but still he blocked our path. *Should I go forward, or run back?* With one eye on us, and the other on the idling car, Dad threw his arms wide for an embrace. *Like a net.* And then, he knelt.

"Get in," my father ordered as Mags's sock slid below her knee. "Margaret," he repeated, "get in the back behind the driver's seat."

Hesitating only momentarily, my sister pulled up her sock and hopped in.

"In front," he directed me.

"No," I countered, "I'm going to school."

"I'll give you a lift," he insisted.

"You don't know where it is." Maybe I could still make it in time to carry Sister Adrienne's bag if he drove me.

"You can show me."

"Sacred Heart?" I doubted him.

"Okay." He nodded. "Yes. I know where that is."

Stay together. Do not separate. What would Mom do? I don't know. She's at home, in bed.

"In the car, Lily," my father instructed again impatiently. *Or I will beat you to death.*

He could, I knew that. Maybe he should. Weren't we responsible, for Mom… all this? Wasn't that what Granddad said? Mags stared straight ahead. I couldn't leave her. Maybe he would really take us to school, and then in the afternoon, I would see Mom again.

I could run like the wind.

He knew that. He watched the car. He already had Artie, now Mags.

He wouldn't catch me.

I looked behind me, around him and back across the street.

What would Mom do if we never came back?

The story that came into my mind was that of the woman standing before Solomon. "Who will cut the baby in half?" The real mother would not. That's what I was thinking when Dad grabbed me and shoved me into the front seat.

"Lock it!" my father commanded, as he slammed the door behind me.

"Straight ahead," I told him. "The school is straight ahead."

Now we'll need late passes.

"Okay." He shifted gear.

"Now turn," I said.

He didn't.

"Turn!" I shouted again and again. "Turn!"

Mags said nothing.

"Turn. Here!" I shouted again as we passed the corner store, where we sometimes spent a nickel each. Then we passed under the railroad bridge, the point beyond which we were not permitted to go.

"That way," I pointed. "We're going to be late."

Touching the passenger door beside me, I memorised everything in sight, every right and left turn, every street sign. As I curled my fingers around the door handle, without warning, my father's hand came flying out across my face. He reached for the handle and locked the door.

Had he intended to hit me?

I wasn't sure. My nose bled profusely, as he gave me a spotless white handkerchief. Mags said nothing, continuing to look straight ahead, almost as if she were driving the car.

"I didn't mean to do that," my father said, "I was going to lock the door. I thought you were trying to jump out."

No one said anything. I tilted my head back.

It was an accident. I sometimes for no reason got nosebleeds. Wasn't I a bleeder?

Everything stilled, except the sound of the mid-morning traffic on the outskirts of Philadelphia.

"We're going to see Artie," Dad offered, "and M. How about that?"

At a silvery phone booth, Dad told me to get out. "Call your grandmother. Nana. Tell her you're all okay."

Leaning over me, he dropped in a slender dime.

"Nana," I said.

"Lily!" She sounded shocked.

"We're with Dad."

"Stay where you are. We will come and get you."

She couldn't. It was too late. My father drew a finger across his throat. *Cut it off.*

"Hang up," he whispered.

"Nana…"

He clicked the receiver.

I never got to say: "I love you, anyway."

Looking down the road, I knew we were way out of our neighbourhood. How would I ever find Mom again? I would watch and wait. We got away once; we would do it again. Where was he taking us? Why didn't we run? Why was Mags so incapable? Why couldn't she make a bed out of a box? All of a sudden, with my mind in a spin, one question after the next, I threw up. Dad still stood by the pay phone, maybe calling M, but Mags stepped out of the car and handed me a Kleenex. I stared at the blood in my breakfast, splattered on my shoes.

Kidnapped, I realised. Why hadn't I seen the clues? Dad would not drive me to school and he would never take us back.

TWENTY-THREE

The drive to St Michael's Military Academy was not as long as I expected, but what was long and tedious was trying to take in that from now on we were no longer to speak about Mom.

"Pretend she's dead," Dad instructed us.

"She's not dead," I retorted.

"In our hearts, she is," he said, lighting up a cigarette.

Not in my *heart.*

"I need evidence so I can divorce her. Anything you can say to help the case. You know she drinks. She's an alcoholic," he reminded us. "Been in and out of the loony bin."

I didn't say anything.

What did *Artie look like now?* I wondered.

A double gate, adorned with wrought-iron eagles, trumpets and a spiralling St Michael, opened slowly. A redheaded cadet saluted my uniformed father and motioned us through. My father returned the salute with two fingers to the side of his head.

"This is it, kids, this is where your brother goes to school."

Sequential drum rolls played off in the distance as a marching band warmed up. My father seemed pleased. This was his version of heaven. He had that look, that smile he always had, after passing through a guarded gate or saluting a sentry. He was on the inside now. He understood how things worked here. I had only to glance at him sideways to be sure of that. He was whistling 'Dixie'.

"What do you think, Lil'?"

"Fine," I replied, "but I'm not going here."

"You can't," my father said, "this is an all boys' school."

Good, I thought, *because first chance I get I am going back to Philadelphia to find Mom. Even if I have to walk in my bare feet, even if Mags won't come and I have to go alone. Mom is my home. You and M will never ever be my home and I am not going on the rack for your benefit. You will not hurt me the way you hurt Mom. I am a lot stronger than that.*

I just wanted to see Artie.

Someone barked, "About face, right, left."

I wouldn't attend this place even if I already knew all the rules. *Right, left, right, left.*

"At half-time," my father said, "Artie is going to do his drills. He'll be right behind the cadet carrying the flag."

Another cadet, happy with himself, called out to my father: "Good morning, Major." He took the keys to the car, and we got out.

In the entrance hall, one green uniform after the next went in one door or out another.

I'll still recognise Artie, won't I?

I took Mags's hand and she let me. It was like sitting on the bus when I felt sick and she knew it.

How could you ever escape from a place like this? My mother could never break in. Nobody would give her a pass, let her through just for being pretty or Irish. What if Mags vanished through one of these doors? I was not sure she would help me get back to Mom, but I didn't want to lose her anyway.

Mags polished the tips of her shoes against the back of her

calves. She seemed to study the floor. Boys stopped to look at her. Now she was more than just a little girl.

"Artie will be waiting for you in the library on the second floor," my father said.

"Yes," a man in uniform confirmed. "Out this door, turn right at the top of the stairs. Quietly, please. These are study halls."

We took the wide, granite steps two at a time, our breath hanging in the cold air. We burst through the thick double doors and skidded to a stop.

"Artie…" I could barely say it.

Mags hung back.

My brother turned to face us from the window seat where he was waiting. He must have been watching us, too.

"Hi," he said, as he stood up and adjusted the hem of his jacket. "Where's Mom?"

Left far, far behind. But I am going to go back for her. You can help me, I thought.

I looked around the room. The doors to the library were closed. A great hush fell over the three of us, until I broke it.

"She's not dead. Dad wants us to say that…"

Artie nodded. "I know."

"She's in Philadelphia with Nana and Granddad."

She's okay.

I hugged him.

I'm sorry.

Artie started crying first. We both sobbed, but Mags went across the room, sat down and snapped her purse open and closed.

I rested my chin in the hollow of my brother's shoulder. Facing me was a floor-to-ceiling painting of Archangel Michael. He fluttered down from heaven, spear in hand, driving it mercilessly into the back of another winged creature, which I guessed was dead.

Artie was now taller than me. He stepped back and stopped crying, pulled himself together, angled his chest.

Who could miss the resemblance to Dad?

"I've got my own horse here," he said in order to stop his unmanly crying. "I drill her with a team. The Black Guards, we're called."

He wore a strip of gold braid on one shoulder. He was on the third-grade drill team. His hair lifted in a cowlick in front, the way Mom always combed it. He had expected her to show up, I knew that. After a while, a familiar twitch pulled at the corners of his mouth. He smiled. I was relieved. I loved him, and I knew he loved me, even if he had refused to come out of the garage when Mom was taking us away. Seemingly he'd got the better end of the stick. He didn't know a thing about Stone Harbor, or Mom being a secretary, or us trying to make beds out of boxes. He didn't know anything about using a spoon as a tongue depressor or what Mom looked like that last night, blinded and thrashing.

"He kidnapped us," I said. "Dad hit me because he thought I was going to jump out of the car."

"Were you?" my brother asked.

"Yes."

Mags sat calmly in an oversized chair with floral covers, studying the morning sun filtering through the leaded glass. She had her legs crossed at the ankles and twisted to one side. She wasn't laughing. She wasn't crying. I wondered if she was really there at all. We grew quiet, careful. She was waiting. It seemed she could evaporate at any moment, disperse like the dust at the tops of the windows.

"Okay," Artie said, "come on, Mags. Let's go. We have a game to watch."

"Yeah," she said, clasping her purse, "I forgot."

After the football game, my brother changed his clothes and we ate Thanksgiving dinner on the road. This was the good thing about Dad always being on the move: we didn't have to play by the rules. Turkey was a non-essential, as was hanging out with a mother, grandmother or any other family member for that matter, or watching TV. A straight line between A and B was the only rationale, the only way to score a kill. Take that hill. Want rice pudding? Order it. Nothing to do with Thanksgiving? Who cares? It's generic. Dessert is dessert.

No sooner had we arrived back home in Virginia than Dad broke the news.

"Ohio next," he said, "you'll love it."

The divorce would take place there. The laws were more favourable, apparently. Whatever that meant. He was still looking for evidence, anything. Something that would put her away for life. *Have her committed.*

The Big Divorce. Division. Coming soon.

"Artie will remain in military school," Dad explained to me. "You and Mags will live with M until I've bought a new house."

But what about Mom?

No one asked. We knew the refrain.

Do you want to go back there? To Lower Darby? Do you know how fast I could put all of you on the street?

On the street. What did that mean? Something awful. Something that happened to Mom.

With two suitcases between us, we boarded the westbound train.

"Stay in your compartment, stay together," my father ordered. "The porter will come and get you in Columbus, Ohio." After dispensing a sloppy kiss to the top of everyone's head, he turned to me.

"You, Lily, are in charge." I felt embarrassed when he said this. Mags was the oldest, but she seemed to be sleepwalking a little since the big kidnap. Maybe she was thinking about escaping now too. Maybe she also was making secret plans to get back to Mom.

Knowing that M and Aunt Penny and her kids would be meeting us at the other end was not the comfort to us my father expected. It was more like a death sentence, especially the prospect of living with our grandmother.

No one had shown me a map, and I was not that good in

geography, not for anything beyond the original twelve colonies anyway. We were in a *sleeper*.

Should the tracks be a straight line or a dashed one? I don't have a map. What if we have to get off? Who knows what could happen? What if the train breaks down? What if we miss our stop? I am in charge. I am in charge. I must know it all.

The porter pulled out the top bunk, and Artie jumped up. He was having the time of his life. Mags sprawled out on the bottom bed, and I chose the single seat close to the window with the metal ashtray in the armrest. I stayed on duty. How could I take care of them and plan my escape to look after Mom? Things felt more and more complicated. I felt stretched very thin.

Thirty minutes out, we'd gone through the snacks in the plaid hamper, including the soup in the thermos. From the porter, we ordered cheese and crackers, which Mags paid for, straight from her purse, with the money Dad said would be more than enough. After the snack, she put the remainder of the cash back in the secret zip in her pocket.

"The rest is for emergencies. If you want anything else, drink water from those paper cups."

Artie took it upon himself to call the porter. He did it enough times, asking again and again if the next stop was Columbus, that the porter became firm.

"You children go to sleep. Do not ring me every five minutes. I will come and get you before Columbus. The dining car is closed."

Evening turned into night, as we rushed north and west, away from autumn and into endless winter.

I imagined black trees rushing by to either side of the track, maybe a yellow leaf barely still clinging to a branch here and there, and decided the best thing to do was to tell a story.

"Do you want me to tell you a story?" I asked.

"Yes!" Artie called out.

"Okay then."

Artie spread out his blanket, slugged his pillow and then lay quietly on his side. Mags, with her purse tucked under her arm, kicked off her shoes.

"Once upon a time," I said, "there was a woman."

"Mom?" Artie asked.

"No, just a woman. Who found a garden gate, an old wooden one, covered with white roses and ivy. It swung on black hinges made long ago from forged iron. She invited all the children inside her garden. When they arrived she led the way. The path was worn in places and in other spots emerald green with moss. Ducks swam around and around in the water under the weeping willows, and two swans glided by with such majesty that the children easily followed them into the stream's soft current, where they played. Rain fell at the same time as the sun shone, and young boys played bicycle polo under a rainbow.

"At first the children were surprised to find themselves there, but then, one by one, they each found something they truly liked – a Barbie doll, a trumpet, Tootsie Rolls, an Erector Set. The woman was plump-cheeked, smiling and hovered off the ground like a saint. She kept her arms spread wide all the time. Unknown to the children, unknown to anyone but a very few, she had a classified mission – to watch over these children so that no harm would ever, ever come to them – and she was brilliant at it.

"She never failed. She was perfect. If it was too hot, she cooled things with a mere ruffle of her long sleeve; and if it got too cold, she hugged then all in her sheltering arms. If they needed anything, she used her wand, and there it was – right in front of them. Anything. Anything at all. Flowers sprung up at her feet. And her voice was like a song…

"Artie?" I whispered. "Mags?"

No answer.

I listened to them breathe. I mounted guard, occasionally looking out the window into the night.

At last the gloved hand of the porter rattled the door.

"Columbus!" he shouted, banging once. A whistle blew, and the train shuddered, squealed and stopped.

I took a deep breath. I'd been awake all night. And I wondered, as I stepped off the train to meet M, who and in what circumstances would tell me a story.

TWENTY-FOUR

"How was your trip?" M asked.

"Fine," I said, piping up for us all.

"Fine, what?" she responded.

"The trip was fine," I repeated.

"Lily, do I have a name?"

"Yes... Yes, M."

"There, now that's not so bad, so difficult, is it? Try to act like a lady, someone with a modicum of breeding at least, like Aunt Penny. So, let's try that again. How was your trip, Lily?"

"Fine, M," I said.

"That's better. Now into the car with you. Your Aunt Penny and Uncle Ralph have been kind enough to bring me to meet you. We have a lot of work to do. I don't know how I will ever manage it."

"Do what, M?" I asked. I imagined moving in, rearranging furniture, cleaning, planting a garden. Real work.

"Turn a pig's ear into a silk purse."

"Why would you do that?" I asked. How did the ear hang? From a shoulder strap or did it have a neat chain-link handle?

"Lily," M said, "speak only when you are spoken to."

"Yes."

"Yes, what?"

"Yes, M."

"How can I turn a pig's ear into a silk purse? Look at you, listen to you – not even the rudiments! And you're old enough to know better. All of you."

In the wide back seat of the Buick, we sat close together. I sighed in our secret language. I wished we were in Uncle Danny's Mustang again, with the top down, singing 'Downtown'. I wanted to be there with Mom. Mags and Artie pressed in on either side of me. Boy, did I have a big job to do before I could even think of finding Mom. How would I ever escape now? I would have to learn geography for a start.

Well, at least we're all together for now, I thought, squeezing Mags's and Artie's hands at the same time – secretly.

"Did someone say something?" M asked, without turning around.

"No, M," we answered obediently.

"Good. Then here we are. We have a lot of work to do. It will be better if we understand each other from the start."

M's apartment looked as if no one lived there. Not one thing was out of place. The first and primary rule was not to touch anything. The second was: M was always right. There should never be any discussion. The third, and unspoken, rule was that Lauren Rose had been a mistake, and therefore we were also. We would just have to remember and accept that.

M said the job of setting us straight was too big for her; there was too much to make up for. It seemed she never stopped talking: "Don't wash your food down," she told all of us. "Don't swing your hips," directed specifically at Mags. I watched carefully. How could I walk without moving my hips? My sister, M said, was in danger of becoming a *common streetwalker*, which posed another question: If I did not want to become a common streetwalker, how did I become an *uncommon* streetwalker? After all, I did have to walk down the street. Even M, on occasion, had to do that.

I, on the other hand, was a *guttersnipe*. What was that? I envisioned a sort of silverfish, something that might call for an exterminator. I was also a *gold digger*, like Mom had been, according to M. How Mom was a gold digger, I didn't know. I guessed. I saw Mom in her can-can dress in France, when she and her friends dressed up for the party at the officers' club. A gold digger? Was that a pop group like The Temptations or The Supremes, something I might have seen on *The Ed Sullivan Show*? In my mind, the Gold Diggers wore gold lamé. I saw Mom, dressed up, singing and crooning, she and her friends dancing with shovels cocked over their shoulders, having all the fun. M also threatened that I was, like Mom, a schizophrenic, whatever that was.

I missed Mom, I wanted to go home, be where she was, and knew the day would come. Mags didn't want to talk about it, wouldn't even think of looking at a map.

"We are where we are, Lily. Grow up."

"No," I said, "I will never give up."

The good news arrived almost as soon as we did. My father and M had found a house. We would move in very soon. The divorce was almost finalised, or so we were told. The new house was only one mile from M's apartment, and Dad's USAF base was a short distance from it as well. This made the new house perfect, or so M said.

I was told to ride my bicycle from her apartment to the new place, and to make sure to carry something in its wire-mesh basket. I chose M's typewriter. I am not sure why because it was hugely unwieldy, causing the front end of the bicycle to weave first this way and then that. I only knew this typewriter was important. The type, M pointed out, was in script. I wanted to do something important.

My grandmother planned to write a newsletter when she retired. Maybe she would write her memoirs. M loved books. You had to ask, actually beg, to take a book from her library. Leaving a book dog-eared was viewed as a sign of degeneracy. Reading, according to M, was the only legitimate pastime for a lady or a gentleman.

Carefully noting the time, 10:15, I wobbled out the driveway before getting my bearings. M had given me twenty minutes for the journey. Who knew what might happen if I did not show up on time?

Carrying a portable typewriter in a wire-mesh basket is not a great idea, even if you're trying to impress your grandmother. Balancing was difficult. I imagined the worst – an accident occurring that would inflict a dent in the carrying case, a yellow, square, mesh affair. Plus I had a mission she did not need to know about: a stop by the new library, which was not on the route she prescribed but close enough. I urgently needed information.

What if someone stole the typewriter while I was inside? What if they stole it, she recovered it and the police discovered the thief had taken it from outside the public library? What if my grandmother asked me what the typewriter was doing there? What if she asked me what I was doing there? 10:20.

I parked the bike outside the yellow-brick building, next to a cedar in a dry patch of earth. I hoped the spreading branches would hide the typewriter because I wasn't going to carry it inside. I left it, walked around the corner, then quickly went back. Well, I'd rather carry it in than have to explain how I lost it. Two signs directed me: the children's section was left, adult section to the right. I went left.

No one seemed to notice my miniature suitcase. So far, so good. Setting the typewriter on the ground beside the wooden card catalogue, I thumbed through S to *Sk. Ski. Skit. Skitso. Skitzof.* No, nothing I recognised. I would have to ask the librarian, so, picking up the typewriter case, I went to the front desk. Behind it stood a tall, lanky woman, working industriously on cutting something out from a folded stack of newspapers.

A snowflake. She looked up and over her glasses, then down a very long nose at me.

"Yes?" she asked.

I loved librarians. They never once confounded me. They just gave me what I needed – information.

"I'm having trouble finding something in the subject file," I told her.

"The subject?"

"Skitzo."

"Schizophrenia?"

"Yes," I said happily. I hadn't got it quite right, but I recognised this as the right word.

She recoiled ever so slightly. Looking down at her snowflake, she told me, "You need the adult section for that."

The adult section? My heart raced. Could I even reach the card file there? As if I used the adult section all the time, I said, "Thank you," and turned to go. I hesitated, feeling time ticking by. I turned around. "Would you mind giving me the correct spelling, just in case?"

She wrote it calmly, legibly. S-C-H-I-Z-O-P-H-R-E-N-I-A.

10:25. What did it mean when they said my mother had schizophrenia, or that she was a schizophrenic?

From observation, I thought it meant someone who was in the deepest, darkest pain you could feel, someone with a broken heart, someone who only felt free when her husband was not around. I knew this was meant to be my mother's problem, according to my father, but sometimes my grandmother would call *me* the same thing.

"You're a schizophrenic," she'd say, "just like your mother." She never said it when anyone else was around, though. The first time she labelled me this way it took me by surprise. I put my hand before my chest, to protect myself. She was going for my heart, I

149

knew, and I didn't want her to break it. She said it in a dangerous way, and I knew that I needed to be very careful from then on or she would do to me just what she had done to my mother.

10:27. I had to fly. But when would I have another golden opportunity like this to get information I could trust? My grandmother hardly let us out of her sight. *Sc. Sch. Schizo* – bingo! Books. Magazines. *The Journal of the American Medical Association*, page 26. The magazine was in a box. This was really adult stuff. My heart ached.

I was about to find out what my mother was. I spread it out on the table like manna, keeping my grandmother's typewriter between my feet. My God, the words were all as long as my arm, thirteen letters and multiple syllables, but on the left-facing page was a brilliant scene of clouds and sheep, and fields and sky. I forced myself to read the one-page, two-column article from beginning to end. I just barely got the gist of it.

Two people, two in one, seeing two ways. Look at the picture. Focus solely on the clouds and the scene is just the passing sky. Look again, just at the sheep this time... well, it was a pasture. Look again – and see a farmer's face.

So, schizophrenia involves being two things in one, I surmised. What a gift. 10:34. I slammed down the magazine, and apologised to the librarian behind the adult section information desk for not being able to put it away. Two in one. I put the typewriter case back into the mesh basket and hopped on the bicycle, riding for dear life. I should make it just in the nick of time. God knows what could happen if I got there late.

I turned into the driveway of the new home. No one noticed I was behind schedule. The moving van had arrived. Every which way I turned I could see things in different ways. Intentionally. The next time my father or grandmother called my mother a 'schizo', I would smile because I knew the truth. I had the gift – perhaps my mother had it, too – the power to change things: dark into light, hate into love, bad into good.

After all, if I could see fluffy white sheep in the fields, looking at things one way, then pure white clouds in a pale blue sky, looking at them another, what couldn't I do?

Schizophrenia. It was simply approaching things in a different light. I couldn't believe anyone would hold my mother to task for that.

TWENTY-FIVE

"Court," my father said. "We're going to court today, and only Margaret will speak because she's the eldest."

We already knew that because Dad had rehearsed us, especially Mags, for a week, while discussing with M if it would really be to his advantage to put his eldest child on the witness stand. *Remember, you do not love your mother; you want to stay with your father.* Could she get it right?

Mags looked down at her toast, buttering it M's way: held still on the side of the plate, cut neatly in half and smeared with a dab taken from the butter dish, not with her own knife but with the butter knife.

My sister would not look up.

"So," my father said, "what are you going to say?"

She buttered the toast.

"Look at me," he demanded.

"Yes, sir," Mags answered.

"You will tell the truth," M said. "You will tell the judge that you want to stay with your father. Now, that's it. All of you, go brush your teeth. Use the toilet. It might be a long day."

Mags and I stood side by side at the double sink in the bathroom, spitting and rinsing at the same time.

"You can't say you want to stay with Dad if you don't want to," I told her.

"I have to."

"You don't. This is your chance to tell the judge the truth. You have to do it, for all of us. Tell him everything. This is it, Mags. This is how we can get back to Mom."

"Lil'." She said it the way she used to back in Virginia, and I thought for a second she was going to hug me, but she didn't. Instead she pushed past me to the towel rack and wiped her mouth. "Grow up. This is not about the truth. Now get in the car and shut up."

"I won't, and if anyone asks me, I will tell them the truth."

"Don't worry. No one will."

At the courthouse, a tall, solemn building of white granite, Mags went one way, and Artie and I went another.

A dark-haired woman, with bright lipstick, closed the door behind us in what we took to be a playroom. We were free to take any of the toys out of the box or any of the books off the shelves; this included, she pointed out, a set of wooden, multi-coloured blocks stacked in the corner. There were metal chairs meant for adults and a ring of children's chairs arranged as they might be for reading hour in any primary-school classroom.

"Do you love your mother?" the woman asked us, unexpectedly.

I stopped in my tracks, putting *Anne of Green Gables* back on the shelf. Artie got his semi-panicked look and stopped rummaging in the toy box.

"Yes," I said, "I love my mother—"

"More than this much!" Artie stretched his arms out wide. Was this our chance?

"Would you like to see her?" she added.

"Yes, yes, yes," we answered, and turned expectantly to the door.

It opened, and there stood Mom. Smiling. The only one who could do it just like that.

"Mommy!" Artie ran to her and threw his arms around her waist. I stood there, with my mind racing, sorting through a hundred questions I needed to ask. The strange woman disappeared.

"Juicy Fruit?" Mom asked.

"Juicy Fruit!" we shouted.

She managed to hold each of us, together yet separately, crooked in one elbow, draped across her knee or over her lap. I mostly leaned into her side, kissing her quickly on her left cheek. Artie could not stop talking because he had not seen her in a long time, since he would not come out of the garage, since we went on our American Airlines flight. She unwrapped the Juicy Fruit for us, and for one minute, I thought this meant I would go home.

Mom lifted his chin, and I gave them some space.

"You are a big boy now, a little man," she said, turning her son around to face her. "Just look at you."

Artie was full of pride.

Our reflections whirled around us in the mirrored walls. This was the start of something good. I could sense it, from the top of my head to the tips of my toes. We might all go home. I never, ever wanted to let Mom go.

The stranger in the bright lipstick came back in and asked Artie if he wanted some juice.

"No," he answered, and watched balefully as she signalled my mother to go.

"Look, kids," Mom bent down to say, "I will see you again as soon as I can – I promise. I will come back." She was certain of that, and we were, too. I sat there in heaven. I wouldn't need a plan, a bus ticket or a map.

The woman poured two plastic cups of Hawaiian Punch and handed each one of us two cream-filled Oreos.

We met Dad, M and Mags at the car in front of the courthouse. Something *was wrong.*

"What did you say?" I whispered to Mags. Maybe my sister didn't say the right thing: "I do not love my mother, I want to live with my dad." Maybe, after all, she said, "No, I love them both, and I don't know what to do." Or, "I do not love my dad, I want to go with my mother." Maybe that was why Mom just appeared like a fairy. Maybe we really were just going home, to our own house, somewhere.

"What did you say?" I whispered.

She gave me the shut-up look and pushed me into the back seat of the car.

"Well, Lily," my father said after an interminably long silence, "I hope you're proud of yourself." He spoke while he drove, never taking his eyes off the road. He could have looked at me in the mirror but from his tone it seemed he couldn't bear to.

"Not now, Jack," M said, folding one gloved hand over the other. "Wait until we get home."

I looked at Mags, who would not look back at me. Artie shrugged and pressed his hip into mine, a kinder way of saying, "Not now, Lily. Shut up." I didn't get it. Didn't anyone want to talk about Mom, how great she looked, how she just showed up, how everything was going to be alright and how most probably we were going to go straight home to Lower Darby? Didn't anyone notice how wonderful she smelled, of Chanel No. 5, and did anyone know that when she got to the train station in Philly she was going to buy Nana some pink geraniums?

"Dinner is served," my grandmother announced after we'd been back from the courthouse for a while.

I did not want to sit down with them. I did not want to eat for a week.

"So," my father said, picking up where he left off, "you kissed your mother?"

155

"Yes, sir," I answered.

"May I ask why?" He cut the dark end from the wet meatloaf.

"The cat has your tongue?" my grandmother added, ladling peas onto her plate.

"No, M," I answered.

"So what was the point," my father asked, "of allowing your brother to climb all over her lap? Didn't you notice the mirrors all over the goddamned place? Who do you think was on the other side? I was, your grandmother, the judge. All of us. We saw everything."

"Dad, I—"

"Don't Dad me!"

What could I say?

"So," he asked again, "what were you thinking?"

"I wasn't thinking, sir."

"Damned right," he said. "You weren't thinking. You almost blew the divorce. They thought you loved your mother. Do you want to go live with her? Well, be careful or that is just where you will end up." He chewed for a while, and then asked me again in a tone of total disbelief, as if it were impossible: "Do you *really* love your mother?"

I do, sir, I said only to myself, looking at my brother, at Mags. We were trapped. Everyone looked down. Mags chose Dad. I chose Mom. Artie was too young to count. The judge was going to have to weigh things in the balance. Make Solomon's decision.

TWENTY-SIX

We'd heard that Mom would come visit us. M and Dad were surprised. Seemingly they had not moved far enough away. My mother had managed the train fare to Ohio. How long had it been since we had seen her? I drummed my fingers into my left palm. One… two… three… It was a dangerous business, thinking about this.

"Six months," I said out loud, "since we've seen Mom."

"What?" my grandmother asked.

"Nothing." I caught myself.

"Nothing, what?"

"Nothing, M."

"Well, then, stop sighing. I heard you all the way over here. Is that what you intend to wear?"

"Yes, M."

"No, I suggest the herringbone instead. Go and change. Your mother is already late. And remember: no kissing, no hugging. I will be in the other room, listening."

The bell on the front door jangled.

"The children are in the sunroom," I heard her announce, without so much as a hello to my mother. "A cab will pick you up in exactly one hour."

"Thank you, M," my mother said.

I had that burning feeling at the top of my chest. How was I going to tell Mom everything I needed to say in an hour, with M listening from the other room? It was imperative that I make no mistakes. After all, I had – my father said – almost blown the divorce.

"Hi, kids," Mom said, waiting for Mags and me to rush in.

We froze. M settled into her armchair in the next room with a book she had no intention of reading.

"Kids," my mother said again. "Look, Juicy Fruit."

How could I tell her? Only common people, M said, chewed gum. Prestons did not.

"No, thanks," I said, in a way that I hoped Mom would understand meant that the Nasty Sorceress in the next room would kill me if I took some. I signalled with my eyes. I wanted my mother to hold me. I ached to be brave enough to tell the Wicked Witch that we didn't care if her whole family hated her and she had a bad start in life, made even worse decisions and had a hump back from a skating accident. I loved my mother and I longed to squeeze her; jump back in that cab with her and go all the way home to Philadelphia, to see Nana and Granddad, Sean and Danny too.

Mags froze and I felt sorry for her because she'd told the judge the wrong thing. I could see M's foot tapping, just so I could notice it, like a warning, and I don't know what made me do it, but instead of being afraid I bounded across the room anyway, snapping up the piece of Juicy Fruit, and planted a big wet kiss on my mother's lips.

"Will you make me a double braid?" I asked loud enough for M to hear, and my mother sighed with relief. We chattered away about nothing, even if I knew she wanted to know about Artie.

Was he okay? Where was he? I managed to say he was back at military school and had a horse, but then M harrumphed in the next room as she noisily unwrapped one of her sour, eucalyptus throat lozenges. I couldn't say anything, plan my escape with Mom, time just ran out. Taking a risk, like in a Nancy Drew novel, I managed to ask her softly, "Can we go home with you?"

"Not today," she murmured back, "but soon, I hope." Then she called out to Mags who stood, weeping, across the room. I didn't feel sorry for her, but Mom did.

"Come here," Mom said, but Mags just shook her head.

"I'm okay here."

I sensed that Mags might break. I understood why she wanted our mother to go away. Since the divorce had been settled, there was order in our lives. There was never a sound at night, we could sleep straight through, and then there was breakfast with multi-vitamins, and M gave us celery because that, she said, was what they gave children institutionalised with poor mental health. Given our mother's medical problems, we'd also been tested for diabetes, an early sign of alcoholism, or so M had read.

"Lily," my mother said, "save this piece of Juicy Fruit for Mags. She might want it later."

I knew M would throw it in the trash so I nodded and then slipped it up my sleeve. I would save it for later. I didn't want this minute to end. I did not want my mother to walk out that door again without us. Who was I without her? I was a guttersnipe and a streetwalker and a gold digger. I wanted my best friend. I didn't want to walk holding my hips straight. I wanted my Barbie doll, Scout, who Dad said he had given to the USAF K-9 unit for security patrols, and Froot Loops and Cheerios. I wanted to go home, but I couldn't say anything. *Where is home?* I just felt my throat close, and my head hurt and the tears well up. *Mommy, please don't go.*

The cab's horn startled all of us. How could it be here? An hour had gone past so quickly. I smiled as if that could hold back time, as if I had braids that might be plaited forever. Mags had ventured slightly closer to where I sat cross-legged on the floor. My mind raced. *Is Mom thinking what I'm thinking, that we could all sprint right out the door while M chokes on her eucalyptus?*

With the second toot of the horn, M came through into the living room.

"Lauren Rose," she said, "it's time for you to go."

"Okay, girls," Mom said, "walk me to the cab."

"No," M ordered, "they stay right here with me."

My mother buttoned her suit jacket and straightened her skirt. "Well, then, let's just have a big kiss and a hug here."

"Group hug," Mags said shyly, practically the only thing she did say, and I pressed in as tightly as I could.

"I'll see you again soon," our mother promised. "Tell Artie I love him. Maybe I can see him at school."

Fat chance.

M closed and double-locked the door behind Lauren Rose.

I went to the window. My mother came from the side of the house, stepped over the grass where the bright sun shone, dappling the lawn under the trees. The cab idled at the end of the drive in a cloud of its own exhaust. An unexpected rain started to fall. M said something about setting the table, but I continued to watch.

I guessed Nana had given my mother the money for that suit. Or maybe she had another job as a secretary or answering phones. She still looked like Mrs John F Kennedy although she was no longer Mrs Jack E Preston. My grandmother had clung on to that title. I wanted my mother to stop momentarily at the open door of the cab. And she did. No safety pins in that suit. She wore fine nude hose and kidskin heels. That's the last thing I remembered about her. I willed her to turn around, and she did. She lifted her hand just so, and I waved back.

"Lily," my grandmother said, "what are you doing?"

"Waving goodbye."

"Well, that is enough. Put your hand down. We don't want to

encourage her with visitation rights. You should be grateful. She won't be able to afford many trips like this."

Yes, M, I thought, *but I will.* I had made a real promise. I would never let my mother go.

TWENTY-SEVEN

"I'm going to Vietnam," my father announced.

I was actually relieved. At least he would be someplace else, away from us.

Where is Vietnam anyway?

M grew quiet.

I sensed she had seen him like this before. Heard news like this before. I was scared. The divorce was over, Mom was – as we were repeatedly told to say and to write in those school blanks reserved for a mother's occupation – 'deceased'. This was inaccurate and I liked to use words precisely. Sometimes I left the blank empty, and just said in my head, 'Mother'.

Of course, my mother was dead only in M's house. In exchange for our humouring our grandmother in this way, M gave us a leg-up at school. She knew everything: whatever we asked, she had the right answer. Our homework, including the extra credit and then some, was always done, on time if not before, and without errors. This M personally ensured.

"Remember who you are," she would say, "and volunteer

first. Extra credit is not the point – you do it as a matter of course. Remember who you are. A Preston."

She continually raised the bar higher and higher, holding up one hurdle after the next. School, church, community. I continued to jump. It was a matter of survival. Honour classes, Altar Society, Red Cross.

M polished and honed me until I shone, across every subject, and little by little would give me rewards, like going to the library. There I hatched my plans, several of them, just in case one or the other didn't work, or if Mags decided to rat on me.

First I found the maps, and plotted the geography from Columbus, Ohio, to Philadelphia, Pennsylvania. This wasn't terribly difficult, as I'd thought it might be. The train ride had confused me. I'd imagined we were many states apart. In fact, Ohio bordered right on Pennsylvania. *Sheer luck*, I thought. God was on my side. Using my ruler, I reckoned that Columbus to Philadelphia was basically a straight shot. I was getting hot.

Driving, I figured out, would take about eight hours, but whom could I get to do that? Only Mags had Nana's telephone number and she wouldn't give it to me. If I could wring it out of her, I would call Sean or Danny. I sometimes imagined that I did, and when I asked them to rescue me, they said, "Sure, Lil', let me gas up the car. Meet us at the library." We'd hit the open road and be singing 'Downtown' long before anyone could find us. But I knew that was daydreaming and I didn't need M to tell me to stop it.

My next idea was to go by Greyhound. This, the schedules told me, would take about twelve hours, give or take, but I would need money. I wasn't going to steal it, but wondered how I could earn it. I came up with an idea that M and Dad agreed was a good one. We would be paid for chores. I drew up the longest list: sixty-seven chores to do during the week from sweeping, to dishwashing, to polishing silver, to gardening, to anything really. While I wasn't devastated that we would only get three cents a chore, I was broken by the fact that M took my list and tore it in half and gave one half to Mags, who couldn't be bothered with making her own list. She said school gave her enough to do and that she should be paid for that. I ended up with one dollar a week for thirty-three chores, and Mags got the same.

At a dollar a week, who knew how long it would take me to buy a bus ticket, and despite my fantasising, even in dress shoes, I couldn't imagine anyone selling me a ticket or allowing me to board a bus without calling the police. I looked, and was, too young. So I then plotted a walking trail. It was 463 miles. I guessed it would take a month's worth of walking. I would have to cut through West Virginia, or so it seemed, and then back into Pennsylvania. I could do this. It wouldn't take too much money. I could eat at McDonald's. Take other provisions. This might be a plan. Maybe I should let Mom know I was coming.

The first sign that Dad was going to war or to Vietnam, which I learned were synonymous, was that he took to wearing green fatigues and dog tags. Mags pointed out these were not a piece of male jewellery but served a purpose that was much more grim.

"They're to identify the dead," she said, "the wounded... whatever. They put them on the body bags."

One evening, I was working on an extra-credit assignment for World History to try and please M. I thought it might end the endless litany of put-downs to which I was subjected.

You are not bright because your mother is dull. Your teeth are bad because your mother did not take care of them. Your manners are bad because your mother didn't come from the right family. She was a failure and so are you... or you will be... just like her.

I read about Ancient Greece from every source I could find. The school text was thin, just a couple of paragraphs. The junior edition of the *Encyclopedia Britannica* was hardly more informative. However, the white, leather-bound, gold-embossed adult *Encyclopedia Britannica*, with added, full-plate transparencies of the human anatomy, was sure to contain everything anyone could possibly wish to know about Ancient Greece.

It did. I loved Ancient Greece. I liked the sound of it, the strangeness of it. I liked even more the additional entries that the encyclopaedia suggested I read, like Ancient Religion, Greece. The River Styx intrigued me when I saw it on a map. I drew it beyond the Parthenon, coloured it midnight blue. Beside it, I placed a three-headed dog, meant to welcome the dead. I gave him a wagging tail. I imagined the dead crossed the River Styx before coming back in another form.

I concocted this idea because it reassured me. It gave me hope for my mother, who might even now be occupying herself with being dead for real. But according to ancient beliefs I knew we would see each other again – if not in this lifetime, then the next. While I did not know how long a lifetime might be, I put the mathematics of it all out of my head, safe in the knowledge that even if Mom came back in a different shape and size, I would recognise her. I would know her by the geraniums she would grow, the fig bars she would bake and the Chanel No. 5 she would wear. By the smell of all three, possibly. *Yes, I would know her.*

I was happy that M gave me a pass with only two spelling mistakes on the extra credit, and I started to pack my school satchel with the report on Ancient Greece and my secret get-back-to-Mom plan.

"Lily, your work is acceptable, and I might even say I appreciate your attempt to write. You do a good job, considering who your mother was."

Is.

I fiddled with the straps on my book bag, wondering what M wanted next, and then I remembered what I'd forgotten: Science.

"So where is the rest of your homework?"

"I'm so sorry, M, I forgot. May I do it tomorrow?"

"No. Now. Right now. Right here. In front of me."

"Yes, M."

I just wanted to put my head down and think about Mom. I wanted to go back to the twilight in Ancient Greece where I would meet her, recognise her whatever garb she might be in, but with M staring down at me from across the table above the thick book she pretended to read, I knew I had to get started.

Pulling the thin, mimeographed sheet with the Biology assignment from my notebook, I sat back, and read: *Write or draw your understanding of the parts of a plant; this is called botany.* Lining my coloured pencils all up in a row, in the colours of the rainbow – purples, blues, greens, yellows, oranges, reds – fanning them out into an arch, I had no idea what to do.

"Stop playing with your pencils, Lily."

"I need the encyclopaedia," I said, always a good escape tactic.

"Go and come straight back."

In the sunroom, I loitered. I didn't know which fat volume to choose. Plants. Biology. Botany.

Geraniums.

In my mind I saw Nana's back garden, recalled sitting on the stoop with Granddad, and Lauren Rose bringing home two little clay pots with tipsy geraniums from her first day of work. I remembered the small mound outside the stone house in Normandy, the window boxes, and Mom saying, "One white geranium will keep a snake away." For a minute I saw the windowsills in M's sunroom covered in pots of all sizes, with geraniums in all the colours of the rainbow. Some were old, and some were new, and like a mini snow globe someone turned M's house upside down and the petals rained down, swirled all around.

"Lily, what are you doing in there? How long does it take to get the volume marked B for Botany?"

"Sorry, M."

Sitting back at the table, I didn't see anything, even with the book open in front of me. Instead I saw everything I needed in my head. I neatly lined my paper into quarters, with the top left labelled shoot system and bottom left labelled root system. The bottom right would hold the feathery geranium roots, still clumped with dirt, fresh from the earth, and the top right the flowers, leaves and stems – fresh with the smell of lemony rose chocolatey pineapple – bowing in the wind.

M turned her pages, breathing heavily. The wall clock in the kitchen ticked noisily, but I felt safe in my thoughts, with my X-ray vision, seeing straight through every pot in the French kitchen windows where Mom used to say, "Watch out for the kerosene lanterns, children."

I drew the stem, green, straight and strong. Then the roots – primary and secondary – spreading out like a fisherman's net. I shaded over my grey roots with a light brown earth-coloured pen. The scalloped leaves I drew up and out – eight of them in all different sizes, smallest at the bottom, balanced on their petiole, firmly attached at the forking node. I sat back as M hovered over me.

"It's getting late, Lily. Let's go."

"Yes, M."

I shaded leaves, the nodes, the internodes and the petioles as fast as I could, and labelled them all with sharp, black pen. Then, throwing caution to the wind, and I knew this was dangerous, I drew a grouping of eight flowers balanced at the top of the stalk with five petals each. Four small buds I drew underneath.

Finally M sat back down, returning to her endless book.

I took my brightest red pencil and coloured carefully every flower and every bud, then deeply outlined them with my fine-point black biro. I managed to shade the full image and create a sort of see-through clay pot. I imagined it in Mom's hand, and her walking back to the garden shelf to collect her gloves and a small trowel.

"Lily," my grandmother said sharply, waking me up, "that's enough." She closed her book. "Could you not have thought of anything else?"

I put the cap on the black pen.

"It's a geranium," I said with a sense of triumph, bringing Mom back to life once again.

"I know what it is." She sighed.

I smiled.

"Common."

"Look at this," my father said proudly, tossing a sheet of paper in front of me on top of my homework a few weeks later. It was the black-and-white image of a devil's head with horns emerging from a dust funnel. "That's for the patch on our uniforms. Insignias for the helicopters."

I quickly stuffed my hiking map into my satchel, and said, "Wow, Dad."

"Colour it," he ordered.

"Yes, sir."

He smelled of Old Spice. With a foot propped up on one of M's dining-room chairs, he gave me directions.

"Make the face red."

The horns I coloured yellow. The eyes blue. Dad was impatient to see the final effect.

"Beautiful," he said.

I was not sure where he was going or what he might be doing there on the other side of the world. I knew, though, because Mags said so, that he might not come back or might be returned home to us in a body bag. I had no idea about choppers or helicopters, but I did know that my father loved to fly. He did not like having a desk job. I knew he loved his country. I knew he was willing to fight and to die for America, but I wondered what it might be like if he were just the postman, delivering the mail, or maybe the auto repairman, fixing cars. I had a fleeting idea if he were a postman or the ice-cream deliveryman that he might drive me all the way to Philadelphia to see my mom, just for lunch or to say hi. Then I wouldn't need to have a plan, or to walk for hundreds of miles and face all kinds of dangers with only a couple of dollars in my pocket.

Dad held the prototype patch against his bicep.

"What do you think?" he asked. "Dust Devils?"

I didn't answer.

"Good job," he said enthusiastically, my silence not seeming to register with him. He straddled the chair and leaned in very close to me.

Could I ask him to drive me to Philadelphia for my birthday?

"Hey, Lil'," he asked, "what do you think about having a new mom?"

TWENTY-EIGHT

Kinks, our new mom-to-be, was the widow of an ex-military buddy of my father's whose test plane exploded somewhere over central Texas about ten years earlier. Kinks looked like a horse, not a prizewinner, not a thoroughbred, but a horse nevertheless, and we reasoned that this had something to do with living in Texas – cowboys, Indians, cattle, the Alamo.

We first saw her in the flesh one hot day. Her ankles, fat and encased in stockings a few shades lighter than her skin, appeared first as she stepped out of a cab. I recalled Mom's ankles, her nude hose and stylish heels. What a difference. *Is this really what my father traded my mother for?*

Kinks trotted right up to the bedroom that had been my own, now temporarily – I was told – converted to a guest room. From behind that door, she giggled loudly, as I imagined Dad tickling her. *What for?* There was her heavy breathing, and Dad snorting like a pig. They seemed to scurry around after we were in bed, clinking wine glasses, lighting a fire and saying things like, "Won't that be grand?"

Despite my pointing out the grunting, giggling and see-through pink nightgown, Mags would have none of it. She fantasised aloud that we'd all get along together like something out of *The Sound of Music*, with Kinks making dresses for us out of a heavy piece of drapery, but this was not to be. She wouldn't be giving me any advice about beauty or boys. There was no dancing, and certainly no singing.

When Kinks left I drew a sigh of relief together with M. It was the one and only time we saw eye to eye. We merely sighed as we looked at each other and placed the jewellery box over the cigarette burn Kinks had left behind on the dresser.

M's worst nightmares were coming true. At least Lauren Rose didn't smoke, and she'd never been married before. The plan was to merge two families – all the rage on TV – each saddened by the loss of one parent/spouse: our (not really) dead mother, and their (really) dead father. We were to acquire a new sibling, a girl – my age. My optimistic father saw this as an opportunity to blend all sorts of talents and interests.

No one really cared what I thought about acquiring a stepmother, least of all my father. His mind was already made up. It was love, and since no one really wanted him to marry her, he would. And, of course, because we were his children, we would fall in with his plans as well.

"Texas," he said, making it sound as interesting as France, Rhode Island, Virginia or any of the other places we had lived. Didn't we want to go? Hit the road?

No, I wanted to go to Philadelphia, check Mom was still alive or, my deepest fear, if our writing 'deceased' so many times had made it come true.

Our father did not just want to drive across one of the largest continents in the world in a couple of days; he wanted to do it overnight, with us in tow, twenty-four hours – maximum. He wanted to set and break his own records. Wouldn't this prove his commitment to his new love, his I-can't-get-there-fast-enough

reason for being? My father moved mountains, men, children…
nothing was allowed to stand in his way.

Dad sang the Air Force, Army and Navy songs. Artie sang
along, happy to escape from the military academy. Mags drummed
her fingers on the car door handle, and I memorised the map
again. Who knew, maybe with this new mother, M would even
look good. I doubted it. Two witches. I did not sing. I read the
map, staying several exits and towns ahead. I would have to start
my hiking plan all over again, and even if I didn't know the exact
details, and Texas was a very long way from Philadelphia, there
had to be a way.

Mags started popping her chewing gum. I am not sure why. It
was something M disallowed, and it was not something my sister
had ever done before. Artie leaned over the back of Dad's seat,
looking just a bit odd out of his school uniform, but happy and
trying desperately to fit in.

Dad was making one mistake after the next that I could not fix,
but I would never give up. I had made a forever promise. Texas had
libraries and maps, and I could get a real job, maybe babysitting,
and then I could take a bus, couldn't I?

"No shoes?" Artie asked, as we unpacked the car and met
Toots, our new stepsister. "We don't have to wear shoes?"

"No shoes," Kinks told him, "this is Texas."

While no shoes came as a surprise, Kinks' announcement
that night that we didn't have to have a bath seemed outright
irreligious. Was M aware of this? What would I do? For me a bath
was a daily necessity, akin to brushing my teeth or using the toilet.
Didn't everyone, everywhere, take a bath every day? Maybe not. If
people didn't wear shoes, why should they bathe?

"Lily," Kinks said to me, seeing my confusion, "if it is important
to you, then certainly, by all means, take a bath."

I could not imagine M ever agreeing that not bathing was okay.
My only job now was to figure out how to convince Toots that

bathing could be fun, because she slept not just in my room, but also in the same big, brand-new double bed. The problem seemed to be that running a bath took a long time. Of course, everything is relative including time. The best I could do was suggest that I take a quick dip, hop in and hop out, and then she could use the recently drawn water. It would take no time at all, I told her. I had seen that done in the movies, especially cowboy movies, in places where water was scarce.

Toots shrugged at the proposal. "Okay," she agreed.

Kinks flew to meet my father in Hawaii. I tried to imagine how romantic that might be. I could only imagine my mother in Hawaii. Wind in her hair. Waiting for my father, flowers around her neck. Happy. She belonged in Hawaii, not Kinks. I tried to imagine my father cosying up with Kinks. And I could only imagine him closing his eyes and pretending she was someone else. Who could possibly kiss *Kinks*? I understood now what a face that could stop a clock meant.

The best part of her going away was the arrival of Kinks' cousin Betsy to look after us. She was young and raven-haired like Mom. She wore shorts with cuffs and button-down blouses in small gingham checks. She wore nail polish and lipstick, and sat with her legs arranged to the side like a mermaid. We sat together on Mom and Dad's bed, the one that was now Kinks and Dad's bed – which was mostly Kinks' these days – and I remembered my mother. I think Betsy even wore Chanel No. 5. However, she was not from Philadelphia, had never been to France. She was, as she said, 'strictly from Texas'.

She tucked aside her perfect siren's legs. "How do y'all like Texas?" she asked.

I trusted her. She wore make-up like my mother did, lipstick, perfume. She was pretty. She might be able to teach me things. That this was a trick question never entered my mind.

"It's tough," I said.

"Oh, poor baby," she cooed, tucking a strand of my hair behind my ear. I wanted to be her favourite, petted and sympathised with.

"Kinks doesn't always feed us, especially Artie. She even beats him." I was certain Betsy's home was as orderly as M's. She would have her gowns in dry cleaning bags like Mom always did. Her bathroom would be spotless, with a special place for all her feminine things. Her dusting powder would also be like Mom's: Chanel No. 5. She might even, if I was lucky, dust the tip of my nose with the puff. I could almost smell it.

"Beats Artie?"

"Yes."

"Why?"

"I don't know, really. I think she's jealous and angry."

Betsy unfolded her legs and folded them the other way. "What is she jealous of, Lily?"

"Everything," I answered, happy to have someone to confide in about the move.

"Everything?"

"Yes."

"Like what?"

"Toots is not very bright. You know she's been held back a grade? She doesn't really know anything. Just watches a lot of television. I don't watch unless it's a very special occasion. I love to read, to think. I think school is more important than anything else. The other thing that bothers me, Betsy" – I said it like I would say 'Mom' – "is that Toots and Kinks don't bathe. I have to get Toots to use my bathwater or she won't at all. I don't think they even brush their teeth."

Betsy changed the television channels until she came to *Ed Sullivan*. She slid away and sat on the floor to stare at the screen.

"Betsy?" I said.

"What?"

I could tell she'd lost interest, but I just carried on spilling out everything that had gone wrong in my life. "Sometimes I am so lonely, I wish I was with my mother. You would like her. She is beautiful. You look a bit like her. She has two brothers that sing as well as anyone. They are so much fun. I wish my parents had never been divorced, and if that is too much to wish for then I'd settle for living with my grandmother M and all her rules and regulations. I just feel so lost here, and I'm afraid for Artie and Mags. I have a feeling something awful is going to happen to them, and I won't be able to prevent it."

Then it dawned on me. I almost choked on the words as they spilled out. "Betsy, would you at all be able to help me with a telephone number or an address for my mom?"

Betsy remained unmoved. She was eating popcorn out of a bowl that had belonged to my mother, white on the inside, blue on the outside. She drank beer straight out of the bottle. I watched her tilt her chin and swallow. In profile she looked nothing like my mother. She looked like Kinks. I had made a terrible mistake. I looked more closely. The nail polish was chipped. The black hair was not her natural colour. At first I hadn't seen the cigarettes in her shorts pocket, or the gold chain around her ankle. I wanted to take it all back.

"Betsy…" I began, not sure how to take it all back, how to say something nice about Kinks, her kid, the house.

"Don't you ever shut up?" she said.

She was definitely not my mother. I moved slowly off the bed. "Okay," I said.

"Okay is right," she said. "You remember one thing: Kinks is family. Toots is my cousin. You are nobody here – nothing. And you better watch your ass! Kinks might just kill you or your brother, if I don't do it myself. Don't think for one minute that I won't tell her every word you just said. You two-bit liar! Telephone number? For your mother? Lily, you're a joke."

Kinks called me into the living room a day or two after she was back from Honolulu. She stood by the television set, flipping from

175

one channel to the next. She seemed more interested in watching the screen than in looking at me, but I could feel a chill creep over me with her next words.

"Is it true you think we know nothing about washing up here?" She tapped some of the blue-black ash from her cigarette into the callused palm of her free hand.

I focused on the tips of her golden, Aladdin-style house slippers. She wore them on quick shopping trips, or on the daily trek to and from school.

Washing up? I thought rapidly. It might be a trick question. Kinks was big on those. I forced myself to think. Did she mean laundry? If I answered incorrectly, or in a tone she did not like, she would claim I was attempting to demean her. Had Betsy spoken to her? Yes, that had to be it. *Washing up.* Soap and water. It dawned on me then like a thousand fireworks. *Grooming.* That was how M would have put it.

"Grooming," I said.

"Grooming?" Kinks stared at me.

"No," I answered. "I mean, yes, I know you do… wash up. You know, we were just trying to save time. Four children, two baths. Why not share water?"

"Okay," she said vacantly, caught off guard by Walter Cronkite and the latest fatality count in Vietnam.

I watched as well. The black-and-white screen showed a newspaper image come to life. The body bags were stacked the way I always imagined sandbags would be if you needed to hold back a flood.

"No news," said Kinks, and turned off the television.

It was Christmas. I wore a green velvet dress in the same pattern as Mags's. Hers was red, and Toots wore the same pattern in blue. I quietly left the party as it wound down to watching television, Artie sneaking off to his room, Mags back in hers and Kinks smoking cigarette after cigarette, kicking off her gold slippers. Out the back door, unnoticed by anyone, I climbed the one and only tree on the property, a windblown cypress.

The moon was full, blank against the night sky. I thought about my father, about his helmet, the weight and the sheer size of it. When they flew his birds, the Jolly Green Giants, into Texas from Ohio, he opened them up to the public. I sat in his seat, in the cockpit, and wore the helmet with the dust-devil insignia. I tried to imagine him at war, flying over the Pacific Ocean, running forays – what were they? But I failed. I could only smell sweat, men and gasoline.

From the top of the cypress, I pretended to fly. I flew all the way from Texas to Philadelphia. I was up high, alone, with a clear view. I saw the new map I'd found at school and was busy memorising. I knew it was twenty-four hours by car, with no buses or trains direct, and weeks to walk. I toyed with the idea of going by bicycle and imagined that would take at least a week, round the clock.

So instead of finding the solution, I pretended to fly. I could spot any number of things unseen from the ground. It was different up here; I felt untouchable. I hovered finally after hitting headwinds and then floating on tailwinds over Nana's house. She was in the garden, with white washing snapping tautly. Sean and Danny were washing the car while spraying each other with a green garden hose. There was my mom, as beautiful as ever and happy. She was grinning ear to ear, walking to her mom with the largest red geranium I'd ever seen. At that moment, a train rattled by and petals fell until it was a blizzard of geranium in white, pink, orange, red and purple. I sent a wish to the moon for my mother, and I pictured her catching it. Lauren Rose would look up on this Christmas night, and think of me, think of us. I imagined her waving and blowing me a kiss, just like when I was a baby.

M would arrive in Texas the following day and stay through the New Year – 1969.

I was still thinking about Mom and the fact that M was about to arrive here when Kinks came into my room very late. She sat on the edge of the bed and whispered so as not to wake up her daughter.

"Lily, listen up. I didn't get to set you straight before, but I am now. I don't know what you're playin' and plottin', but Cousin B told me everythin' – your whole pack of lies. You try that again, and I will have your tongue. You ever speak to anyone about anythin' that goes on in this house, I can guarantee you will never speak again! Think about that. You think beating Artie was bad, honey? Think again. Push me far enough…"

I lay still, sniffed the air. The woman had not even been drinking.

"Lily," she crooned, tucking my hair behind my ear, just like Betsy had done, and pretending to tuck me in, "what were you thinkin', Little Missy?"

Of my mom and a way to get out of here.

Kinks left as fast as she had come in the minute she heard her daughter stir and mumble in her sleep.

I'm not sure why, but M didn't arrive. Kinks told us that she was very busy at work and that our grandmother would have to come another time. I think in order to make up for it, she took us to Lake Waco, and I can genuinely say that I was thrilled, not just for myself because it was the closest I'd been to anything like the ocean since Dad stole us from Mom, but because Artie could fish and I liked to believe that was Kinks's way of saying 'sorry'.

We used the old plaid hamper from long ago, and I made all the sandwiches and Mags made the drinks. Artie sorted all the fishing equipment, and we were more than surprised when Kinks rented a boat.

"You don't want to fish from the shore, do you?"

"No," Artie said, "I don't. Thank you. In the deep, I might catch a largemouth bass."

"That's right," Kinks said, swirling the ice in her frosted glass.

"We don't need a boat," I said.

"And why is that, Miss Lily?"

"We like the shore, the hot sand."

"This is not a beach, like back East, girl."

"We like staying on the shore."

"No, we don't," Artie said. "I'd like to fish for white bass and crappie."

"Yes, that sounds good," Mags joined in, cutting me off, giving me the 'be quiet' signal.

The terror rose in me as soon as Kinks quipped about the boat rental, but tripled when she insisted on taking Artie out alone. Too many people in the boat will disturb the fishing, she said, and Artie had agreed. I watched as they turned into one large dot, just about as far out as I could see. I recalled that time I lost hold of his hand under the water. I calculated how far I could swim.

Kinks' daughter kept quiet as I paced the shore nervously. The water was so deep and so blue, but it wasn't anything like the Atlantic Ocean, the Jersey Shore, and the day wasn't anything like a picnic with Mom.

"Don't worry, Worry Wart. Nothing is going to happen," Mags said.

Artie started to look different and to act like someone other than himself. He hadn't eaten in two weeks apart from the scraps we and, sweetly, Toots had smuggled to him. "Punishment," Kinks called it. Discipline. Sometimes it was just called a beating. On the surface, it was for foul language, not picking up his socks, talking back, not doing homework, but in reality it was because Kinks now hated Dad for, as she saw it, deserting her. It was as simple as that. Artie looked like Jack, and Kinks was, as Mags liked to say, 'really mad'.

"Who can blame her?" my sister said. "One minute love, and the next Vietnam. One minute one kid – now four. You tell me why she's wild at us."

"She doesn't seem to know Dad very well."

"And he doesn't know her," Mags said. "She keeps two bank accounts. Haven't you noticed? She's pocketing his cash. Do you see her spending anything here? It will all end in divorce, and we'll start over again with nothing."

"Well," I said, "that might not be so bad."

"She said she didn't know Dad was going to Vietnam. That he lied to her."

"Well, he didn't tell her the whole truth. She thought he was being posted here."

"But don't you find it amazing, what women do for love? For Dad?"

I was the smart one at school, but when it came to survival Mags was a genius.

I think the three of us knew something needed to be done and wondered what would happen when M eventually arrived. Artie had been in hospital overnight after one beating, and nearly lost his eye. Kinks had found his secret hiding place at the bottom of the garden. She found a wounded raccoon that he'd been feeding scraps he took from the garbage, things like banana skins and orange peels. Sometimes I wondered if he ate them himself.

When Kinks found his whole menagerie, including a one-eyed armadillo and a homemade red ant farm, she went berserk. She took the garden hoe and without warning broke it across his back. I got there just as I heard him roar and turn on her. He seemed to rise up to twice his height despite the skin stretched taut across his collarbones.

"You bitch," he said loud and clear, as she smashed an incubator he'd rigged up with an old battery. As he hurried to save the yet-to-be-hatched hens' eggs and the new chicks, including a bobwhite, Kinks picked up a handful of red earth and threw it in his face.

I called the police and they arrived just as Kinks had poured herself a whiskey and soda, which she threw down the sink. She then stubbed out her cigarette with the speed of a demon.

"Disturbance reported here," I heard the officer say.

"Just a young man flying off the top bunk, out of control." Kinks shook her head. "Boys, these days."

"Let's take a look," the officer said, clearly not believing her, and within minutes an ambulance arrived, which took Artie away. They wanted to know where Jack Preston was and who was our next of kin. Mags told them everything as Kinks smirked and pretended concern.

She came on the prowl for us as soon as the medics and the police left.

"Who called the police?" she asked us together and individually, but no one spilt the beans, not even Toots. My heart pounded in my chest, and I was grateful for the odd sound of a freight train piercing the air with its shrill whistle.

Not me, not me, not me.

Thankfully, Kinks had more important things to do and went out with her cousin Betsy for a drink.

M arrived earlier than expected and in a mood, and without more than two words to Kinks, immediately took all of us away from the house with a police escort. We stayed in a hotel in Dallas because M felt that at least it was a major city and not someplace out in the boondocks. Within another week my father joined us at the Adolphus Hotel. "Compassionate leave," M said.

As we dined, my father and grandmother chatted. They were, like it or not, joined at the hip, shared an odd commitment that dated way back. *What was it?* For better or for worse, they relied on each other. Dad would never truly leave home, even if he was miles away, no matter how old he got.

"Look at you, children," M said. "Why didn't you call me?"

"We were afraid, M," Mags said. Artie and I nodded.

"Well, you were very lucky this time," she said before ordering a coffee and asking her son what he wanted for dessert before excusing herself for bed. Dad ordered a drink as soon as she left and enthralled me once again with any old story.

"Yes," he reminisced, "M acted as mother and father. She brought Penny and me up with tough standards. I would be an officer and a gentleman – no matter what." He laughed and swallowed his drink. "She had her sights set on West Point, but I joined the Navy instead. I don't know if she ever got over it. She's a real nightmare sometimes, but I feel sorry for her: no father, no husband. God, I am all she has."

Mags and I left Artie commiserating with Dad and made our way to our own adjoining hotel room, and in our own spanking fresh sheets and new nightgowns we talked.

What a miracle to escape Texas!

We were relieved on so many counts that it was hard to think straight. M had called Dad's superior at the Pentagon, and he might permanently come back to the USA or at least have a new assignment – no more Vietnam; she'd taken Artie to a surgeon who told us his eye would be okay; and we had had an awfully good dinner at a table with napkins, a full menu and baked Alaska for dessert. Full of hope and happiness, I couldn't sleep. I thought now might be the right time to ask Mags for Mom's number.

"Snowball in hell," she said before she pulled out from her satchel my folder with the rainbow drawings, the precise daisies and the multiplication table done backward and forward from zero to fifteen in my own unique way.

Where did she get that?

"And Lil', if anyone else ever sees any of your ridiculous hiking plans back to Philadelphia, you will find yourself in deep doo-doo. Not only is it impossible, and you would die trying, but also you will find yourself locked up, just like Mom. Get it? Give it up or I will tell M, and what do you think will happen then? How did you even think you would manage to walk across Texas scrubland in ninety-degree heat? Promise me. Give it up," she said, as she tore all my notes and plans into tiny shreds and let them sail out the Adolphus window into the night sky.

I watched in horror, but didn't say anything, except to myself.

"Give up?" she asked, as if she had me in a vice grip.

Never.

TWENTY-NINE

"The Panama Canal," my father said, as he pointed out the engineering feat below. "Fifty-one miles from Atlantic to Pacific, three sets of locks, the Gatun, the Pedro Miguel and the Miraflores."

"Yes," I said, taking it all in, my forehead pressed against the window. I was thinking of France. I was thinking of Mom in Philadelphia. How would I find my way back from Panama – not just a different state, but a separate country? I wore the blue, dotted Swiss dress I had made in Texas from a Butterick pattern. Mags wore the yellow, double-breasted blazer she made from an advanced *Vogue* pattern.

"Learning how to sew," she said, "might be the only good thing we get out of Texas."

Artie, dressed in blue jeans, also sat pressed against the window on the opposite side of the plane, alone, chewing the knuckles on his left hand. Although he'd fattened up and his hair no longer grew in patches, he didn't seem to belong to us anymore. He was like a bushel basket baby someone had just left on the steps, at the front door. Except for his love of animals, his beloved animals, I hardly recognised him anymore. Happily, already, he could reel off the names of the birds and animals he hoped to see in our new home: jaguars, hammerheads, iguanas, toucans and hummingbirds.

I wasn't sure how free Artie would ever be. He might get over Kinks, his bruises heal, but he would never get over Mom, the fact he had never come out of the garage and that he might never see her again. He seemed to think that he had failed over and over again, except for with his animals that he could raise, heal and often send back into the wild again.

We watched a ship below transiting the locks, growing larger and larger as the plane descended. Finally we veered off and landed miles away from the actual canal.

We respected Dad for probably the first and only time. Technically, M had liberated us from Kinks, but Dad had come to Texas as quickly as he was called and kicked down the door to that house. He had turned white when he realised it was empty. Kinks had taken him for everything, except a few photos of himself that she had left propped up in the centre of the living-room floor.

"We're going to start over," he'd said as we dined with M in the great dining room of the magnificent Adolphus Hotel. "I'm going to lose everything, but I don't care. I just want you kids." He ruffled Artie's hair. Plied us with questions. How many times had Artie been beaten? Did you, Lily, call the police? He already knew. Weren't we lucky the retina did not detach?

"No one will ever take you away from me," he vowed. "She can have everything else."

Ghost of a chance of her wanting us, I wanted to say, but didn't. After all, he had saved us and the touchdown was a soft one. We were safe. Every time Kinks came to mind, I calmed myself by working out how many miles away she was: 802. Texas was a long way from Panama. Thank God.

I understood why my father liked flying and divorce. They were like ice-skating or sailing. It was all about being free.

"Uncle Sam will take care of us now," he promised.

I was never sure who Uncle Sam was. Even when my father

explained about the military and its pivotal role in preserving the American way of life, I did not really understand. All sorts of things materialised at the behest of Uncle Sam: temporary housing, permanent housing, teak furniture with red cushions and new schools. I had persistent trouble with one small detail: a zip code. Did the Canal Zone, the CZ, have one? My mother would never find us without one, and I would never find my way back just by remembering the route in reverse. We'd cut the cord, as my father liked to say. Maybe that was a good thing. I was having such a difficult time remembering everything.

We were in a very different place suddenly. Definitely not American. Everyone spoke mostly Spanish. Panamanian, properly. We were aliens, living in the Zone where we could speak English with others just like us.

"APO," Dad explained. "We don't have a zip code; we have an APO."

"What's that?"

"Army Post Office," he said in a firm way, as if he were saying: "Have no fear, the doors are locked."

"Okay," I said, "APO. What's the rest?"

"Lil', what are you expecting – mail?" He laughed at me.

Yes, I wanted to say. *Did you tell Mom so she could at least write to us here?* I would never ask him if we could write to her. She was dead to him. I said nothing because the subject remained a minefield, and even I could tell that the man who came home, the man who rescued us, was not quite himself. At first, I chalked it up to divorce, maybe two divorces, but a large box displayed in the airport bathroom caught my attention.

"Marijuana, Drugs and Other Paraphernalia," I read out to Mags as we dried our hands on rough paper towels. "Amnesty," I finished. "What's that mean?"

"It means put your drugs in that box if you don't want to get caught."

We walked right by the poster that read: "Are you suffering

from Post-Traumatic Stress Syndrome? If so, the Army is here to help." I didn't bother to ask Mags about that because we had enough to worry about.

Dad hired a woman called Fiore to help with the house he was assigned on the Air Force base. I loved the green jungle encroaching all around it almost as much as Artie did, and the odd animals he brought home that he found crawling in and out of the trees or crossing the lawn, including a sloth that moved at a decidedly slow pace. I especially loved the rainbow-coloured birds that Artie brought in from the jungle. They cawed and he squawked back. They often landed on his arm or right where he sat, outside the louvred windows on the patio or my balcony.

Fiore, a bright light, sang when she was cooking, whistled when she cleaned and watched Panamanian TV when she ironed. She liked all of us, and called Artie *niño*, *muchacho*, *chico* and *pequeño*. I was so relieved my brother was coming out of himself, slowly but surely. Fiore was a bit like a mother to him and a sister to us girls. Artie became more like his old self with a joke and a ready smile, maybe the best part of his inheritance from Dad. I might have guessed it would not last forever, but one night when I heard a tap on my bedroom door and Fiore's nervous voice enquiring, "*Señorita* Lily, *por favor*, please help me?" I was sure of it.

She pointed to her bedroom, where Dad lay on the floor snoring.

"Dad!" I shouted. "You're in the wrong room."

He woke with a start. "Oh," he said apologetically, "wrong turn."

Wrong turn? Technically, he was correct. His bedroom was right next door to Fiore's, and he did always come up the stairs in the dark. Maybe he had made a mistake. However, since he was in his underwear, he would have had to go into his room to undress and then back out and into her room. I tried to remember, were his clothes on her floor? *No*, I thought, *just him in his underwear*.

I sat on the edge of my bed and looked at the curtains, patterned with blue iris. I was mostly angry for Artie's sake. Now Fiore would have to go – sooner or later. The streetlight shone in through the louvres and the tender green stems of the elongated iris. The seasonal rain started to pour. I wanted to rush out the door onto my balcony, put both hands on the railing and jump over the side, shouting, *"Emergency. Emergency. SOS."*

But who would hear?

THIRTY

Mags started creating and sewing even more complicated dress patterns than she had in Texas: *Designer Vogue*. She also started working after school at the library, tracking and stacking books.

"I dust them," she said, "but the most interesting bit, Lil', is the fact that the library makes an enormous amount of money by doing absolutely nothing. They just collect and count fines on overdue books!"

I nodded. I could imagine Mags counting out pennies, nickels, dimes, putting them in those drab paper sleeves. I saw her flattening out the bills and using rubber bands and paper clips to secure them. They would give her a desk. She would be important. Her numbers would be in clear, straight columns with everything honestly totalled up, and she wouldn't have a clue what was happening at home with Artie or me. I wanted her to focus on us. I wanted to say, "Mags, you have a family here," but I didn't because she seemed to be more awake than any of us and repeatedly told us so, especially me.

"You have to get a job, too," she would say, "a step up from babysitting, or you will never – and I mean never, ever – go to college. Wake up! Don't fool yourself. Dad will never pay for anything. We are on our own. *You* are on your own!"

At home, Artie looked after his ever-growing menagerie, which had gotten so big that even the local kids paid him a nickel to have a peek. On two occasions folk from the Smithsonian Tropical Research Institute came by to see Artie's wounded tapir and golden tree frog. Mags went to the library, and I made the many different dinners that M had drilled into me. An hour for just about any menu, including Dad's favourite Worcestershire meatloaf, mashed potatoes, salad and green beans. I wanted everyone to eat, and Fiore taught me Spanish as well as how to sing.

"*Mañana*," I said to her, "*empanadas.*"

"*Sí.*" She winked.

I thought I might write Mom or Nana and Granddad. Maybe I could find a phone number from the directories in the library, since Mags definitely would not help me. Fiore's singing grew contagious. Happy and hopeful, I guessed life could be good.

Setting the table, I checked and rechecked the meatloaf, the potatoes and string beans; tossed the salad and prodded the refrigerated quick-mix pudding for dessert.

Dad roared in through the door. "Jim Beam."

First, I froze, but then calmly measured whiskey, plunked ice into the short glass and ran the tap to cold.

"Dad?" I asked. *Is this a good time?*

"Yes, Lil'?"

"Nothing." I pretended I forgot.

Can I call Mom? It had been such a long time and we were so far away from Philadelphia that maybe I thought he might just say, "Yes, of course, hon, why not?" "Chance in a million," Mags would say. Even Artie would shake his head. He would no longer be an accomplice. He had given up. "She's dead," he once said when I showed him my plan to take a ship that went through the locks and up the East Coast to New York, then by train down to

Philly. I agreed there were obstacles, but nothing that couldn't be conquered.

"We won again," my father said, wolfing down his food. That's what men in the armed forces did, bolted their food when they were on twenty-four-hour alert. It was a habit, he once said.

"Good," I celebrated.

"Operation Black Hawk-Eagles won. Left Riptide Rangers belly-up. We swarmed all over their backs."

"Okay." I nodded.

It was one of those days when Dad felt good, wore his flight suit instead of the khaki uniform.

THIRTY-ONE

3:45pm?

Why was Dad's car parked in the open garage? Something was wrong. My heart sank. What now? Had Artie been caught, skipping school again to track a frigate bird or spider monkey? Walking slowly up the drive, I scanned the horizon for clues. I heard his voice, and then I heard another that filled me with dread.

"Ja-ack," M crackled, "what did you expect?"

Please make it only a short break, a holiday.

"Lil'," my father said, smiling, as I swung open the door, "look who's here."

The enemy.

"Hi," I said.

"Hi, what?" came the instantaneous demand.

"Hi, M," I said.

"Give your grandmother a kiss. She's come to live with us. She had her last day of work and has left the civil service reeling. I don't know what they will ever do without her, but I'm definitely happy she's here."

Live with us?

"You kids need her, too."

"Children, Ja-ack. Not kids," M corrected him.

Dixie cup in two hands.

This was Artie's fault. Some narcotics officer had taken photos of kids buying and selling a strain of Panama Red at the Goethals Monument during lunch, and he'd just happened to be there. Dad said they had photographs of all of us, though I didn't believe it. I had never even been to the fountain, sat on the rim of the basin. Who had time? Artie peddling drugs? Hard to imagine. Mags? No way. She was college-bound. Nothing would be allowed to get in her way.

So M was back. At least now I wouldn't have to pull Dad out of Fiore's bed, but I could count the minutes until M would send the maid flying. There would be a trumped-up reason, and it would most likely kill Artie.

Fiore had mothered Artie back to laughing, even crying, and helped him out after the odd prank or two, but I could hear M warning against: "Such close proximity to a young, vulnerable man." Dad or Artie, I knew the real truth, which wasn't always easy with Emma Preston.

After dinner the first night that M came to stay, with all the lights off, I slipped out onto my balcony. Leaning far out onto the simple railing, I looked up and down the road, first one way and then the other. Jungle everywhere. *La selva.* A steady buzz of air-conditioning units underpinned the odd caw of a tropical night bird and the pleasant syncopation of the tree frogs. These roads hacked through the jungle, linked base with base, with multiple checkpoints in between.

If I jumped this balustrade now, where would I go? Panama City? I could get lost there. Every time I imagined my story was finally beginning, it ended.

M.

Just then, someone tapped sharply, throwing open my bedroom door in the same instant.

"Wha-at? What are you doing out there?" my grandmother shrieked.

"Thinking, M," I answered. "I am thinking."

"In your pyjamas? Without a robe?"

"Yes, M."

"Well, get inside at once. Who do you think you are? What will the neighbours say? Are you out of your mind? That's not even a real balcony. It's decorative, only for effect. Tomorrow you're changing rooms. This one is now mine."

The loss of my room aside, M's arrival didn't start off too badly.

"She's retired," Dad said, as if announcing she had won a prize. I was never quite sure what M did, though I knew she worked for the government. I'm not sure how many times she told me her story of pulling herself up by her bootstraps, which I could never quite visualise. The point was she had taken care of herself, and we were expected to do the same.

I understood this change was meant to be good for us all. Perhaps M had retired her old ways as well, along with her job as spy, grandmaster or whatever else she wanted us to believe. I envisioned having a real grandmother, one who would help me sort out the garden as it appeared I had made a disaster out of it with a variety of hopeless tropical plants, along with helping me with Dad, Fiore, Artie and even Mags. Maybe having a real grandmother would make up for no longer having a mother.

M instead of Lauren Rose?

If nothing else, M was good at scheduling, organisation. Everyone went to sleep and awoke at the same time, ate breakfast together and dinner in the evening. Everyone was required to speak, talk about his or her day – what did and didn't work – before being excused to do homework. While the conversation was heavily monitored and we knew what to say and what not to say, I actually enjoyed the ritual, the orderliness.

While I winced at the loss of my room, my own personal, thinking space, I was more than happy to be sharing again with Mags. It wasn't all bad. We'd been drifting apart since going to different schools, and with her working at the library in the afternoons and weekends. While she worked and stockpiled her cash, she still worried about the future, about college, or at least the fact that she believed Dad wouldn't pay a dime towards it. She had a recurring nightmare: she would be a bag lady, pushing a trolley on the street. Mags suggested I read Ayn Rand's *Atlas Shrugged* and learn to count on myself, nobody else.

"No fantasies," she warned repeatedly, "about Mom, M, Artie, Dad or anybody else. And don't hold your breath – Fiore is going, eventually, whether you like it or not. You know M: anyone who catches Dad's eye, including you, me or Mom, has got to go. She's so intimidated, insecure. She never understood that in the end a mom is meant to let her kid go."

M did get rid of Fiore. Without any advance warning, any goodbye, she just disappeared. I pictured her slipping back into the jungle, somewhere between Panama and Colombia, with her doe eyes blinking and her short legs stepping out lightly in her white bellbottom trousers and her navy blazer into the tall blades of lime-green grass. She would be wearing her gold, hooped earrings and bright pink lipstick because she wasn't at work.

I would miss her cooking, her *sanchoco, empanadas* and *ropa vieja*. M, guaranteed, would not be making *tostones*. Artie would not stand for it. *What now?* How could Dad and M be so clueless? Fiore had brought Artie out of himself. She offered the motherly love he'd lost. She sang, she danced and she could also communicate with animals, just like he did.

What would I do without Fiore? I couldn't imagine M and I sharing a laugh. *Did M ever laugh?* What about the odd article of clothing? I couldn't imagine borrowing anything from M's wardrobe, and I had been so close to getting my ears pierced, something that now would be verboten, branded as low-class, cheap and common.

"I don't think so," M would say, "not on my watch."

Where she found Hernanda, who didn't seem to speak English, I did not know. She hardly spoke at all. She cleaned, ironed and did exactly what she was told. Her hulking presence shocked me. In her tight uniform, I thought she'd be better suited to a nursing home or insane asylum – maybe Corazón – Hernanda's presence proved to be a sort of corrective. The ground shifted. Dad, at least, I was sure, would not be hopping into this woman's bed.

THIRTY-TWO

Dad popped the cork and even let us have a sip of champagne.

"A year in Panama," he celebrated, "and M here to keep us afloat."

His mother smiled demurely, pretending not to have orchestrated the whole thing, clapping her hands together once and beaming.

Mags leaned over and mouthed, "I know who wife number three will be."

"Who?" I asked.

"Silvie Tierney, head receptionist at the library."

"No?"

"Yes."

"Mother of the infamous Candy?"

"That's the one. Dad met her while collecting me. He takes her out for long lunches, but she avoids me. She would do anything to be an officer's wife, and apparently has," Mags snorted. "She'd kill to live in officers' quarters. Beware of her. She will get rid of all of us, one by one, if we get in her way."

"I don't believe it."

"Trust me. Kinks couldn't hold a candle to Silvie T. She and her kid are on the prowl for an officer, according to the rumours, and the daughter is... well, let's just say the entire football team knows her intimately."

Artie joined in. "Well, that should set M's hair on fire."

"It's not funny," I said.

Everyone fell silent. How many times had we seen this before? M rescues Dad, he marries to escape M, who helps him engineer a divorce to save him again. *Merry-go-round.*

"Yep. M'll threaten him with leaving, hoping that will dissuade him from marrying yet another ne'er-do-well."

"But if not her, it'll be someone else," Artie said.

"Who?" I asked.

"Anyone." Artie laughed a little too much.

Is he high?

"Yes," Mags agreed. "Anyone. I've got to catch the bus to the library or I'll be late."

Wait, I wanted to say to her. *Mags, please, don't leave us. Let's hang out together like we did with Mom. Stay with Artie. Stay with me. Let's all hop in one bed and have a good long Saturday-morning sleep heap.*

"You're dreaming again," she said as she hitched books onto one hip before going out the door. "I can see it. Remember what I said. 'Survival of the fittest'."

The next weekend, Artie sat across the table from me, the house empty but the atmosphere thick with suspense. *What next?*

"Where are M and Dad?" I asked.

"Mother's Day," he answered. "Brunch at the officers' club."

"Yes. I forgot." *Why would I remember Mother's Day?*

"They said so last night. Apparently they want to talk. We know what this means. Secret pow-wow. On to Act Two, where she leaves, and against all odds – flying in the face of everything for the woman he loves – Ja-ack marries Silvie." My brother paused.

"Do you want something to eat?" I asked.

"You don't have to worry, Lil'," Artie said in a Latino accent. "Everything is under control. *Todo bajo control*. Colonel Jack Preston uses condoms. At least there won't be more kids for you to look after!"

Reaching into his pocket, my brother pulled out a package of three prophylactics and threw them on the kitchen table.

"Where did you get those?"

"In the glove box. I was scrounging change for a Coke."

"He has them in the car?"

"Never know," Artie said, again in his Latino accent, "when you might have to have a bit of automobile lurve... and I don't mean with Silvie."

"...with your new intern?" I added.

Artie smiled at the suggestion.

I didn't know which was worse: Dad tying the knot with Silvie, the Zone's most notorious librarian, or picturing him in the back seat of our car with his most recent intern, one of Mags's classmates.

We'd all seen the photo in *Stars and Bars*, the one with Dad smiling narrow-eyed as if he were JFK and Charlotte the classmate was Marilyn Monroe. That grin had disturbed me. It didn't mean: job well done, here's your cheque for Intern of the Year. It definitely meant something else. I knew M had seen it and sensed trouble. The other officer in the photo, balding and fat, holding the opposite end of the presentation cheque, didn't smirk like that. He didn't look like he was twice divorced and had just swallowed... what? Charlotte's panties? Perhaps that was what M and Jack were talking about over brunch: Charlotte and that *Stars and Bars* photo. I only hoped.

M and Jack eventually came home. The news was simple and not sweet. They didn't mention Silvie Tierney, Charlotte or long-gone Fiore.

"I'm leaving," M said, with her nose-in-the-air, 'I'm offended' look.

Yes. Act Two.

I swayed at the edge of the kitchen counter as if I were at the top of the Miraflores locks, seeing the water churn below. Kinks II? Impossible. Artie had begun disappearing for days at a time, and Dad, while no one said it, was drinking more and more. Who knew what had happened to him in Vietnam, but it was beginning to dawn on me that his compassionate leave might not have been granted solely so he could rescue his children from an abusive second wife.

"When?" I managed to say.

"Next week," M answered.

No protest. I wanted M to go, but who would come to stay next?

"You tell Artie and Mags," my father instructed.

"Yes, sir," I said, as I saw his own failure dimly register on his face and a flicker of furious rejection on M's.

Same thing over and over again. Insane, I thought. *Red alert. Red alert. Breathe.*

As soon as Mags returned from counting overdue fines and stacking library books and Artie blew in from who knows where, I sat them down.

"Good news," I stated. "M is going."

"So it's true?" Mags said.

"Most probably."

"Silvie Tierney?" Artie went off like a Geiger counter. "You know what this flippin' means?"

"Yes," I answered. *You will take the brunt.*

"Listen," Mags piped up, "we've been here before and we can do it again. We are older, and if I guess correctly, it's only a matter of time before we end up with M, like it or not, in the great State of Arkansas."

"How do you know that?" I asked.

"I'm going there in August. U of A. Dad's plan. He bought land there – so he can retire. A farm, I think. M is going to wangle her way in. Where else does she have to go? You think Aunt Penelope and her family want her? We are the scapegoats. She'll probably get Dad to buy her a house there. Who knows? I am not counting on anybody for anything. Neither of you should either."

Artie stood up, staring at Mags. "You both know what's going to happen. You're going to leave me behind! This week, next week, next fall. You will be gone and I'll be left alone with that... that dumbass monster! I'm too young to join the military and he's already pushing for that. And Silvie Tierney... and the daughter. Frickin' nightmare."

"No, Artie," I protested.

"Yes, Artie!" he mimicked me, walking out, slamming the door so loud that even his parrots seemed to say, "Jeezus."

M's exit didn't even register on Dad. *What did she think? That her imperious departure would shock her son into reality? Had it ever?* Jack Preston did not miss a beat. Hope sprang eternal in him. At a home barbecue, he introduced us to Silvie and her daughter Candy, whose reputation preceded her.

With red highlighted hair, Silvie, like her daughter, stood out anywhere. They both wore bold colours – yellow for mom and lime green for daughter. The vinyl boots took me by surprise, along with the short shorts and the stretchy, knit tops. *If only M could see us now.*

"Delicious," Dad said, as he sawed through the crust of the stale meringue they'd brought.

"Yes," Mags agreed.

What did my sister have to lose? She was leaving, and the look she'd exchanged with Silvie said everything anyone needed to know about how they felt about each other. Mags was not up to the game of helping Dad win a bride or us a mother. Those days were over.

"You two must have gotten to know each other," he said while eating another helping of powder-dry meringue.

"Sadly, we don't work on the same floor," Silvie whined, throwing back her motionless hair. "I'm at reception, checking the books in and out."

Artie didn't stay for the dessert, said he was busy, needed to check on his science project, his fer-de-lance, the most dangerous snake in the Panamanian jungle.

At this, Candy cooed, "Can I come, too?"

"No," he said a bit too quickly, with terror writ large across his face.

Does Artie know Candy? Where is he really going? Does he even have a fer-de-lance?

"Next time," Silvie said, and patted her daughter's knee.

"Next time," my father said, afraid Artie may have upset his romantic strategy. *Does anyone know how hard it is to woo a woman when you're twice divorced and have three kids in tow?*

Mags bailed to her room when Artie left, but I remained to prop Dad up.

Silvie, showing off for Jack, slinked over, wrapped a bony arm around me, and while I momentarily thought she was going to ask if I wanted a Kool cigarette, she asked if I wanted to go shopping.

"Have you ever been shopping in Panama City?" she cooed, taking away her arm with the twelve jiggling silver bangles.

"No."

"I know all the best shops. Where to get a good deal. We could buy some material, some patterns, maybe sandals, and how about some gold hoop earrings like these?" She modelled her own.

Pierced ears.

"Absolutely." I smiled at Dad.

Candy snickered, sipping the piña colada she'd made for herself without asking. *Maybe she's seen it all before, too.*

"Okay, then." Silvie batted her eyelids. "I will collect you at nine tomorrow morning. Saturday is the best, and we want to go early before the traffic and the heat gets too much."

"Okay," I said, leaving Dad to neck with his long-throated wench, while her daughter helped herself again from the refrigerator and bar, to anything else she wanted.

Silvie honked her horn outside the house. This was another of M's 'no-nos'. *A sign? Who needs a sign? This has disaster written all over it.* Only Dad seemed oblivious, gesturing from the door, blowing kisses to his new love as I made my way to her Ford Escort that looked as if it had just come off the Great South American Road Rally.

"So Lily, tell me all about yourself," she asked as we got underway, bumping along empty streets, with those same bangles jangling. "I understand you're very popular at school. Get good marks. Candy thinks you are super stellar."

"She's pretty popular herself," I said.

Minefield. Third wife. Hunting for info.

"So you design and make your own clothes?"

"No," I answered, "Mags is the seamstress. Fiore was also really good."

"Fiore?" she asked slowly. "Tell me about her."

I'm not sure why, but I did; I opened up. What did I have to lose? "She was an amazing cook," I said, and Silvie relaxed. "Made the best *empanadas*. Perfect. Dad swallowed them whole."

"He did?" She stiffened.

"He hired her; M fired her."

Silvie chortled like Kinks. The rusty hum of the car, the dust and the equatorial light bouncing off the asphalt, with the jungle leaning in on both sides, lulled me into some faraway fantasy: going shopping with Lauren Rose.

"Tell me about Mom Number Two."

"Kinks?"

"Yes," Silvie said huskily, in a voice like one from a midnight radio show. "Yes. That's the one."

"A nightmare," I said, throwing caution to the wind. "From beginning to end. A mismatch. Cigarettes burning wherever she left them."

Silvie flicked her ash out the window and then stubbed her cigarette out, slamming in the ashtray. "Really?"

"When we finally got to Texas and Dad flew to Vietnam, she changed. Not nice. All but killed Artie. Nearly starved him to death."

I could not stop talking. Maybe Silvie wasn't so bad after all; maybe she was a sympathetic woman, and that's why all the men liked her. She was a good listener.

Third time lucky?

"Tell me about your own mother, Lauren Rose?"

"Mom?" I repeated. No one ever asked that. That was definitely forbidden. "She was beautiful. Is beautiful."

"I thought she was dead."

"No, she's not. We are just meant to say that."

Silvie almost hit the car in front of us, before laying on the horn and looking at me sideways, raising one eyebrow. Clearly she doubted me.

"She's amazing. She can grow anything. Anything."

"Oh?"

"Geraniums like you've never seen before. Roses, even orchids. She has a green thumb. I miss her terribly."

Maybe if I can convince Silvie that Mom isn't dead she'll help me. She can get an address from the library, a phone number. She'd understand. What if Candy were looking for her?

"So," Silvie asked, "what do you think about a stepmom?"

"A stepmother? Never," I answered, no longer sedated by the hum of the car, dust or the tropical light.

"Never?" she repeated before instantly turning her rattletrap of a car around, lighting a cigarette and turning up the radio.

Never.

We didn't make it into Panama City, or the best shops with the finest deals. Those bolts of fabric remained on the shelves, especially the one I imagined with the mustard background and the tiny white flowers, as did the natural leather sandals all my friends wore at the weekend, as well as the gold hoop earrings that I guessed might catch the light when I auditioned for cheerleader.

Silvie dumped me off unceremoniously, not even pulling into the drive. *Wife number three.* In my room, I waited, practised breathing and reworked homework I did not need to do. Dad's Oldsmobile Cutlass with the prophylactics in the dashboard screeched to a halt outside, sending the parrots and the parakeets squawking.

Jeezus.

His heavy, measured tread shook the house as he came up the stairwell. The metal buckle of his Air Force belt made a seatbelt sound. *Unclicking.*

He didn't knock. Inside my room, he pulled the soft, dark navy cotton weave straight out of his belt loops with a swishing sound. I imagined a sabre slickly pulled from a scabbard.

"Enjoy lying?" asked my father, who could make a weapon out of anything. With the folded cloth belt gripped in one hand, he slapped it against the other.

"I didn't," I said, not looking up from the Biology textbook I was reading on my bed.

"You did. You said you didn't want me to marry Silvie."

"No, Dad, I didn't say that."

"Turn over," he said. "I asked her to marry me and she said 'yes' and now she won't because of you and your lies."

I counted fifteen strikes but didn't feel anything. I was still wearing the thin skirt I dressed in to go to Panama City. *Something easy to put on, to take off, for shopping.* My legs and feet were bare so I could try on sandals.

Afterwards he shouted, "Stand up. That's for lying!"

205

"I didn't," I said.

"You did."

It was hard to tell who was beaten, him or me. He backed away and then walked down the stairs, to the carved bar to make a Scotch on the rocks.

Maybe he'll call Silvie?

Sitting on the side of my bed, I took stock. Fifteen welts shone bright and sharp as when beef is scored. I thought about Mom. *Is that how you deal with it? Decide to feel nothing? What kind of magic, what kind of superpower do I possess?*

Mags slipped into the bedroom and with a cold cloth touched the back of my legs.

"I am so sorry, Lily. This can't happen again."

"It will."

"I promise it won't."

"You can't swear anything," I shouted at her, pushing her away.

None of this would be happening if you could have just made a bed out of a box, a tablecloth out of a skirt and collected soda bottles for the deposit.

Then my legs began to sting, the welts widened and I collapsed in tears.

When M flew off, she left Hernanda in charge to run the house. Even I knew the real reason M fired Fiore, despite telling us that 'that lovely young slip of a thing was going back to finish her education'. We knew it was to stop Dad's inappropriately flirtatious behaviour and to stop Artie thinking Fiore was like his mother.

Neither of them would be attracted to Hernanda, but I was. I liked her. We co-conspired. Being just shy of fat and over-the-top friendly, she blossomed when M left. Her cooking filled the house with sweet aromas and her housekeeping skills proved better than M's. Her English turned out to be surprisingly good, and she taught me Spanish on the go. Possibly confiding in her more than

M would find appropriate, I asked very specifically for her help, especially with Dad, whose demons seemed to be getting the better of him.

"It's normal. A man goes to war. What else do you expect, Lily? Tranquillity?" She blessed herself. "Any trouble, you come and knock on my door. I will help you with him."

The first time I asked for help, Dad was staring glassy-eyed, commanding his bedroom wall. In the past a cold glass of water and soft assurances that he was in Panama and not Vietnam would put him back to sleep, but this time it didn't work, and Artie and Mags refused to help.

"Call the police," Mags said. "It's too big for me."

"Call his commanding officer." Artie rolled over.

This particular night, Dad's groaning and muted talk began to worsen.

"Gook," he kept saying, "gook."

Slipping on my bathrobe, padding to his door, I stopped in the doorway and studied him. My father, the colonel, lay curled up small. I went into the room. Before I had a chance to feel sorry for him or turn around to get Hernanda, he had two fingers plugged into the side of my neck and the other hand slammed sideways across my chest.

"Who are you?" he demanded.

"Dad, it's me, Lily. Wake up."

"Lily?"

"Yes."

"I'm going to break your neck, Lily. How do you like that?"

Paralysed against the wall, I couldn't call out. My mind raced. Dad's fingers pushed against the thumping aorta in my neck. The pain, unbearable, kept me nailed to the wall, and I only dropped to the floor when Hernanda opened the door and in a low, quiet voice spoke to my father.

"Colonel Preston."

"Yes, sir," my father answered, turning away from me.

"I have the papers you need to sign. The insurgents have been rounded up. I will take this one with me. Be back shortly. Stand down."

It was as if Hernanda had turned on a lullaby. My father went back to sleep as if nothing had happened. She quickly steered me out of the room and into the kitchen, where she soothed me and made me promise never to take him on again alone.

"I am here." She made the sign of the cross. "Ask me if you need help."

I made the sign of the cross, too, and she walked me back to my room.

"Lock the door. Get me when your *padre* is ill. *Promesa?*"

"*Prometo*," I swore.

In the months that followed I was able to observe each phase of my sister's withdrawal from us and, finally, it became too much for me. Despite everything I had said to Artie about not leaving him alone with Dad, I told Mags that when she left for the USA, I was going too.

"Lily, you can't leave," she protested. "There's school—"

"I have to."

"But you don't have any place to go."

"Doesn't matter. I'll find something."

"You can't leave Artie."

"Mags, I cannot stay here."

"You can."

"I can't go through another marriage. Silvie is worse than Kinks ever thought of being. Silvie's daughter is the school—"

"Be careful, Lily. Be very careful," my sister warned, her eyes swivelling towards the door in case we were overheard.

"I can't do it," I whispered. "I have tried every which way I can to figure out how I can stay, help Dad, help Artie, but all I can see is disaster heading straight for me."

Mags gave up arguing. "I know. I know," she sighed.

"So I'm going with you," I declared. Every time I said it, I believed it a little bit more.

"You can't! I'm going to college, Lily. M doesn't want you—"

"But Dad told her to buy two houses. I can live with you in yours."

"She didn't. She bought one big one. I guess she wants to die in style. And remember, she always wins. You're setting yourself up for trouble. I'm going into a university dormitory. I am not counting on anyone but myself and you should, too."

"I am. I am not staying here," I insisted.

Mags stared at me for what seemed like forever and then back at her new suitcase, the one she'd bought for herself with the monogram and shoulder strap. She flipped the handle back and forth.

"Okay, but don't say I didn't warn you. They're gunning for you, both Silvie and M. I can't understand it, but they are. M is going after you like you were Mom, and Silvie... well, for her it's just par for the course. You're another woman and you're prettier than she is... and don't even mention her daughter. She asked me a million questions, too! She's evil, Lily. She's just a pair of tits and a great big mean streak in a skinny rib sweater. That's why I keep my head down and stay out of the way."

Mags kept flipping the handle back and forth.

"Look," she admitted, "I've gunned for you myself before now."

I felt like the girl on the school bus who years ago used to vomit every day because she was so afraid of what would happen next. Did my sister mean she hated me?

Mags reached out and touched my cheek, shaking her head slightly.

"Sometimes, it's just so hard to take, you know? You're beautiful and kind, and you have a mind – a rich one, a unique one – and you are ballsier than I could ever even think about being. I know you are never going to have to work in a canteen or even

209

a library. I know you are going to be rich, and you are going to do it with your writing. You might just be like Ayn Rand, Lily. Think about that. And you know what? I'll read everything you write." She smiled at me, willing me to reconsider my decision. "I just can't understand how you can give everything up here – cheerleading… class vice president… all your friends."

"Because I want to stay alive!"

"He is beaten, Lily. He's lost everything. Wives, his friends in Vietnam. Even M is gone."

"There's still Artie," I said, hating my own cowardice. "And M will always return, at some point, to rescue him."

"Silvie and her daughter will destroy Artie and bleed Dad dry. Who needs a crystal ball and who could we even call for help?"

"I want you to know that I have tried to get Artie to come with us. I even spoke to Dad about it. Artie is the one that wants to stay. His exact words were, 'And who is going to save that son of a bitch from himself?' He said he sees himself as the heat for a heat-seeking missile. He wants to take the hit. I couldn't talk any sense into him. He wants to stay."

"Reminds me of that day in the garage," Mags said, getting to her feet, "remember? He loves the old man. Despite everything."

"He does."

"Lily, I've seen your plans. Pure make-believe. You have to give up on this. Be wise. Look after yourself, like I am. Get into college. Mom has never been, nor will ever be, any help to us. Get that through your thick head. When was the last time you heard from her? Yes? Tell me."

"That's not exactly fair." Didn't Mags remember how it felt when we escaped with Mom from Virginia to Philadelphia?

"It is true. Tell me again the last time she telephoned or wrote us a letter."

Mags had a point, but I didn't respond. I couldn't give her details, but I knew in my gut that Mom was still alive but maybe not able to get in touch. I couldn't explain to Mags that Mom had been flattened by Dad and might have a hard time standing up. I wanted to say that if she sent a letter or made a call, do you think Dad would be receptive to that? Instead, because having a discussion about Mom with Mags seemed pointless, I just said, "Why can't Dad ever find a nice woman? Maybe one with no kids and a real zest for life, or at least not so hard-bitten. Maybe we should have been more open to some of the others."

Mags nodded. "Maybe. Still, there's one good thing, Lil'."

"What's that?"

"At least he's not stationed in Fayetteville, Arkansas."

THIRTY-THREE

As the plane arrived in Arkansas, Mags and I held hands. It was the first time in a long time, and it was the last. She knew she was going on to college, *saving herself*, while I was walking into hell.

The house M had bought with Dad's money was a gracious ante-bellum home. Mags and I were shown to our rooms by our sombre-faced grandmother. So far, I thought, this was a good move, right into the geographic heart of the USA. At least here I was closer to Mom. Would M let me stay? For how long? Her turf now, her rules. What little protection my father had offered was at an end. He had at least forced her to take me on, to make room in the house he'd paid for.

M said with great elaboration that she had sorted a local high school for me, and as she handed Mags the thick terry cloth towels, emphasised the word *guest* as she showed my sister to the *guest* room.

"M," Mags said with no hesitation, "the room is lovely. But tomorrow, I'm going to the university. My dorm room is meant to be ready, and my job in the cafeteria starts then, too. I start even before the other kids arrive."

"Students, Margaret – even before the other students arrive."

"Even before the other students arrive." Mags grimaced behind M's back. To me she mouthed, "I can't wait to get out of here."

Lucky bitch.

I heard the relief in her voice. *Even before the other students arrive.* I was mortified. Mags would do anything to escape. She would gladly wear a catering worker's unflattering hairnet. She would voluntarily sit in front of hundreds of her fellow students for the whole lunch or dinner period, hours at a time, hair scraped back, face shiny, smelling of food. She would smile while wearing a white lab coat and clicking a number punch. She *would* do anything to escape. *She had escaped.* Almost.

I wondered if, in the guest bedroom later, she would toss and turn, worrying that her dream would crumble to dust overnight. But I knew this would most likely not be the outcome. One more night and Mags would be free. This gave me hope, even if it was a long game.

M turned to me, as if to a chance visitor. "And this is the upstairs sitting room."

The sitting room. Not 'your room'. Am I supposed to sit in it?

"Is this going to be my room?" I asked.

"Lily," M said quietly, out of earshot of Mags, "you weren't invited here. This was meant to be my private sitting room, but for now I am allowing you to use it."

I got the message but I had prepared my argument on the plane for just such a moment. I could defend myself. There should be a place for me. I opened my mouth to protest. *Dad sent you here to purchase two separate houses or a duplex. One would be for Mags and me to live in while we were at university, and the other for you.*

"The sofa converts into a bed," M said, pre-empting my reply.

I stared at the bed. *A sofa bed? A bed I have to put away every morning and must pull out every night? An uncomfortable bed, meant to be for a few nights only.*

Bad news.

But I would grit my teeth and be on my best behaviour. In two years I would go to college. I could do this. I would do absolutely nothing wrong, or anything that M could remotely construe as wrong. If Mags could wear a hairnet, I could live with my grandmother. I could make it work. I could pray to God. I could always tell the truth. Be a saint.

"Here are the sheets," M said. "You can use the lingerie chest and the closets," she pointed, "over there."

M hated having me to stay. Mags was right. My accommodation here was makeshift, not permanent. Trouble was already hanging in the air. I sat down amidst the carefully embroidered pillows, looking out at the eaves that covered the veranda. The August breeze stirred, rocking a heavy lampstand. Mags knocked, then walked in.

"Don't give up," she told me. "I know this is shit, but think of Artie. If he can do that... You can do anything if you keep your cool and don't let M get to you. We've seen worse."

"Yes," I agreed, not believing it for one minute. I would try to get to Mom, but I didn't tell my sister that. She still believed it was nonsense. Maybe she even believed Mom was 'deceased'. I never did or would.

Oddly, a small vanity, built into the wall, stood between two banks of closets. I was reminded of a vanity from what seemed like an eon ago in New Jersey. I recalled being angry at Mags because she would not make a bed out of a box. I was livid then because I thought she'd sold us out. I was sad now because nobody wanted me. But Mom still did, didn't she? I was irritated because I had no magic formula to get myself to Mom or Mom to me. I couldn't keep calm because I knew M and surely she would hurt me. I could feel it. For the time being, I had to endure whatever she dished out, but I could also plan.

Arkansas to Philadelphia? 1,285 miles.

"Think about it," Mags said almost gaily, "which is worse, M or Mom Number Three?"

We smiled, looking at our reflections in the mirror over the vanity. We were practically grown up. She was as dark as I was light. I placed a comb on the counter, and my brush.

Can't be that tough, I thought, as Mags brushed a kiss across my forehead before leaving. *I can hack it for a night or two. Maybe I can make it last for three weeks or four. Someday*, I thought to myself, *I will look back and tell my daughter: "I had a vanity, a beautiful vanity, a place where I could sit and brush my hair. It was a place where I could dream of big things." Who knows? Maybe I will be able to tell her that I had a lovely time in my new school. That if my daughter ever has a vanity of her own then the best thing she can put on it is hope because that was all I had.*

I hoped against hope that M would leave me alone.

The school bus was like any other yellow school bus I had ever sat on, except that here the students were segregated. Not in any overt way. Nobody told anybody where to sit, but all the black kids seemed to sit in front, then there were a few empty seats, and all the white kids sat in the back. The Zone had been a melting pot. I never noticed colour there, black or white. I appreciated black men, girls with blonde hair and boys with blue eyes. A real mix and match. French, Spanish, American. To me they were no different. Was I colour blind or culture blind?

Who was I kidding? I had been the new girl long enough to know that every different place has its own rules and regulations. I was going to have to act like a rabbit again, busily sniffing out all the unwritten codes.

The yellow-brick high school rose up, new and different, the way they all were on my first day there. I readied myself for the old role of new girl. I missed the wind in Panama. Probably it would be raining now, stiff and hard, refreshingly cool. Then, just like that, the downpour would be over, with the sun shining and everyone soaked. I never recalled seeing umbrellas or raincoats there. Just the rain, then the steamy sun. I missed Artie, and M was already banging on about his marijuana use: "Just like your mother and alcohol… sleeping pills."

Apparently, Artie, in amongst his rescued animals, grew pots of marijuana. Evidently he and Candy had both missed the civil ceremony, which left Dad and Silvie fuming. *Didn't anyone care?*

My survival now depended entirely on M. It was a cat-and-mouse game, delicate in the extreme. She'd had it with Dad, her departure from Panama a humiliation too far. And now he had forced me on her, despite its technically being my home, and was allowing Artie to run wild.

I pretended total allegiance to M. *Yes, M… what a shame Mags this and Mags that. Yes, M, what a disgrace. Right you are. That Silvie, what a harpy, a gold digger, a woman hunting for an officer! What a shame for Artie, too, you should have brought him here.* We had to dissect Mags's behaviour over and over. *Yes, M. That's right, who knows what will become of her?*

I walked a tightrope. The critical bit was always to agree with M, no matter what she said – keep nodding and not get up until she said, "You may go." Additionally, I had to feign rapt attention, hang on her every word, even if I had heard them many, many times before. She would always start out with something minor, like, "What did you do at school today?" Then you had to be on your guard. Any attempt at conversation by M was a bugle call, an initiation into some sort of subterfuge that might blow up in your face or someone else's.

The trick was not to let the game get to you.

"I had a nice day, you?"

Then I had to wait. Any false move would be classed as impudence or worse. Would she ask another question? Reveal some awful news? Ask me to sit up, put my shoulders back, not to eat like an animal. Just pass her the saccharin, no matter where her conversation might stray. 'Rain this afternoon' might end up with a critique of Mags, Artie or me. Criticism of myself, I could take, of Mags to some degree, but when she started on Artie I began to twitch. And, of course, almost without exception, every conversation led to a complete denigration of my mother.

"Lauren Rose..." she would commence.

"Yes, M?"

"I knew from the beginning she was no good. I tried to warn your father."

"Yes, M." I would sit through an entire cup of my grandmother's instant coffee, which she could drink in the longest-lasting way, sometimes even topping it up with a bit more water.

Didn't she have anything else to do?

"Sit down," she'd say. "Stop wriggling."

That spelled disaster. It meant I wasn't interested or, worse, maybe I disagreed. It meant I had to listen to another diatribe, maybe about Aunt Penny and her recalcitrant husband – now dead. Aunt Penny was sheer perfection. Her deceased spouse, of course, had not been. Penny's daughters, M's 'other grandchildren', were all-star, and compared to us, well... there was no comparison. They were clean, well-groomed, scholars and beauties, both advancing nicely in life – unlike us. We were all headed for the gutter, just like our mother.

"Yes, M, yes."

When my grandmother finally let me go, to tiptoe from the breakfast room through the dining room, living room and up the stairs to my borrowed sitting room, without calling me back for another abusive remark, I would notice the photographs. Her daughter. Her son. A photo of Artie in his old military school uniform. Mags in a prom dress M had generously paid for in Panama. But there was no photograph of me. Most probably, she didn't have one. Perhaps I could right that, but on the other hand perhaps it would start World War III.

That was my motive for going into M's room. I didn't want to believe that in the whole house there was not a single photograph of me. I recalled a many-branched whatnot that used to sit on her dresser, right beside her Pietà, the Preston family tree, with at the top a photo of Dad in his bomber jacket taken when he was seventeen.

I crept across the carpet and into her forbidden room. I just wanted to look. *There has to be a photograph of me.* I looked at Penny and her two twin girls; they both had my eyes and chin. As I dared to touch it, M pounced.

"Lily," she shouted, "what in God's name are you doing in my room?"

"Nothing, M. Nothing."

I had too much pride to say 'looking for a picture of myself'.

"If I ever catch you in here again, I will call the police."

I could hear the story now – Lily the Thief – she'd tell Dad, Aunt Penny, Mags, if my sister ever came over, which she never did. In fact, Mags never even telephoned, and I didn't blame her. If I could, I would get as far away as possible.

M would make emergency calls:

"Yes, Ja-ack, I caught her red-handed going through my things. Everything rummaged. Your daughter has left me no choice but to call the authorities."

"Yes, Pen-ney, she shoved me so hard I cracked my head against the wall. Yes, the whole jewellery box. I have no idea. Should I call the police?"

Lily the Thief would become a more and more elaborate tale, embellished with facts from different times and places.

"A hobgoblin, a banshee... I don't know what you brought into this house. You should have seen her eyes dart and stare. I am frightened of her, Ja-ack. Scared."

As I listened in my sitting room, I shook my head. Was it any wonder that neither of M's children ever called her unless she rang them with some trumped-up emergency?

Tag; for the moment, I was 'it'.

I missed Artie. I ached for Panama, the certain knowledge that the Pacific Ocean lay only minutes away, that the winds were eternal, that they blew every day. I missed everything about the

Canal Zone, wondered who'd taken over my place as cheerleader and the vice presidency of the junior class. I missed my friends, *empanadas* and speaking Spanish with Fiore, and with Hernanda, who had refused to work for Dad and Silvie.

August in Arkansas held no hint of rain. Walking in the closest entrance to the school bus stop, I was immediately accosted by a tall, dark-eyed boy, who reminded me of Panama and everything I'd left behind, especially Artie.

"Piece of information," he said, "that door is for the blacks."

"Blacks?"

"Negroes."

"Negroes?"

"Where you from, girl?"

"Panama," I said, shifting into New Girl persona.

"Oh, well," he said with some relief, "international."

Global, I mused. Finally, trailing after him, I reached room HH3 – my homeroom. And there was my dark-eyed boy again sitting right beside me, grinning as if I had made his whole day.

"Ever smoke any Panama Red?"

"No," I answered, but momentarily thought about saying, "Maybe."

He whistled, and then shouted, "I got dibs on the new girl."

I was still thinking about blacks and Negroes and separate doors and spaces on the bus when he leaned over and said, "My name is Geronimo, what's yours?"

"Lily," I answered. "If I'm not meant to come through that back door because I am white, why did you?"

"Because I am brown."

"What?"

"Yep," he said, "here that means black."

"Too confusing. Pointless. I'll come through the most convenient door. Where are you from?"

"Costa Rica," he laughed, "my *prima* from Panama."

"What?"

"The name is really Guillermo."

"William."

"Yes, but generally around here they can't pronounce it so they just call me Geronimo, like the American Indian."

"Guillermo, I love it."

Just saying my new friend's name was like a taste of honey from Boquete bees, from home, or the last one anyway.

"Guillermo."

Between classes, down one hall and up the other, I read posters about the upcoming student elections. In a toilet stall, I rested my forehead against the door. 'Cindy for class vice president'. Who cared that *I* used to be vice president – in a larger school, maybe a better one. I had been elected a senior cheerleader, but here I was returned to nobody status.

Behind the school, Guillermo met me in the smoking area and was surprised I didn't smoke.

"It's the new girl," he announced. "Tell us about Panama."

"Well," I answered, "it's a country in Central America. It's that tiny bridge of land that connects North and South America, and it's most famous for the Panama Canal, which cuts right through the middle, but what I love best is the beauty of the land and the people, the music and the birds—"

"No, not that stuff. The pot, drugs, marijuana. Does it just grow on trees?"

"No, but they do have an amnesty box at the airport. When they've collected enough dope, they incinerate it. It's near an area where a lot of kids go. They sit down and get high off the fumes."

"Guess you won't find that in the guidebook."

"No."

Guillermo considered. "Listen, I don't know a lot about most things, but I am going to give you some advice, New Girl. You don't belong here, or at least it will take you a while to belong here.

That's the way it works. Smile. Look beautiful… and the rest of it… smarts, been places… hide it. And if anyone asks if you have met Jesus, just say 'Amen'."

Guillermo invited me to meet his family, play pool in the basement and sit around the flagstone swimming pool while generally berating life in Fayetteville. While we sipped what his mother called sweet tea, an engine gunned in the driveway.

"That will be Diego," Guillermo said.

"Diego?"

"My twin. I think you will be perfect for him."

"What do you mean?" I asked.

Before Guillermo had a chance to answer, Diego walked in. Tall, handsome, better-looking than his brother, I felt momentarily swept away by him. For no reason, he lifted my glass of iced tea, pulled out the lemon wedge with two fingers, rattled the ice and downed it in one long gulp. He smiled, showing me a perfect set of teeth.

"Are you Diablo?" I said. "I think I heard you on the roll call in Environmental Science."

"Diablo." He chuckled. "Diablo and Geronimo, *sí*?"

Guillermo piped up, "It's Diego, Lily. People here can't pronounce it so they say Diablo."

"Okay. That's weird, but I get it."

"*Nueva Chica?*" Diego asked.

"*Sí*," I answered, "*soy el.*"

Diego smiled, and said, "You're the one."

THIRTY-FOUR

"A seamstress?" I asked, aware of M's many deceptions and tricks. The word seemed to be from another century. I imagined heavy fabric, the rustle of floor-length skirts, hatboxes, tubular muffs, the clack of carriages and steamer trunks.

"A dressmaker," M translated. "She can make anything – without a pattern. Choose anything you desire, something from a magazine."

My heart held its wish in check, but there was one gown – just a drawing, a sidebar, a page in *Seventeen* magazine I'd seen in school. The model held a thick velvet skirt up and to the side – just like Olivia Hussey in *Romeo and Juliet*. Had M said 'yes' to my going to the prom?

She stood there, right in front of me, waving her arms as if flourishing a wand, telling me, "Anything, whatsoever, choose anything at all."

Racing up the stairs, two steps at a time, I already saw myself dancing – in Diego's arms.

"Slowly, Lily." M's voice rang out. "Don't run in the house."

With the picture of my prom dress from *Seventeen* on the dining-room table, I waited patiently as I listened to M and the seamstress busily discuss where to position the cushioned pad into the shoulder of her new dress that helped to disguise M's twisted spine from 'the dancing accident'. "You see," she explained to the other woman, who nodded with a mouthful of pins, "then no one notices the hump."

The dressmaker, towering over M, cocked her head, zeroing in on the picture of my dress. She could see it: me as Juliet. A smile tugged at the corners of her mouth as she slipped a pin into M's upholstered hump.

"That dress," she finally said to me, "would look good on you."

The dressmaker measured and hemmed and hawed and finally asked if we had the fabric.

"Yes," I answered, waiting for M to give me permission to go and collect the royal blue satin for the gown, the blue velvet for the floor-length pinafore and the white eyelet lace from the closet in her room.

"The back of the pinafore," the woman said, "should be slightly longer than the front so as to produce the illusion of a train. What do you think, Miss Lily?"

"Perfect."

"The neckline like this?" She demonstrated and my grandmother agreed. "Your hair must be styled, nails polished and with just a touch of make-up?"

M nodded.

I danced with the moon; Mom must have been hovering somewhere. *Make-up.*

I couldn't breathe for three weeks, certain that if I put a foot wrong, sanctions would be taken and the prom and the Juliet dress would be whisked away.

The banner over the gymnasium read 'Here Comes the Sun', and I felt as bright as daylight. While winter was on the way and I still worried about Artie, especially with no word from Dad or

Silvie, hadn't I thrown off the shackles of Divorce I, Divorce II and Mom War III? I had hope. I had a ball gown that weighed a ton, and I felt like a girl in a medieval dance, or at least straight out of a Franco Zeffirelli film.

I hummed 'Here Comes the Sun' as the band played the theme. The transformed gym looked like a beach, and I could only think of Panama, the San Blas Islands. In his tuxedo and starched white shirt Diego stopped time. I thought of him as mine, but so, it appeared, did a number of other girls. I folded my thin, white gloves and tucked them into my small bag, embroidered with seed pearls. I danced along with everyone, pretending not to mind when Diego was shared around, and, like most of the girls, I held my breath when the name of the Prom Queen was announced.

"Susie Handy!"

As she was a new best friend, it felt a bit as if I'd been crowned myself, but when she kissed Diego on the lips, I stepped back, pretended not to notice and instead started the conga line that snaked its way around the polished floor. Everyone shouted more than sang 'Here Comes the Sun', and at the end of the night everyone started to head home, mostly sober, especially me. I had to toe the line. *Survival.*

Diego sang to me in Spanish, and we talked about Panama and Costa Rica. It seemed a bit 'fairy dust' that his dad, being a physicist at the university, had brought him to Fayetteville, and my dad, looking for a place for a farm and a university for Mags, had brought me. Cuddling in the park, not far from M's house, I smiled. Could life get any better? First, I had a life that didn't include pulling my father off a maid, I had a boyfriend, a school that seemed cool and M, who might actually start being kind, treat me as her own and help me understand life, grow, achieve, do things I imagined a loving grandmother would.

Momentarily, I deliberated over whether or not to tell Diego about Mom, but when he pulled me close, it went straight out of my mind. Who wanted to go home?

We did make it home by M's curfew: one o'clock.

"*Señorita*." Diego bowed to me as he opened the car door.

"*Señor*," I replied.

The lamp beside the front door shone like our own private moon. Filled with dreams of Verona, Panama and even Diego's Costa Rica, stars in velvet night, a breeze, a balcony…

"Lily," M called out just as Diego's lips grazed mine. "Is that you?"

"Yes," I answered nervously.

"Yes, what?"

"Yes, M."

As M unlocked the front door, she swept everything away – Verona, the perfumed darkness, all of it.

"Goodnight, Diego," M said, closing and relocking the door after I stepped inside. "You look like Lauren Rose," she remarked.

I beamed.

"It wasn't a compliment." She paused. "Your mother was a whore."

Moving carefully past her, with my gloves and my beaded bag, I held my skirts up and out like the model in *Seventeen*. "Goodnight, M," I said, "thank you."

M might have thought I was insolent, but I truly was grateful for my blue dress, the prom and Diego. Thankful for the evening, an introduction to adult behaviour, a new outlook, I began to understand something that Mags already did. A whole wide world awaited and I doubted M's ability to shape and control all of it.

Your mother was a whore.

Sad old M. What was it that she hated? Me? Mom? Herself? She didn't make a dent in my joy. As I twirled slowly just inside my bedroom door, the sitting room, I heard a little yawn.

"Mags?" I leaned in.

"Lil'?" Mags stretched, rolled over and opened one eye. "You look amazing."

"I do?"

"Yes."

"Thanks," I said. "But what are you doing here?"

"I tried to make it before you left. Wanted to see you, take a photo, but I couldn't get out of the canteen. Had an extra shift."

"Oh, thank you, Mags. I had a brilliant time. Better than ever. I get it, Mags. I've got to take care of myself. Start thinking about myself, *for* myself. But just for tonight, do you know what I wish?"

"You had Mom's number?"

My sister placed a folded piece of paper in my palm, folding my fingers over it.

"I don't intend to ever call her, but I know you might."

I sat up for ages, long after Mags had gone to bed, until the sun came up, in my dress, thinking, dreaming, speechless, terrified and at the same time brave, with that number in my hand.

Diego gave me a ride home from school every day, which raised a few eyebrows. M would never have approved, so he dropped me off at least a block from home.

"One day," he said, as we sat feeding the swans in the park before I had to be home, "your grandmother will be history."

"I can't really imagine it."

"Doesn't matter. One day she'll be gone."

My ball and chain.

"Diego, my mom is not really dead."

"I didn't think so."

"Why not?"

"Sixth sense or something."

"Really?"

"No, actually it was my mom. She said you didn't act like a kid with a dead mom." Diego stopped pitching crumbs to the swans and turned towards me. "Say it again."

"My mom's not dead."

"Again."

"My mom's not dead."

"How about, she's alive."

"My mom's alive."

"Okay, so where is she?"

"Philadelphia."

"*Nueva Chica*, that's a long way away."

"Yes, but I have the telephone number."

"On you?"

"Yes."

"Well, please, pass it over."

From my purse, I withdrew my wallet, and from the secret compartment, I took out the small folded piece of paper.

"Lily," he looked at me, "this is illegible. The crease runs right through the number."

"That's okay." I smiled. "I have it memorised."

"Perfect then. Let's go. We can use the phone at my house."

"Wait. I need to be home in fifteen minutes. What about M?"

"What about her? What's she going to do? Get you committed?"

Yes, I think she might just be capable of that.

"Diego, we only have fifteen minutes. I need to be home. M will kill me."

"I think that's against the law."

"Trust me."

"I think you're afraid to call your mom."

THIRTY-FIVE

Was I afraid to call Mom?

She might hate me, have a new family, other children. Why didn't she ever write, or make an effort to come to Texas or Panama? Maybe she knew I lived in Arkansas, or maybe she had just had enough. Maybe she, too, was afraid of Dad and M. Maybe I just wanted her to materialise in her kidskin heels, Chanel No. 5 and nude stockings.

I didn't need Diego to call Lauren Rose. I could call her on my own. I could call from the school phone booth. What had I been waiting for? Didn't I have the number memorised? I counted out the exact amount of money, dialled the number, dropped in the change and waited.

Would it be Nana's voice or Granddad's? Mom's?

It turned out to be none of those. I tried three times and still got the same message: "The number you have reached is not in service, or temporarily disconnected. This is a recording."

I stood for just one moment as the thought ran through my mind that maybe Mom was dead after all. My life seemed to drain from the top of my head, sucked down through the earth, through the soles of my feet. What had I been thinking? Mom would just pick up the phone and recognise me? I hugged my books to my chest. Yes, I did. I expected she would pick up the phone and recognise me.

A few weeks later when I least expected it and was knee deep in preparing for exams, Diego found me in the school library.

"It's a ring," he said before even handing me the small box to unwrap. "Will you?"

"What?"

"Wear it."

"Me? What about Susie Handy?" I asked. By now I knew how popular he was at the school. He had friends everywhere, boys, girls, young and old. There was a rumour that even young Mrs Bright, the English substitute, was one of his admirers.

"Never. Susan Handy? You've got to be kidding me."

"Yes, Susan Handy, why not?"

"Because I want to be with you."

"I can't accept a ring, Diego. M would kill me…"

"Why does she even have to know?"

I laughed out loud. "You're right. She doesn't."

Diego finally opened the box for me and slipped the brightly coloured Costa Rican ring on my finger. "With this ring," he said, "I promise to help you find your mother, which clearly you intend to do with or without me."

"I do," I said, and felt infinitely normal for the first time since the prom.

"By the way," I asked one day after school, "will you teach me to drive?"

Of course Diego agreed, and we worked at it every afternoon. M, now charmed by Diego, bought a car, and he, beguiled a bit by her, took her to run errands. Always surprised by M's ability to hypnotise, I wondered how she did it. How could she dupe people so easily? Even I could be taken in. I always hoped to get along with her, that when we had a good patch the harmony would last forever. I desperately wanted someone to love me.

I knew what Diego was up to when he danced her around the kitchen, opened and closed doors for her, took her shopping at the Piggly Wiggly, asked her about her career, let her tell the same stories over and over again. He took her to church, and even sat with her. He anticipated her every move; whatever she needed, he did. He complimented her children, her other grandchildren, and intuitively avoided any subject that made her wince. He handled M like quicksilver, pouring her from one hand to the other.

Without M's permission, there would be no Diego and me. Saying that, I always waited for the other shoe to drop. There would come a moment when the tide would turn. Suddenly, Diego the Demigod would become Diego dead man. M's personality would change. I enjoyed the upside while it lasted. She was for now the keeper of the keys, and I would stay onside.

The day I passed my driver's test, Diego suggested dinner. He'd bought me flowers and chocolate.

"I bribed the examiner," he joked.

We drove all over Fayetteville. It was a town I was beginning to love. It was becoming home to me, and Diego and his family had played no small part in that.

"Park over there." He pointed, fumbling with the contents of his backpack.

As I turned off the engine, having shown off a nice parallel park, Diego grinned and handed me an envelope.

"What's this?" I asked.

"Open it."

"No, it can't be. To Costa Rica?" I asked, staring at the air ticket in my hand.

"M has already agreed because my mom's coming too, of course. How else?" He laughed.

At the front door, no sooner had Diego given me a goodbye kiss than we heard M's voice.

"Lily!" She came out the side door. "Stop making a public spectacle of yourself."

"Sorry," Diego said without missing a beat, "you should be first in line to congratulate your granddaughter. She passed."

While Diego smiled, M glared at me, but at least for now I was off the hook and a plan was just starting to grow in my mind.

In Atlanta Diego and his mother flew on to San José and I changed planes for Philadelphia, Pennsylvania. It had taken all my fast-talking powers of persuasion to get Diego and his mother to sign up to my scheme, but I was not going to let this opportunity pass. When would I ever get a chance like this again?

Diego's mother offered no resistance, merely turned to her son and said, "I told you she's got something ticking." What could possibly go wrong? I'd meet them back in Atlanta, and for now everyone else thought I was in Costa Rica.

After landing in Philadelphia I ran out the arrivals hall and into a taxi. I imagined Diego in San José, and for a brief moment wished I could be in two places at once. I only had the old address, which I gave the driver, who said, "Ten minutes, twenty max."

His accent was music to my ears, sounding a bit like Uncle Sean or Danny. I tried to contain myself – all the 'what-ifs'. What if she really was dead? What if she really was crazy or no one wanted to see me? What if she didn't recognise me or didn't want me?

As the cab pulled up to a small row house, I stepped back in time. The porch remained the same, with pots of geraniums everywhere. I paid the driver and collected my bag with nothing in it except pyjamas and a pair of blue jeans. As the taxi driver departed with a toot of his horn, he called out, "Enjoy the family."

Walking up the short flight of stairs I had last gone down the

231

day Dad kidnapped us on the way to school, I faltered. *Why hadn't I run?* Nana opened first one door and then the next before I'd even rung the bell.

"Lily!" She closed her eyes and took me into her familiar arms. "What are you doing here?"

"Mom..." I said.

Anna moved me deftly off the porch and into the front room, seating me on the sofa. "Does your grandmother know you are here?"

"No."

"Okay," she said, "let me get some tea. Are you hungry?"

Everything was just as it was years back. Through the archway, on the sideboard my mother's graduation photo still had pride of place. *Where is she?* Obviously, not at 402 Sycamore Street.

Beside the teapot, Nana's prized Irish butter shortbread biscuits fanned out, neatly formed and cut into three- and four-leaf clovers. I studied the dusted sugar. I couldn't seem to hear what she was saying.

"Lily, your mother had a nervous breakdown. She's not here, I'm so sorry."

"Where is she?"

"Not far. Lily, your mother is safe. She's getting good care."

"May I see her?"

"No. Your mother is just getting back on her feet. She held out for so long. We kept expecting you kids to call. She wrote every day – letters to Ohio, Texas and Panama. She only knew you'd moved on when the letters came back 'return to sender'. Then she'd call her lawyer, and it would all start again. One day she just stopped – stopped everything, writing you, working, saving money."

I remembered her seizure under the illuminated statuette of Jesus. "Nana, I never had any letters. May I please see her, know where she is?"

"Not now, Lily. It would be too shocking for her nerves just now. I will tell her that you came. It will make her happy."

"Will she get well?"

"I think so. The doctors think so. She's starting to make plans, which is a good sign. She's moving to Connecticut. I promise she will contact you when the time is right. Now I need to call your grandmother."

"No, Nana, please don't do that."

"She really doesn't know you are here?"

"No."

"Lily, I am really sorry that you've come all this way. I know what a risk you've taken with your father and grandmother, but your mother is not well. This is not a good time. I think a better one will come, and I know I have no business asking you to be patient, but please try. And I am sorry that I cannot take you in. You cannot imagine how hard everything has been. Your father and your grandmother have caused extraordinary pain and damage. Do you understand what would happen if you came to live here?"

"I do."

I didn't want to admit it, but I understood. We both did.

Nana held me for a long time, saying nothing at first and then telling me that she loved me and that I looked so much like Lauren Rose at this age, my smile in particular.

"In the future we will all be together again," she swore to me.

THIRTY-SIX

"I can't take it anymore," M sobbed down the phone. "Lily is up to her old tricks. It will be the death of me! She's sleeping with that boy, may even be pregnant for all I know."

I'd woken up. It was midnight.

Who is she speaking to?

"How do I know? *He* told me," she emphasised, "said she threw herself at him. People in this town don't take to this sort of behaviour. She's just like her mother…

"The decision's been made. There's to be no further discussion. She cannot go on living under my roof. It will be the death of me. Ja-ack, Penny will not have me exposed to this sort of unpleasantness. I will not have it, and you shouldn't either."

Sitting in the stairwell, stunned by what she was saying, I listened to the rantings of this madwoman, who could one minute let me go off with Diego to Costa Rica with her blessing and the next throw me out with her curses.

I stood, poised for flight, but reluctant to leave until I'd heard it all: the lies, threats, perversions of the truth.

"Well, of course it's your house! But I believe you said I was to look on it as my home as well."

I slumped back on my sofa bed. *Dad kick his own mother out? No chance.* The veranda light reflected off the ceiling and the walls. Did she know about Philadelphia, that I hadn't gone to Costa Rica? I didn't care. I had four valuable pieces of information: Mom was alive, didn't hate me or have a new family. And she was planning to move to Connecticut.

In the morning, I acted polite and pretended I was unaware of last night's conversation. From M's behaviour to me, it might never have happened.

"Orange juice?"

"Yes, please."

"Toast?"

"No, thank you."

Except for Diego and his mother, I kept the joy of what I had learned in Philadelphia to myself. It fortified me. Maybe M sensed something, because after 'Costa Rica', Diego was banished. Without offering any reason, M merely said 'that boy' was forbidden to come on the property or she would call the police. So I met him in secret. I didn't even bother to ask M why because that was an opening gambit that would lead to nothing but trouble and insane thinking.

M insisted I take the bus to school and back. I did everything she asked, and listened carefully and with great patience to her unwavering litany of abuse, the never-ending list of all the shortcomings I'd inherited from my mother. If this was the price I needed to pay to stay in Fayetteville, to be close to Diego and see Mom soon, I decided I would pay it.

One evening while I was confined to the house, with only memories of Philadelphia, drives with Diego and a ring I couldn't wear, I sat down with M. She had a cup of tea and offered me a glass of milk and two Oreos from the tin decorated with a picture

235

of a Dutch girl. I listened to the clock tick. She studied her watch. We talked about nothing in particular until she asked me to lock up.

"Take the keys, I am going to bed. They're in the sideboard."

"Yes, M," I said. "Sweet dreams."

Maybe things were flipping again. Maybe Diego could come over again. She was letting me lock up. This was a first. I was on my toes, but ever hopeful. Maybe we could still be a normal family.

Why didn't I ever give up on my pipe dreams?

I didn't notice it when I took the keys out to lock the front door and the back, but I spotted the letter after checking all the first-floor windows and pulling the blinds when I went to put the keys back.

The letter was in an envelope neatly sliced open. The piece of paper was pulled half out. *Could it be from Mom?* No. The thin airmail stationery, addressed to M, carried Silvie Tierney's looping scrawl, with her signature daisies for dotted I's. Feeling sick in a way that dated way back, I forced myself to read the note. *What next?* I could hear M's voice now: "Reading my mail, going through my things…"

Dearest Emma,

My heart aches for you. I can only imagine how you feel. I have known for ages that Lily, like her mother, is schizophrenic. Jack didn't need to tell me anything. In my work as a librarian I have helped innumerable patrons research and understand the nature of the illness: the quick changes in personality, the manic behaviour, the follow-up lethargy. I knew as soon as I met her that she was devious, and I am not at all surprised that you say that the school now labels her incorrigible. Poor you!

I am so happy that you called us. Yes, your son must do something. I support you fully. Jack will be there to get help for Lily. I know the promiscuous behaviour must be

terribly unsettling and remind you of the disaster of your
son's first marriage. Lily must, if your plan does not work,
be institutionalised. Sadly, that is the way these things go.
Like mother, like daughter. Remember, before taking my
degree in Library Studies, I was an assistant nurse at the
Corazón Psychiatric Institute.

On this note, and please believe I do not want to alarm
you, I have recommended to Jack that Artie be assessed. I
think it is too early to tell, but he may have similar problems.

Thank you for asking about my daughter Candy. She is
a dream, as always. Jack loves her as his own. She remains a
good influence on us all.

Your loving daughter-in-law,
Silvie

"One by one," I said aloud. A sort of cold steel slithered its way
through the ribs in my chest. Mags had been right. Silvie and M
were natural allies. I slipped the letter back into the envelope.

Nothing had changed.

The other shoe would drop, and I was afraid.

THIRTY-SEVEN

M didn't tell me where I was going until the night Dad arrived from Panama. She left that job to him.

"Your grandmother has chosen a girls' school for you."

"Father Dominic suggested it?"

I knew M set great store by the opinion and guidance of her parish priest.

"Yes, he said it was the right sort of place for you."

I ate the Worcestershire meatloaf. I looked at Mags, whom I hadn't seen since the night of the prom. Dad had arrived mid-day. It was Saturday. We guessed he might be coming as M cleaned the house in a particular way, made foods that only he ate.

After a second, thick slice of meatloaf, dripping in gravy, my father announced we would be leaving in the morning for St Savior's.

"That way you can start class on Monday, with the rest of the girls."

No time for me to see Diego, much less call him. Mags would have to let him know where they were taking me.

I couldn't eat. *St Savior's? What exactly has M told the priest?*

"What do you expect," my father said over his green, pistachio-perfumed pudding, "when you can't keep your clothes on? This started in Texas. Didn't you have some issue there? In Panama it was drugs. Doesn't matter where you go, there you are in trouble, eh? Just like your mother."

All lies.

After finishing the toxic-green pudding so M would not be offended, I asked to be excused.

"Lovely dinner, M."

"Yes," she said, "thank you. You'd better start packing."

Upstairs, I sat for a minute, thinking about how I could escape. This had to stop. How long ago had she started to talk to Father Dominic? It had to pre-date the interrupted kiss in the driveway, passing my driving test and the trip to Philadelphia. God, I hated all this. The lies, deceit, subterfuge. There was a way out, and I was going to find it. My grandmother was a nutcase, a madwoman, deranged. I pulled a small case from the top shelf.

"Hey." Mags crept into the bedroom, and I jumped.

"You scared me, Mags."

"I'm not surprised. This house is booby trapped."

"Where have you been all this time?"

"Living my life."

"You should have called."

"I did."

"When I was here."

"Lil', I have and I did. She wouldn't put you on, every time. She's a bitch, but you will never convince Dad that she is a total psycho. Don't try on your long ride to St Savior's. He knows it; he just doesn't want to deal with it. Remember, he grew up with it. Same with Aunt Penny. No matter what the cost, they'll keep their heads buried in the sand."

"Yes," I sighed, "I just want to know when this is going to end."

"Soon," my sister said, "when you turn eighteen."

"I'll be dead by then. I want to run away now. March right out of here tonight. Can't you help me? Please."

"No, Lily, I can't, and it kills me that I can't. That bitch will call the police and have me incarcerated. She will work a larger drama so all the world can know her terrible martyrdom and then even old Penny will come running, not to help, though – just to count the cash. M's been a sociopath for so long – she's always one sick step ahead."

I started crying uncontrollably, even if I knew sobbing was forbidden in the Preston household. No tears, no anger, no love.

"I'm sorry," Mags said. "Really sorry. But it's not so long to wait now. You will be eighteen soon – a year? You can do this. You have to do this. Be brave."

I stopped whimpering and let Mags stroke my head, promise me a future. What were my options? Zero.

"Look," Mags finally said, after I calmed down, "you must really try to be strong. I'm not sure what's on the horizon."

"Mags, I don't want to do this. I don't want to go away again. Do you know anything about St Savior's?"

"I don't know a thing. You know M. It's always broadside. Please keep your chin up and I will get word to Diego."

"Thanks."

Looking at Mags, I felt proud of her. She was perky, happy, standing upright, even able to joke about her meal clicker and hairnet. *Self-made.* She gave me hope, even if I knew St Savior's would not be my moment in time.

Dad drove M's car past fields of wheat and corn, most of them harvested and left barren for the spring planting, through Arkansas and into Missouri. Across the Rand McNally road map, he'd written in his attacking, clean black hand 'St Savior's' and underscored it twice. While I navigated the simple straight route north, I listened to the car engine and the tires against the road. At a roadside café, I couldn't help but think of our long drive to Texas years before.

"Milk," he ordered for us both.

"Dad," I began, "I am not promiscuous. I don't smoke pot. I don't drink."

"I don't want to talk about any of this. Let's go."

M lies to you. She makes this stuff up so you will call her, come see her. Your sister, too. No one ever calls M because they want to. Not unless there is some crisis she can drum up. This time I am the crisis. Don't you get it? She's just telling lies.

I heard Mags's voice saying, "Don't try to tell him anything."

"Let's go," my father said again.

I would have, if I could have.

St Savior's, at first hidden behind a dense wood of red cedar, rose up slowly from behind one locked gate after the next, one intercom after the next. With the windows down, the spicy wood smell reminded me of Christmas, after which time I promised myself I would be out of here. I don't know how but I swore to myself I would be back in Fayetteville or with Mom. A nineteenth-century Gothic building stood brick-solid in front of me. My hope seesawed. An immaculate reception area, except for the odd curled leaf from a bare dogwood, greeted me, but it wasn't until I rounded the corner, past the Victorian polychrome façade, that the grand public face of St Savior's dwindled into a clutch of temporary buildings made from aluminium siding. Someone, it appeared, had run out of funding.

"You might like it here," my father offered, ever the optimist as we pulled into the turning circle at the top of the drive. "Never know. But, Lily, you must make something of yourself."

"Is this a hospital?" I asked.

"Of course not," he said quietly.

Softening up? Maybe he'll turn around. Take me back. I'd even consider Panama. Anything but this: Nueva Chica *yet again.*

A black-clad nun met us at the front door, immediately ushered my father into one room and me into another.

"Wait here," she ordered.

"Good afternoon," I could hear my father saying to the headmistress, the mother superior, holding his Air Force hat in his hand. "Thank you for seeing me on such short notice."

The rest I knew by heart: conquering war hero needs help. Father and mother to three small children, now teenagers. Didn't everyone owe him something?

I imagined my father parroting M and the letter from Silvie. *Sadly, Lily's mother was a schizophrenic... promiscuous... an alcoholic. It appears that Lily is going in the same direction. You are our only hope. My daughter is incorrigible – my mother says.*

I pondered the tiled floor. I studied the wavering reflections of my father and the mother superior through the frosted glass of her office door, craning to hear murmurs and trying to make out the intermittent shrieks I heard coming from the main house. *What was that?* I couldn't decide, much less figure a way out, so instead I decided to wander. *Where am I?* Every doorknob I turned was locked, every glass reinforced with wire or bars. This whole place had the feel of a prison. Loony bin, Artie would say.

"Lily," my father called out.

"Here."

"I've got to go."

Dad. I am a good girl. May I have a kiss, please?

He just wanted to leave.

It must kill him to say things about me that he cannot believe are true. Why would M make him do this? Some fealty, some payment for imagined sins. If he weren't my father, I could kill him.

"Bye, Dad," I sang out.

He didn't turn around, shoulders hunched uneasily.

Well, that's that then, I said to myself. *Let's get on with it, New Girl.*

"Miss Preston," the mother superior motioned to me, "come this way." Two other nuns joined her and one slightly overweight man in trousers a size too small for him. They seemed to be prepared for something. *Am I meant to run away?* The man did not have a butterfly net, but I felt he might. As we passed through room after room I noticed an antique lintel which read 'Catholic Reformatory and Hospital for Young Offenders 1895'.

"This school must have been many things in its time," I ventured, but no one responded.

"Best not to speak unless spoken to here, Miss Preston," the mother superior said. Her rosary and keys rattled as she walked.

In what appeared to be a nurse's office, I gave blood, had my blood pressure taken and my temperature recorded. After ten minutes with a lanky, nondescript doctor, who scribbled notes in a plain file with my name hastily scrawled on the front, I found myself in a sort of storeroom, where I handed over my own clothes in exchange for a skirt, blouse, shoes, underwear, sweater and faded pyjamas.

"Where are my things?" I asked.

"They've been put in storage," a uniformed attendant laughed.

"You can do anything," I heard Mags say.

Self-made.

I guessed this is where it started.

At the top of the stairs, on a well-polished landing, as I looked out from the fortress window, I imagined my father, the colonel, turning M's car at the top of the drive and quickly hitting the high road, singing the US Air Force Song 'Wild Blue Yonder'.

"Off we go…"

Guilty as sin. Cowardly bastard.

Mother Superior motioned to the others to leave and then rested one hand on my shoulder. I tried to assess if its weight was intended to comfort or intimidate.

I can do anything. In a year I will be eighteen.

"You may call me Mother or you may call me Sister Mary

Agnes. As you can tell from my lovely Irish accent," she leaned in, "I am a long way from home here, as you are. You will want to go home, as I do. Listen to me carefully. I am a fair judge of character. I will make that decision for you as and when necessary. It is my hope that you will go home, and sooner rather than later."

Thank you. Wherever home is.

I shared a room with five other girls. Sleeping hospital-style with all five white-painted, wrought-iron beds running parallel, we might have been in an orphanage. When Sister Mary Agnes and the goon squad left, a closet door on the far side of the room swung open. A large girl emerged dressed in the same grey uniform that I had just been given. She smiled at me.

"Want some?" She offered me a slice of black forest cake from out of a hatbox.

"Not now," I answered. "Thanks."

While Artie would call her coco-loco, I just felt pity. Did she have an irredeemable, lying, scheming, psycho grandmother, too?

Two more girls walked in, accompanied by escorts and babbling to each other. They were redheaded twins.

"What are you in for?" the prettier of the two asked.

"What?" I answered.

"Mental or criminal?"

"Neither."

"It's always one or the other here."

"Neither. I'm just finishing high school here," I said, or *until I can get back home or to Mom.*

They both started laughing, at which their attendants gave them warning looks.

"We are Beatrice and Barbara."

"Where are you from?" I asked.

"New York, New York," Beatrice said.

"Don't believe a word she says. We are actually from Chicago. Good, rich Irish Catholics," Barbara, the shorter of the two, added.

Their bodyguards left, and both girls sat down on the beds opposite mine. The pieces of the jigsaw finally fell into place for me. M had outdone herself this time, could twitter away about this with Aunt Penny and Ja-ack for months. Bars on the windows and lock after lock. I put a few things in the bedside table and hung what I'd been given from the storeroom in the closet.

"I'm going to try to call my boyfriend, and maybe go for a walk. Want to join me?"

Beatrice and Barbara laughed. Even the girl eating what appeared to be stolen cake joined in, and another girl, sitting on her bed on the far side of the room, cracked a toothy smile and broke her silence.

"You've got to be kidding me, right?"

"Maybe not," I sensed was the right answer.

"This is someone's enlightened idea of a hospital reformatory for teenage girls," Beatrice said, serious now.

Barbara added, "You are in here, under lock and key, because someone somewhere decided things weren't stacking up with you. You either have a drug or an alcohol issue. Maybe you're promiscuous. Or you've committed a crime, but you are still underage so classed as a 'juvenile offender'. And the other bit is that you may or may not have the issue or have committed the crime but someone somewhere thinks you will, sooner or later."

"I haven't done anything—"

Again, the girls started to laugh, and the one who had cracked a smile asked, "Not even marijuana? That's what they all say, 'I haven't done anything.' By the time you leave here, you will."

"No, not even marijuana. I am going for a walk."

"Good, you try that," Beatrice said.

Straightening the thin wool blanket on my bed where I had been sitting, I turned towards the door. All eyes followed me. We were locked in.

Would M stop at nothing? She'd pulled out all the stops this time: caged me. I sat comatose for how long I don't know, but then it dawned on me. That's what M would want, for me to waste my time figuring out why she was a monster, her son a minion, get depressed and give up; so – no – instead, I sat up, straight, had a rethink and did exactly what she and Dad had taught me: consider the endgame.

A few locked doors? Steel bars? Nothing can keep me from getting back to Mom.

The last shock of the day in a long line of shockwaves took me by surprise. Who would have thought that I would be made to take a sleeping pill before bed?

I learned early to keep the pill dryly under my tongue and at the first possible moment to throw it away. As a result, I sat awake night after night, when the others had drifted into a chemical oblivion. Then, I'd listen to the mammoth clock tick, behind its impenetrable wire mesh, second by second, on the dormitory wall. All around me the thick, drugged blanket of sleep lay heavy. Through the arched windows I followed the path of the moon. On clear nights the stars shone and frost crept in.

On most nights I imagined escaping. I came up with different ideas, but fleeing was exactly what M would hope I would do so that her ridiculous label for me of 'incorrigible' would stick. Some girls actually had fled, but mostly as a lark. They essentially called St Savior's 'home', and were happy to have been caught – rounded up by the police and brought back, with another black mark on their record. I had to play by the rules, whatever that meant, and use my gut instinct to somehow prove to the mother superior that I was in fact of sound mind. It seemed like it should be easy since it was true, but I wasn't about to start fooling myself. I knew what could happen.

Other nights, I played memories like movies, backward and forward, or in slow motion. I might start off with Mom, then move to Mags and Artie. Maybe I would go to France or Panama. I skipped the painful parts or I rewrote them. Of course, I always ended up with Diego, and a normal family, an ordinary life, having proper fun, instead of a father I pitied and a grandmother who conspired to imprison me. I saw myself in high school, wearing cute clothes, meeting friends, driving with Diego, the boy who loved me – and no one putting me in prison for doing so.

I knew Mags put her Preston faith in the fact we had already gotten through many bad things, but I knew just keeping my head down until I was eighteen would not magically make everything okay. I could do that and *still* stay locked up. Sister Mary Agnes, my gut told me, was my ticket out. I made believe she already knew an injustice had been done because she had that Irish thing, that Irish Catholic factor to be specific. An extra-sensory awareness of a fellow countryman in trouble, call it mindreading if you like, that had enabled Mom, Mags and me to flee once before.

Now, how would I prove my innocence? I knew, as before, it would be a waiting game. M would have to slip up before I did.

Christmas came and went, largely unobserved apart from with extra services in the chapel. It was thought best that I remain at school in order not to lose touch with my new, more settled way of life. I wondered if Diego had forgotten me by now. Maybe Mags hadn't told him where I was. I didn't expect to hear from M or Dad, but where was Mags? St Savior's was a fight for survival every day, amongst people who were waging war for their very lives in a different sort of way, or so it seemed. I was surprised to learn that most were orphans, had no one to care for them, except, in a funny way, each other.

My only escape was English class, which Sister Mary Agnes taught. I had always escaped into books, and now was no exception. Being teacher's pet had been a survival trick of mine for many years; it was also a way to pretend I had a mother. No matter, I would do anything, agree anything, just to get on the right side of the woman who had basically said to me: I am your key to getting out of here.

At night, down the hall or a floor up, I would hear a commotion break out, sometimes a siren. Someone was giving up or else fighting back. I learned the names of all the issues my fellow inmates suffered from. Beatrice was a manic-depressive; Barbara co-dependent on Beatrice, which seemed pretty natural to me, considering they were twins. By comparison with the problems faced by other girls these seemed like relatively minor ones and my dorm felt safer than most.

I thought often about what I heard Dad say to Sister Mary Agnes that first day – 'incorrigible and promiscuous'. Diego and I had not slept together so that was false; I was not promiscuous. Incorrigible? Because I could not please M? Was I being locked away for being nothing more than my mother's daughter? The truth was that I did want to punch somebody, something – burn the house down – but that would not achieve anything. Someday, for whatever reason, I believed I would get to be properly angry, I would be able to right the wrong that had been done to me.

I knew my father had painted a false picture of me and I thought even Sister Mary Agnes did, too. I read profusely, hid out in the library and steered clear as much as possible from one girl's phobia-induced screaming or another's manic episode.

My weekly group therapy and one-on-one support wanted to put a label on me: depressive, self-harmer, paranoiac, anorexic/bulimic, passive aggressive. Everyone agreed I wasn't the promiscuous type, not a 'bunny'.

"I just want to go home," I pretended to the group and the counsellor they brought in week after week. I began to understand the lay of the land – who got released and who didn't. That desire and the way I expressed it, calmly and repeatedly, caused everyone no end of amusement; even the therapist smirked.

"Add something constructive to the conversation," I'd be instructed.

"I'm going to see my mom again."

Once, on an especially nice evening when I was enjoying the cloudless sky and a full moon, which I was told could be a particularly tricky time at St Savior's, Beatrice sat straight up in her bed, speaking to no one, but talking all the same.

"You aren't leaving." She turned and stared right through me. "You are *not* leaving."

Lowering myself down in my bed so as not to spook her, I scanned the room, knowing exactly where the red emergency button hung some distance away. Our drugged roommates would not wake up. All fast asleep. "In candy land," they called it. They gobbled up their sedation, some seemed to live for it. The idea of running away or even going home brought down the house when I aired it to them.

"Ha-ha, where would we go?"

Without warning, Beatrice flew out of her bed and seized me by the throat. Her strength pinned me to my mattress.

"Die, bitch!"

I clutched on to Beatrice's wrists as I felt blood begin to trickle down my neck.

"No," I managed to say, struggling to copy Hernanda's smooth, unthreatening intonation. "You are going to let go of my throat."

Beatrice laughed.

"Beatrice, relax. Everything is okay. It's dinnertime."

By then Barbara was awake and shouting, "Beatrice! Stop it… Get off Lily! Get off her!"

Even if Beatrice had released me when Barbara shouted, waking her up, it still set off a number of alarms, lights and a night nurse, who came barrelling down the corridor outside. Immediately, I crossed the room and hammered the emergency button, until someone had to stop me.

Damn my bloody, fucking grandmother!

It was M I pounded each time I slammed the button.

Damn my bloody fucking grandmother!

Being the best fucking little girl in the world would get me nowhere.

Damn my bloody fucking grandmother, and her son, and her daughter who never did a goddamned thing to help!

"Stop slamming the alarm. It's over," an orderly instructed me, as he dropped to his knees and started to attend to my throat.

A young doctor appeared. "Trachea uncompromised," he confirmed as he knelt beside me and conducted a brusque examination. "Superficial injury only. Scratches."

By then, the regular staff had rounded up the rest of the girls in the dorm room and directed them back to their beds, some requiring a second dose of sedation. The orderly continued to restrain me from slamming the alarm while the doctor staunched the bleeding, but though the excitement was over for Beatrice, it was not yet over for me. Sister Mary Agnes sailed in from out of nowhere, like a steamer picking up a refugee.

"Look at me." She pulled my chin level with hers, fixed her eyes on me. "Calm yourself." Then, waving everyone else away, she said, "Lily's coming with me."

With surprising strength, she slipped one arm behind my back and the other under my legs and lifted me up like a small child. We seemed to glide together down a long, polished corridor, with her habit rustling, billowing, until we came to a small, unlocked room, where she set me on a low bed. Flowers filled a vase on the night table. She sat beside me, held on to me until my ragged breathing subsided and the sobbing stopped, until every terror I'd felt since I could remember had spilled out of me.

"I'm sorry," she said finally, and I recognised that this was someone who meant whatever she said. "Tell me where you come from," she said in a soothing tone. "In the old country."

The old country?

"Your mother," she prompted me. "What was her family name?"

"Ryan."

"That would be O'Riain then. *Rí* means king, Lily. So you are of royal origin." One arm encircled me still, protecting me. "So you must originally hail from Tipperary, not far from my own family in Limerick."

She said this like a blessing, like a door unlocking to who knows where, but I didn't care. Irish mumbo-jumbo or not, it was the first time in what seemed like forever that I felt safe in someone else's arms.

"Tell me," she said quietly, "all about your mother."

After that night when things could have gone horribly wrong, Sister Mary Agnes gave me my own room. I was still under lock and key and observed at regular intervals, but kept away from Barbara in particular, who thought I had somehow provoked her sister. Apparently Father Dominic had been called and had offered his opinion that I was an attention-seeker – something that didn't sit well with anyone else except M, who agreed I was clearly the culprit and gave the perceptive priest another neatly written cheque.

Hasn't she been right all along?

"I am concerned for your health, Lily," Mother Superior said to me one afternoon.

At least she had not added 'and mental wellbeing', and that was my first real glimmer of hope.

Self-harm predominated at St Savior's. Prior to being incarcerated I didn't know it even existed – along with a number of other phenomena like girls who wanted to be boys, to the collective horror and outrage of their parents and parish priests. I knew girls could be attracted to other girls, but for the most part at St Savior's everyone had a radar that read who was interested and who was not. I slept in my own room after the night Beatrice attacked me, and I kept trying to think of a way out. The only possibility seemed to be ingratiating myself further with Sister Mary Agnes, which was not difficult, and of course getting along as well as I could manage with my mercurial classmates.

Eleanor, who had been at St Savior's for two years, and whom Mother Superior thought might be ready to go home, became a sort of 'twin' to me. Sister Mary Agnes described to me the St Savior buddy system or 'twin' programme that was created for girls who were believed to be approaching the end of their time there.

"You look after her, she looks after you. A sort of mutual support system. Friendship, even."

"Okay," I agreed, as I subscribed to *anything* that brought me one step closer to Mom, before dashing off to do my daily chore, dusting the library before locking it back up – which I enjoyed. I liked reading *Time* magazine, sitting for a minute and imagining myself at whatever cost back in M's library or anywhere else, really. A few times the nun in charge caught me not doing the clean-up, but she only laughed, happy someone was reading, although she warned me all the same that if the library grew any dustier I'd be sent to the attic to soak stamps off envelopes.

"Remember," Sister Mary Agnes directed me, "Eleanor's healthy, but delicate. One of our success stories, if you will."

Having earned the right to walk in the school's park, from the front drive with its single file of dogwood trees to the main road, with its wall of red cedars, I asked frail Eleanor to join me. She came along gingerly, both because she had a genuine fear of the outdoors and because I'd become known as 'the one who did it to Beatrice'.

"Where are you from?" I asked.

"St Louis."

"Happy to know you are on your way home soon?" I stopped and snapped a twig. "Smell this. Freedom."

Nutmeg, cedar, earth.

"I don't want to go home."

"Why not?"

"I don't want to go home," she repeated more urgently.

Is she growing agitated? Sister Mary Agnes would not approve.

"Okay, Eleanor," I said, trying to calm her.

"I want to stay here."

"Why don't you want to go home?"

"Because there I am raped repeatedly by my stepfather and his two brothers."

"Eleanor, I didn't know. I—"

"They are drug addicts and alcoholics."

"What about your mother?"

"Mother?" Eleanor started laughing. "Don't have one," she said, and before I understood what had happened, my new friend had taken a razor from her sleeve and sliced a perfect X into the palm of her left hand. Cool and collected now, she smiled at me beatifically.

"I'm not going home," she said.

In the mother superior's office, I waited. An hour grew to two, and I wondered how I would be disciplined for Eleanor's latest episode. Wasn't I, her 'twin', meant to safeguard her? Had I pushed her over the edge with a walk in the park, the smell of cedar, talk of freedom and asking about her mother?

Sitting behind that same icy glass with the reinforced wire, I listened to time tick by. Where was Sister Mary Agnes? On the desk, my file lay open. Seeing 'Lily Preston', typed neatly in the upper-left corner, was too much for me to resist. I was up and out of my chair, opening the report. Stamped across the first page at a diagonal, all in caps and in red ink, danced the word 'released' along with another word, quickly scrawled in blue, 'success'.

Before I could take this in, one of the younger nuns, not much older than me, came in with my bag and the clothes I'd arrived in six months earlier.

"Change here," she told me. "Mother Superior is on her way."

"What?"

"You're going home."

The words came at me in slow motion.

You're going home.

I fumbled with the bag and pulled out clothes that I hardly recognised. I didn't ask questions. My heart raced, and as she kept

253

her back to me, I dressed as fast as I could. It felt like an escape. While my skirt hung loose on my body and my jacket was missing, I kept quiet. I didn't know who'd given the green light, but I was not asking; I was walking out that door. Just as a car pulled up on the front drive, Sister Mary Agnes rushed in, motioning in the same instant for the younger nun to wait outside.

First, Sister Mary Agnes closed the door and told me to sit.

"If you can bear to." She sat down too, smiled at me and leaned forward with her elbows poised on her desk, chin resting lightly atop her interlaced fingers. "Maybe I'll see you in Ireland then one day."

"Maybe." I crossed my arms over my chest, hoping to contain my tears. "Am I really being released?"

"Yes," she said. "Lily, you have a good future ahead of you, and I for one will not keep you shut up here any longer. You are brave and bright and intelligent. I expect great things from you. I want you to stay in touch, and I want you to know that, if you need me, I am here for you always, and if by some lucky chance I am ever able to go back to Limerick, I will have left a forwarding address."

I nodded, afraid that careless speech would bring everything down on my head like a house of cards. That this moment of release, so longed for, would suddenly evaporate.

Sister Mary Agnes stood up, delved into her skirts to find her bulky set of keys and said, "Let's go."

As she unlocked the front door and walked me to the car, I saw Diego in the driver's seat.

Diego? Why would M send Diego? I didn't care. I was two steps away from freedom, and Diego never looked better – tall, bright-eyed, dark-haired and with that quirky 'alright then, I love you' half grin I had been recreating in my mind for far too long. His faded blue jeans, work shirt and Costa Rican ring marked him out as someone who belonged to this century – while St Savior's, with its fussy brickwork, hand-polished floors and stale musty air, was a throwback to the last.

Beside the car, he signed the paperwork neatly secured to the younger nun's clipboard: he would take responsibility for me. Yes, he was the family friend Mrs Jack Preston had sent.

"I'll take that," he told the youthful sister, as he lifted my small bag and placed it carefully in the trunk.

Before I had a chance to think about what I must look like to him in clothes now two sizes too large for me, Sister Mary Agnes had swept me up into her arms and kissed the top of my head.

"Be strong, Lily," were her parting words.

"Just go," I said to him, still wondering why M had allowed this.

Diego drove with precision, managing top speed in M's car. I laughed aloud. For now I didn't want to know anything about how this had been arranged. I was back on the 'outside' and nothing would stop me from finding some kind of sanity, somewhere, somehow.

Nothing will stop me from finding Mom.

We drove until I felt far enough away from St Savior's. By a field of young wheat, Diego stopped. I felt as if I'd died and gone to heaven. The horizon stretched forever, and I wasn't quite sure it was real. Diego spread out a picnic blanket at the edge of the field and pulled out the same plaid hamper I had packed all those years ago for our picnic lunch when we visited Mom in hospital.

"Wait. Do you have any money?" I asked, tossing the blanket and hamper into the back seat.

"Yes," he said.

"Good," I answered, "we are going for a proper meal, in a restaurant, and I am going to eat like a free person. Do you understand? And I want that red plaid hamper ditched in the nearest trashcan."

"*Sí.*" He grinned, pulling me closer. "*Nueva Chica, yo entiendo.*"

"Oh, Diego," I said before breaking down and crying. "That was the worst six months of my life. You cannot imagine... I was almost killed in there. Medicated... sedated. I thought I would never get out. I actually wondered if I might go mad, and who would care, and would it all end up the way M wanted: mad granddaughter – just like her no-good mother. And M saying to anyone who would listen, 'I told you so.'"

"But you are here right now, *conmigo*."

"Yes."

"And you must have friends in high places."

"Yes," I laughed. "Irish ones."

Thank you, Sister Mary Agnes.

THIRTY-EIGHT

Diego explained during the drive back that he was as surprised as I was that M had asked him to collect me.

"Well, I'm out now," I said, "and I will do whatever it takes to stay out until I'm eighteen and can do whatever I want."

"Good. Me, too," he laughed. "But get ready for the biggest surprise yet."

"Artie!" I shrieked even before Diego brought the car to a stop in M's driveway. I flew from the car to hug my brother. Taller, leaner, lankier, with his shoulder-length blond hair turned white by the tropical sun, I could hardly let him go. His smile, so like Mom's, made me cry.

"Lil' sister," he sang out, wiping that tear away, as only he could, swinging me off the ground and around three times. The eight months apart felt more like eight years. He couldn't quite fool me with his wide grin, though. I saw the wear and tear he'd suffered while we were apart. In an instant, just as I knew all about him, I felt he knew all about me: Diego, Philadelphia, the horror of St Savior's, the red X sliced into Eleanor's hand.

"You look great," I said.

"You, too," he roared. "Not bad, huh – for two freed inmates?"

"What do you mean?" I asked, at the same time remembering Silvie's smug, self-congratulatory letter to M.

"You didn't know?" My brother paused to light himself a cigarette. "*Corazón*. They put me in the *Corazón*, the psycho ward. You know – like mother, like son? Never mind that Dad's lost it completely. Surprised he's not lining up M60 machine guns on swivel mounts at every window. And Mom Number Three is lost in space with the exception of following the plan M laid out to her – getting rid of us one by one. She'll even ditch Dad, I think, if she can keep his housing and pension."

"*Corazón*?" I heard myself ask, then I swayed momentarily until Diego came to support me. With his other hand, he shook Artie's.

"Good to see you again, man," he said. "The trip was easy, and your sister was ready to go."

"I bet." Artie gave a lop-sided smile, taking a long inhale on his cigarette.

"Is M letting you smoke?" I asked.

"Sure, little sister. I'm the mini-man Ja-ack. And you can thank me for M allowing Diego to collect you. That took a lot of coaxing from me – fancy footwork. So you owe me."

"I do, thank you."

Diego gave me a kiss and handed Artie my bag. "Things will only get better for you from now on," he whispered to me.

"Yes," I told him before he left, "I know."

I will never, ever let my guard down around my grandmother again.

After dinner with M, who made light conversation as if nothing had ever happened and who seemed to be on the right side of sanity, I helped put the dishes away and excused myself. Sitting with Artie in M's library, evermore aware of her presence in the house, he turned on the TV and we spoke in low voices.

"Corazón was Silvie's idea. Dad's so easy to manipulate. She had friends on the staff there. She found Candy in my bed and decided to get me neatly out of the way, 'for my own good'."

"What are you going to do now?"

"Live here," he said, "with my fairy godmother, M. After all, I owe her for getting me out of Panama."

"You think?"

"No, seriously. She sprung me – her mini-Ja-ack. Or maybe, Lil', have you ever thought about this… maybe, to her, I'm a mini-Father of Jack?"

"Dad's dad?" I hesitated. "I forgot he even had one. You can cross that off your list. No one is permitted to mention him."

"Precisely. Wouldn't you like to get to the bottom of that story?"

"No," I answered, speaking quickly. "I don't have time to think about the past. I want to think only of the future, like Mags said I must. Did you notice how she never tried to change anything or wasted time thinking about the past? St Savior's was no picnic, Artie. I can't go back there, or any place like it. I have one more year left at school. Please help me get through that and then I can take myself out of M's way for good."

"You got it," he told me. "I've got your back and you've got mine. Two smart kids and one evil old cow. What else could she possibly do?"

THIRTY-NINE

The summer heat hovered around eighty degrees.

While the house seemed relatively calm, Artie reminded me constantly 'to sleep with one eye open', which he had learned in Corazón and I had understood since forever. Artie's new personality seemed a strange, patchwork affair. One minute he was his old self, finding the odd stray animal, usually wounded and bringing it back to health, and the next revelling in sharing with me his latest exploits – picking some girl up, evading the police and having sex at the top of the water tower.

"Can't rely on anything," he'd say while smoking in the carport or in the back garden. He twitched constantly, often looking behind himself, even in the house – especially in the house. He'd gotten his driver's licence and sometimes was out all night. Strangely, M never said much about this, except that my influence on my brother was negative. His favourite phrase, always delivered with a smile, proved to be: "Catch me if you can."

Mags never phoned or visited. She wanted to stay out of M's reach. She was okay – going from strength to strength, it seemed, volunteering in a children's camp in Maine. Messages came through Diego, whom M allowed me to see intermittently and capriciously on the odd Saturday afternoon, if she were at home and in the next room, reading. Diego and I found each other at school, meeting when we could at lunchtime, despite clashing schedules and my terror of being caught and sent back to St Savior's or worse.

"Don't trust M," Artie warned me. "Can't you just smell trouble brewing?"

Sometime in September, just after my final year of high school started, I'd discovered I'd forgotten a paper for my Economics class and had to return home to collect it. I hoped that M would not be home and I would not have to explain why on a Wednesday in the middle of the day I was not at school. A forgotten assignment would not suffice. She would imagine all sorts of deceit on my part. I could already hear the midnight calls to Aunt Penny and Ja-ack.

As soon as I turned the glass doorknob on the front door, the brass security bells jangled. *Intruder.*

"What are you doing, sneaking in like this?" my grandmother shouted instantly.

"I forgot my—"

"You didn't forget anything. This is more of the same, isn't it?"

She surprised me more than I surprised her. Dressed in her best silk dress, designer shoes, serious pearls, navy jacket and with her hair immaculately coiffed, she looked as if she'd just stepped out of that court hearing back in Columbus, Ohio.

"...Economics paper," I finished.

"Why didn't you say hello, let me know that you were in the house?"

"I just opened the door."

"You had time."

"M, I forgot a paper I need for this afternoon."

"Who's that out there?"

"A friend from school."

"Diego?"

"No."

M looked out the window, then opened the front door.

Bounding up the stairs, grabbing the paper, I sailed past her on the doorstep and jumped into the waiting car.

Escape.

I pretended normalcy for the sake of the friend who had been kind enough to drive me, but my heart raced like any fugitive's. What was M up to? She'd just come in from somewhere, an appointment she had not mentioned over breakfast. Or was she going out? She wasn't dressed for volunteer work or for a Right to Life meeting.

Something was up. I could read the signs. She'd been stewing ever since Sister Mary Agnes had foiled her plans. "What nerve," M had said, "and from a foreigner too, Irish." M even severed her relationship with Father Dominic.

I thought back over the events of the last few days. There had been the odd phone call when M spoke in muted tones. Was it with Aunt Penny? M had no friends. I located Artie at school, which was beginning to be a rarity since, with my brother, girls, smoking and drinking took priority over anything else.

"Old Preston subterfuge," he said while rolling himself a cigarette, "best be on your toes."

"You think?"

"I do. Bull's eye on your back."

"Please don't say that."

The following morning, at breakfast, an elongated, crisp, white envelope addressed to me lay at my place.

"What's this?" I asked.

"I don't know," M answered, dabbing her lips precisely with her napkin.

"Where'd it come from?" Artie joined in as I opened the legal-looking packet.

"Hand-delivered," M said, "yesterday."

Could a seventeen-year-old call her grandmother a liar? I went cold.

This was it.

M was going to come after me the way she went after Mom. The orange juice turned the blue glass a sort of pale green. The One-a-Day vitamin pills stood beside the dark bread, which stood beside the platter of potent, calcium-packed Velveeta cheese.

A healthy breakfast in an elegant room. A minefield waiting for me to take just one unwary step.

"It's a summons," I whispered, unable to speak clearly.

"Oh." M patted the corners of her mouth again.

"Someone has made allegations that I am a juvenile delinquent."

M stirred her coffee.

Artie jumped up from the table. "Jeez! Get it on, Louise."

I took the bus to school only half aware of what I was doing.

Juvenile delinquent… What is a juvenile delinquent?

This was Arkansas. I'd moved here from Panama, a country known to produce and export drugs. I had publicly mentioned pot. I wore a long ethnic-style skirt, designed by myself, from fabric made by the San Blas Indians. *Is that enough to have me labelled a danger to society?*

At school, Diego found me.

"You know your name is in the newspaper? My mom saw it."

"What?" I asked before he threw a protective arm around me.

"Your grandmother and apparently your father are not responsible for your bills anymore."

"What bills?"

"It's in the Classifieds."

Two strikes in one day? M meant business. She'd worked overtime on this. I felt blindsided.

It was unbearably warm, and as soon as Diego hugged me and left for his class, I thought I would faint. The walls seemed

263

to collapse, and the floor felt uneven. Artie had said he was hitchhiking to the lake this afternoon. In the library, I asked for yesterday's paper and flicked through to the Classifieds.

Mrs Emma Ewen Preston and Col. J. Preston of No. 1 Crescent Way will no longer be responsible for any debts incurred by Miss Lily Preston.

I read the notification twenty times. Did I have any debts? I never charged anything, always paying with cash. None of this made any sense. Recently M had bought me several frivolous things from a local store. Would she claim I had done this myself and expected her to pay for them? Wasn't that fraud? Where did juvenile delinquency come into it?

From my San Blas Island woven bag, my little piece of Panama, I retrieved the summons.

Allegations have been made that Miss Lily Preston of No. 1 Crescent Way is a juvenile delinquent. Miss Preston is to appear in court on Friday, September 28th, 1973, at 2:45pm.

Smith Caney, Juvenile Judge, had signed the document.

Who can I call? Panama is so far away. And how likely is it that Dad will help since his name has been included in the legal notice in the newspaper? Diego, his mom... who else is there to help me? I don't really know anyone else here. The school counsellor? Could I tell her what M and Dad did to my mother? Could I call Nana, would the Ryans help? Would Mom? Who could I tell that I was being set up in exactly the same way as my mother had been, and that I was deeply afraid?

Finding a dollar's worth of change, and not knowing what else to do, I called the number at the bottom of the summons. I decided I would not passively let my grandmother do this to me. I would do whatever I could to take things into my own hands.

"Juvenile," a woman's voice announced.

"Please can I speak to Smith Caney?" I said.

"He's in court. No, wait a minute… No, no, sorry. He's here."

I prayed for the change to last.

Proper people don't use public phones. The last public phone I'd used was when I said goodbye to Nana, when I couldn't recall the way back anymore, when the roads were well beyond our neighbourhood, when I was being kidnapped.

"Caney," an abrupt voice declared.

"Mr Caney," I started, "this is Lily Preston. You don't know me but there's been a mistake. I received a letter from you today."

"No mistake about it," he said curtly.

"May I see you?"

"No… Yes. Tomorrow. Right before the hearing."

I stayed silent, unable to voice all I needed to say. *How am I a juvenile delinquent? What will happen to me? Did you know that Emma Preston is crazy?*

"That's it. Take it or leave it," the judge said, waking me up.

"I'll take it, sir. I will take it."

"Tomorrow then, two-thirty. Ask for me at the courthouse. And don't be late."

After getting permission to leave school early the next day, I felt a surge of confidence. *Taking things into my own hands.* While gossip flew – who hadn't seen the classified ad? – Diego said to me, "Don't worry about it. What anyone else thinks of you is none of your business. What *you* think of you is." Both receptionists in the school's front office covered their mouths while reading the summons, which I had to show in order to get a pass out. I wanted to defend myself to them, but didn't. What did they know of my troubled life to date?

In the evening, in the bathtub, I cried. Artie had not returned from the lake – sometimes he didn't look in at the house for two or three days in a row. Shouldn't M be worried about that?

Couldn't she smell him in the night smoking marijuana on the roof, right outside her bedroom window?

I put my seventeen-year-old's dreams – boyfriends, girlfriends, good grades, university, maybe becoming a writer, if that wasn't a dream too far – on hold for the millionth time. I needed to prepare for Smith Caney. I needed to defend myself, push back, but how did I do that when the person I most needed to convince was a highly trained lawyer and I was struggling to complete twelfth grade?

Just as I was attempting to make a mental list of 'things I've done right', the brass bells on the front door clanged.

"Ja-ack," M squawked.

Dad. What is he doing here? Just in time!

Throwing on my bathrobe and racing down the stairs, two at a time, I flung myself into his arms.

"Don't touch me," he said. "I had to fly from Panama for this? First Artie, now you. You're all just as screwed up as your mother."

"For what?" I asked. "Why are you here?" I didn't care what I said to him now. What did I have left to lose?

"Don't speak to me like that! It's all over between us."

What's all over? What does he mean? After everything he let M do to me, to Mom, what's left that could be 'all over'?

Back upstairs, the fear of being incarcerated again in even worse circumstances sank into me. I tied my robe tightly and sat on the edge of the bathtub.

God help me.

I couldn't call Mags, Diego, anybody. Artie came home unexpectedly, speaking with Dad downstairs, carefully trying to defend me without calling M a crazy bitch.

"Useless," my brother whispered through the bathroom door, "he's on one of his blind missions. M's got him all wound up. He's just here to please his mommy and take the enemy out."

"That would be me?"

"Yes, that would be you."

"Ja-ack," M called out, "how about a bite to eat?"

The wind whistled that night, and I stayed awake, listening, cataloguing the things in my bedroom. When would I see them again?

How many times was Mom taken out in the middle of the night to who knows where? How many times did I set up a room of my own only to dismantle it and move on? How many times did I count on a new life lasting? How many times did I think I'd found someone who would be on my side, only to find that they weren't?

I imagined Mom saying, "Come, Lily, come live with me." Well, that hadn't ever happened and it wasn't going to happen now. *Stop dreaming.* M had planned this attempted incarceration ever since my unwelcome return from St Savior's. Thanks to some less than upright citizens at school I now knew what happened to juvenile delinquents – they were sent to juvenile jail or else the nut ward. I'd been there already and wasn't ever going back. Instead I would go and talk to Juvenile Judge Smith Caney. Finally I would stand up and speak for myself.

The next morning, we sat around the breakfast table. The same blue glasses turned green by the orange juice stood by the already dispensed One-a-Day vitamins by the health-bringing black bread, but instead of cheese there was fried eggs and bacon.

"Ja-ack, I am so lucky you could come." A smiling M held court. She relished moments like these. While I fought to pretend it was a normal school day, I knew it wasn't.

M sparkled like a young girl. "More eggs, Ja-ack?"

Had she concocted all this just to have her son show up? It dawned on me then that pot-smoking Artie had been right: "What do you expect when a woman marries her son?"

Light spilled through the trees in the park. A light fog covered the ground. I didn't go to school that morning. Instead I walked and walked to kill the time before I was due to see the judge.

The courthouse smelled of wood, wax and polished linoleum.

Old and well used, the pre-Civil War building seemed to be slowly melting into its own front lawn. I thought I could be sucked under with it. The echo of footsteps ran the length of the corridors, distant voices called back and forth and a clattering elevator dwarfed all sound. Finally, I found a nameplate that read 'Smith Caney, Juvenile Judge'.

"Come in," he said the moment I knocked.

We looked each other up and down. He seemed pleasantly surprised by the sight of me. So much so, in fact, that he removed his black-rimmed glasses, stood up and shook my hand.

"Please," he said, "sit down."

Smith Caney, on the other hand, was just what I'd expected. His suit, a bit rumpled, had once been smart, maybe even expensive, and a shirt just this side of white signalled unmarried. He wasn't portly but might soon be. His hair wasn't unduly short but suggested he might have been a military man but now worked diligently to be a civilian. His grin suggested a passion for his job.

"I don't know why I'm here," I said.

"Because you have a hearing before me in fifteen minutes."

"I am *not* delinquent. I don't know who made that claim, or why."

"Emma Ewen Preston did."

"Who delivered the papers?"

"She did. Took them with her on Wednesday after we met."

"But what have I done?"

"Apparently, a whole lot." He chuckled.

"I am not going to the penitentiary. I have not committed any crime. I have been up against this persecution and campaign of lies about me for a long time."

"Breathe, Miss Preston. Slowly. Tell me."

"My grandmother is devious. She is mean."

"Mean?"

"Yes, sir, she is. She will use you and this court to get what she wants, and that is to crush the child of the woman she considered unfit to marry her son."

Smith Caney picked up a black file, stepped out from behind his desk and paused to look me up and down. "I'll say one thing," he commented, throwing his frayed robe over his crumpled suit, "you don't look like any delinquent I've seen before. I can count on one finger the juvenile lawbreakers who have had enough nerve to call me up. Also, as you've arrived without a lawyer, I am guessing you intend to defend yourself."

"Yes, sir, I do," I told him, with no idea how I would handle myself in court.

Entering the courtroom with Judge Caney proved to be something of a coup for me. Dad in his full dress uniform, including a chest full of ribbons, and M in her green silk, pearl earrings and diamond brooch, stared at me with visible outrage.

"Mrs Preston," Judge Smith commenced, "you have made allegations that your granddaughter, Lily Preston, is a juvenile delinquent. On what grounds exactly do you make these allegations?"

"First," my grandmother harrumphed, "she has sex."

Smith Caney shot me a glance.

"She goes out," M continued, "at all times of the day and night…"

I studied the courtroom window, coated with a thick film of dust. The hum of the air conditioner partly drowned out my grandmother's denunciation of me. I'd heard it all before in any case, tried to fight it all before.

"She's been kicked out of every school she's ever attended for deviant behaviour…"

Still Smith Caney would not let me speak. Sitting mute in my straight-backed, wooden chair before his desk, I lost the thread of M's words, her lies. Jack Preston, erect beside his mother, leaned forward. M's feet, crossed at the ankle, barely touching the floor, swung back and forth like a little child's.

"Recess," a clerk announced.

My father stood up, helped his mother to stand. "Thank you," he said, nodding gravely at Smith Caney, only to stop at the door to issue his parting shot. "Your Honour, if this doesn't work, I will have Lily committed, just like I did her mother."

In an empty meeting room, with a white paper cup full of water before me, I sat – my mind scrambling to make sense of it all, deciding the right thing to do. Before me lay a boardroom table with pens and tablets of paper, a telephone. I didn't worry about calling anyone. I would help myself. I started writing. I had fifteen minutes, but it would only take me five. I wrote the worst of it down in clear, sharp bullet points – Dad's brutality to Mom, stepmother one, stepmother two, my own beating, Artie's frequent beatings, a young man in many ways now almost beyond recognition – can you help him? – my time at St Savior's, that I hadn't seen my mother in almost a decade, that I had to say she was dead when she wasn't, that I had been left for ten years not actually knowing whether my mother was, in fact, dead or alive.

Whether Smith Caney had had the time to read my notes or not, I did not know. When the court reconvened he came out from behind his desk, motioned to M's representative to introduce himself since he'd arrived during the recess, but then cautioned the three of them to sit down and be silent.

"I want to thank you, Mrs Preston, and Colonel Preston, for bringing Lily Preston to the attention of my court. I've now heard enough from you and it is my desire to hear something from the defendant."

M and Dad blanched.

"Please stand," Smith Caney addressed me.

"Yes, Your Honour," I answered, fearful of encountering a landmine at any moment. How did I do this? No one had ever asked me to speak up for myself: to tell the truth. This was stepping off the edge for me. This was death or glory. How many years had I been told that what I felt was not real? Could I turn the tide?

"Miss Preston?"

"Yes, Your Honour," I said for a second time.

"Your Honour," M interrupted, after clearing her throat, not just for the judge's benefit, but also for mine.

"Mrs Preston, you've had your say. Lily, please continue."

"She has no right to speak," M interrupted again.

"Yes," the judge said, "she does and this court will hear her out. And if you fail to remain silent, Mrs Preston, you will be removed."

Two guards shuffled against the wall. Suddenly M looked very small, as did my father. Miniatures. Balloons with the air let out. *Is someone actually telling M to shut up?*

My turn had come. "Your Honour, this story is a long-running one. I almost don't know where to start. There has never been a time when my grandmother has not interfered in the lives of my family, especially my own. While on the surface her actions appear to be motivated by concern for us, in fact they are not.

"As a young child in France, I was called gifted. I excelled in my studies there. In Panama I was a cheerleader and class vice president. Here, I was pulled out of a school while doing well, thriving in fact, and committed to St Savior's, a reformatory where thankfully the director realised I didn't belong. Diego Quesada is my long-term boyfriend with whom I've not had sex. Every single so-called fact put before you by my grandmother is a lie. She considers me a threat to her. I am not, except to her extraordinary need to prove that my mother and I are…" I hesitated.

"Carry on," Smith Caney directed, as the court stenographer typed away furiously.

"…insane."

"Miss Preston – Lily, if I may call you that?" Judge Caney addressed me gently. "Do you think that you are?"

"No, Your Honour, I do not."

"Neither do I," he said as he turned to M, Dad and their legal representative. "You have wasted my time and the time of this court. I won't mention the time and the life to date of this young woman. I hereby terminate this hearing and urge you to leave this courtroom without making any further comment unless I choose to open a criminal case concerning your actions over what appears to be a good number of years. This child will remain in my custody, as a ward of this court. I find you unfit guardians and record will be made of this finding."

My father whisked his mother out of the room, and their glares caused me not a moment's unease. A 'just wait until you get home' glower no longer frightened me because I knew I was never going 'home' again.

I had thrown the case finally, as I should have years ago. I could still hear my father's voice after I had kissed my mother long ago in a cold room with a two-way mirror: "You almost threw the divorce."

"Approach the bench," Smith Caney instructed me. "I want to have a private conference with you." While I leaned against his desk, for just a second he reminded me of Uncle Danny. He looked like a different man now, softer. "Listen carefully," he said in a quiet voice, "I am going to tell you a story about a king and his wise men."

I paid attention.

"This king had three sage men, and he wanted to know the answer to any problem that might ever befall him or his kingdom. The clever men put their heads together, searching the kingdom for the answer, and guess what, Lily, they found it."

Smith Caney loosened his tie, and then took off the gold ring he wore on his ring finger. Inside, I read the inscription: 'And this too shall pass away'.

"Not much, is it?" he told me, slipping the ring back onto his finger. "But that's the solution, Lily. To every ill that befell the king… and you."

Is he crazy? I've just dodged the most incredible tsunami. Three wise men?

"Now I am going to ask you the most important question of the day." He grinned. "Did you have lunch?"

"Lunch?" I asked. "No."

"Thought not," he answered. "Me neither. Would you like to eat?"

"Yes," I said triumphantly. *As much as I can.*

Slinging his robe over the desk, he turned to the clerk and announced, "Application denied. Miss Preston, I have three more things to say to you before we leave here."

"Yes?"

"First, be clear, you are not a juvenile delinquent, incorrigible, mentally ill or insane; second, have you considered studying Law? – those notes were brilliant, clear and to the point; and finally, we've got to find a safe place for you to live until you are eighteen."

He beamed and then hooted right out loud, along with several of the court staff, who apparently knew and respected his good judgement.

"Some act, that family of yours," he shook his head, frowning, "some act. And I have seen it all in this room." Outside, he steered me straight past my father and grandmother, who stood in the parking lot looking lost. "Let's find a bright, respectable, public spot where a juvenile court judge and his new ward can eat a late lunch together."

FORTY

Both pear-shaped, Zachary and Sara Bell looked like brother and sister rather than a married couple approved by the court to host foster children. They welcomed me into their home on the same day M lost her case and I was acquitted. Straight from lunch, Smith Caney drove me to my new foster home, which he promised would have all the odds and ends I needed for a few days, including a toothbrush. Without hesitation, the Bells moved their two sons out of their bedroom and into the master bedroom.

"Top, bottom or both are yours," Zachary joked, pointing to the bunk beds.

"Thank you," I said.

What miracle was this? I had landed on my feet here. I would not have shock treatment, be locked up, sent back to St Savior's or the state penitentiary. Someone had listened to me.

"If you stay here long enough," Zachary added, "you'll have a room of your own. Just off the kitchen, I'm building an addition."

If I stay here long enough I can finish school. My smile started to hurt.

"Smithy's right. You're not like the usual kids they send us.

Don't worry, everything will turn out all right. You're safe now," my foster dad assured me. "I've got your back."

After Zachary showed me their little farm, and his sons told me tall tales of frogs and unicorns, I undressed, showered and put on the soft gown Sara had left on my bed. Sitting on the lower bunk, I patted the sheets to see if they were real. Just a few hours ago my life hung in the balance. A child's astronaut and skyrocket motif encircled me. Two gerbils, busy in their cage by the window, burrowed in deeply, pushing wood shavings and hay around. A sweet potato plant overflowed the windowsill and bookshelf, creeping towards the floor. A streetlight poured through the blue curtain, where a spaceman landed on the moon.

Zachary laughed at everything, not as if it were a joke, but as if he were Buddha himself, and wasn't life funny? With his thick glasses in their square black frames, Zachary Bell would have been the kid in class whose shirt never stayed quite tucked in, and the one who, despite your wanting to say no to him, you agreed to dance with when he asked. No matter what, he kept coming back at you with good news: the dweeb.

"Do you believe in God?" he asked me one day.

"Yes," I answered, "why not?" I thought of Guillermo's advice when I first arrived in Arkansas – if anyone asks if you know Jesus, just say yes.

Chuckling softly, he added, "You don't have to. I believe Christ Jesus is my Saviour, but don't let that put you off. Any idea of God will allow us to sing off the same page."

"Yes," I agreed.

He paused and then continued, "You've gotten a bum rap, Lily. You're lucky Smith Caney dealt with the application. Your grandmother is crazy. No, God bless her, I shouldn't say that. Demented, maybe. Nasty. Mean. Who knows what went down with her when she was a kid? But don't worry. We are going to help you now."

"Thank you," I told him.

"Do you want to go to college, Lily?"

"Yes, I do."

The Bells' refrigerator kicked on and off all night. Their young sons giggled in their parents' bedroom before falling asleep. They camped out for weeks, sleeping on the floor, used to giving their beds away.

"To the poor," the youngest told me one morning over buttered toast, "you have to give it all away: your bed, your clothes, your food, everything. That's what Jesus wants."

"Oh," I said.

A charity case? Suddenly I understood Mags, her years of counting paycheques from the library in Panama and that God-awful, black nylon hairnet that came down past her hairline and over her ears. I respected her, not unlike the stewardesses on that flight from Virginia to Philadelphia had respected Mom.

I sheltered on the bottom bunk: happy, sad, cold, safe, afraid. In a tract house, somewhere outside of Fayetteville, Arkansas, with a plot of land big enough to plant potatoes, I'd escaped Emma Preston.

Was Sara Bell serious when she suggested I write to my mom? Could Zachary really have her address?

"Why not?" he laughed. "This is America, not a war zone. It's the twentieth century. Of course you can contact your mom."

"Coffee!" Zachary rapped on my bedroom door.

"No, thanks," I answered, "I don't drink it."

"What kind of incorrigible are you anyway?"

"A caffeine-free one."

"We're in luck, children," he said, bellowing, "Lily still has a sense of humour." Then, a bit less loudly, he added, "Hit the shower, get ready for bacon, toast and pancakes – most of it raised and made right here by me – us."

276

"Thank you," I said, "I'll be right out."

"Did you hear the rooster, Lily?" he asked.

"No," I answered.

"Then listen up."

Zachary crowed on the other side of the door, and, despite myself, I laughed.

What a dweeb. How well-off could one girl be?

"Now it is like this," Zach told me a day or so later. "We are going to your grandmother's house to pick up your clothes. You are not going in alone. Remember, there's nothing much she can throw at me that will knock me down. Being a rehab counsellor and country pastor, I have seen it all. She will attempt to humiliate you. She is an angry old bitch."

"Did you say bitch?"

"Would you prefer witch?"

"Neither," Sara weighed in.

"Be prepared for the black trash bags routine," he instructed.

"Excuse me?"

"That's a favourite."

"For what?"

"To send your clothes out in."

Emma Preston dropped three black plastic trash bags over the railing from the second-floor landing. They thudded on to the hall floor. Zachary and I exchanged glances as we stood at the open front door.

"She's not to come into this house, Penny," M made clear in a shrill voice.

When did Aunt Penny arrive? Where's Dad?

Aunt Penny refused to meet my eyes and motioned to Zachary to pick up the black bags.

Did she whisper 'sorry'?

If we had been a few minutes later my things would have been out by the garbage cans on the curb. I didn't feel sad, didn't allow myself to suffer humiliation. Instead, I raged inside. I wanted to barge right through that front door with its ridiculous jangling brass bells hung on a drapery cord and tell M and Aunt Penny what I thought: pitiful women. Who were they to try to hurt me, never mind Lauren Rose?

Zachary placed one large hand firmly on my shoulder, and I stepped back, and for some reason I heard my mother's voice asking me to promise her that I would not run around in Mrs Martin's first grade class, not answer every question, read every book, that I would take a nap like the other kids, put my hand down, only go to the bathroom once.

"Thank you, Mrs Preston." He nodded to both women, picking up all three bags in one swoop of his free hand and swinging them over his shoulder.

"I'm sorry," he said as we pulled out of the drive. "Nasty old woman. Mean as the day is long. Just fuming that you got away. I wonder what happened to her. You don't have a clue? Lot of pain in there."

I nodded, which he could take for sympathy if he chose.

"Put your own life into high gear," he instructed me. "Think about that. Forget all the things you can't do anything about. You graduate in less than a year. You're safe with us until then."

While I was sitting, listening to the sound of his truck's engine, not really thinking of anything, Zachary asked if he could take me by his office for a Rorschach test.

"Does it hurt?" I asked.

He laughed his everything-is-funny belly laugh, and said, "No! But it has to be today because we don't have much time to make the application for tuition and books if I can help you get into university. Today is the absolute deadline, even with prayer and me pulling a few strings."

"University?"

"Remember, I'm a rehab counsellor – I get people into school."

"I know, but I'm not in rehab."

"But I can put you down as RTA."

"What is that?"

"Reaction to Adolescence. It means nothing. Everyone reacts to adolescence. In the case of a ward of court it means you get your tuition and books paid for. One despicable grandmother cannot hold a good girl down."

"I'm scared," I said.

"Of what?"

"The test."

"Why?"

What do I have to lose by telling him?

"Because my mother was a schizophrenic."

"And your grandmother says you are one too?"

"How do you know that?"

"Par for the course. I've seen it all before, and besides, she mentioned it in court. Smithy gave me the paperwork."

I was so angry I couldn't speak.

Am I being observed all the time?

"I know schizophrenia, and you don't have it," he assured me.

"Are you certain?"

"No, I'm just trying to make you feel good." He laughed and hit the steering wheel, thinking himself funny, which he was. His rooster crowing could on occasion keep my spirits up all day long.

Zachary parked the car, and as we walked side by side into a small brick building just off the main road through Fayetteville, he nudged me with an elbow.

"Lighten up, the bad part's over. Get into the office and take the test. Gal's name is Amy. She's a sweetheart. Onside, if you catch my drift. Do your best, which I know you will."

Before I could say anything, Amy met me at the door, and handed me a paper cup of water. In front of me stood one of the happiest-looking women I'd seen in a long time. With red hair pulled back neatly from her face and fine wire-rimmed glasses that looked more prop than necessity, she smiled broadly.

"Quick," she demanded, "sit down. We're racing against the clock here. Zach has all the paperwork completed, and I just have to say you're sane by lunchtime."

"Okay," I answered, a bit dazzled by the overly bright incandescent light, slick wood panelling and her enthusiasm.

She lifted a set of cards.

"Go," she sang out.

"Go?"

"Yes. What do you see?"

"Ink stain."

"In the ink."

"Nothing."

"Nothing?"

"Well, anything."

"Like what?"

"Okay, anything. I don't want to sound nuts."

"Don't worry, you won't."

"Pagoda, pelvis, butterfly, lake, diamond, face—"

"Okay, stop!" Amy said as she looked at her watch. "Done! You're definitely not crazy."

"Thank you," I answered.

"What do you want to do?"

"With what?"

"Your life, after school?"

"Write!" I said.

"Okay," she concurred, "that'll do. Future occupation: author."

FORTY-ONE

"Surprise!" Diego said. "Again."

I kissed him, right out in the open, in Zachary and Sara Bell's driveway. The sun shone, and a perfect blustery Sunday beckoned.

"Do you want to drive?" he asked, already tossing me the keys.

"Yes, please," I said, hardly believing that I didn't have to think twice about everything I said or about my every move in advance.

"I love you," he said. "Now put it in reverse," he instructed. "Do you remember how to do it?"

"Yes, I do. Every bit of it."

We waved to the Bells, who both stood at the front window like proud parents. In a sense they were. In a few months they had given me back my pride, some self-esteem, and it looked like they might even have raised enough money for college.

"Reaction to Adolescence," I told Diego, who laughed. "Zach says it means absolutely nothing. It's not like I'll have a record or anything – just books and tuition for school."

"Fantastic."

"Sara thinks I should go east to school, maybe New York, a writing programme."

"New York?"

"You could come with me."

"Let's see. You know I'm looking at California."

"Let's see," I echoed.

The engine of Diego's new convertible hummed, and I found myself lost in the drive, enjoying every hairpin turn from Fayetteville to Eureka Springs. The old Beatles tune 'Here Comes the Sun' came on the radio, and we both smiled and sang along. That prom night seemed a hundred years ago. I remembered it all. Hadn't Mags said I looked like something out of a magazine?

We both knew where we were going and what we were doing. Diego had reserved a room, a suite at the Swan. He bought roses: big, blowzy, double-headed white and ivory roses, and he'd given me another ring, a diamond one this time, something that had belonged to his grandmother.

"Is this legal?" he asked when we arrived.

"Yes, I think so."

"Well, I consent," he said.

"And I do, too," I laughed.

We warmed up with hot cocoa, called room service for food and lit a fire. With my back pressed against his chest, we watched a waterfall just outside the window and beyond that mountains that stretched forever.

I felt safe, as if years and years of running, of ducking and diving, had suddenly come to a halt. I could now move forward on my own terms. Diego kissed the back of my neck, and I turned around.

Nothing was left undone.

Back in the Bells' driveway by ten that evening as requested, I could barely separate from Diego, but I was happy to get 'home', back to my astronaut bedsheets and sweet potato vines.

"Artie!" I said, surprised to find my brother sitting in the living room, chatting away to Sara and Zach.

"New housemate," he laughed, and gave me a deep hug. "You spent the day in Eureka, I hear," my brother said with his ever-present smile.

"That's right," I said. "It's so great to see you, but what are you doing here?"

"Simple. M called Smith Caney with another incorrigible, and he said, 'Skip the court, go straight to the Bells.' Dad was too drunk to weigh in, too busy with his hell-on-wheels wife in Panama."

"Yes," Zach piped up, "never been assigned a boy before, but why not? Now that we have the addition, and Lily has her own room, Artie can take the boys' bunks and they can come back into our room."

"In another few months, if all goes well, as I'm sure it will, Lily will be at NYU and you can have her room," Sara added.

"NYU?" I asked.

Do they already have the paperwork?

"They called this afternoon, while you were in Eureka Springs. At the moment, Lily, you are first alternate for the writing programme."

Diego threw his arms around me, kissed me on the lips in front of everyone and nobody batted an eyelid.

"Now," Zach ordered, "everyone sit down. I have some tougher news."

We sat. Sara left the room.

"Your father is ill. He is being medevac-ed from Panama City to a veterans' facility outside of Fayetteville. Not sure how serious it is, but your aunt arranged it all. I don't have all the details, so I am not sure if it is life or death."

Artie looked first at me, then at Zachary before getting up and heading for the door. "Wishful thinking, Mr Bell," he said. "Death, that is."

FORTY-TWO

Finally Zachary said we had permission to visit Dad.

"Are you sure he wants to see us?" I asked.

"Yes. He is up for it."

When the day came I wanted to go alone. The veterans' hospital sprawled endlessly over grounds that had formerly belonged to an old plantation renowned for its apples. Convalescing soldiers had used the farmstead since the Civil War.

I had no hopes or expectations for my meeting with Dad. He was just a sick, decorated soldier with what I had learned to call post-traumatic stress disorder, and now depression too. I was paying my respects, maybe coming to say goodbye. I had not even decided whether or not to tell him about NYU. I was no longer an alternate. I had not only been accepted, but with a full scholarship, based on a submission of my work.

I was doing this without Jack Preston, or M – no handcuffs, no ball and chain, no manipulation. Not one inch of my new life belonged to either one of them. But still, it seemed dangerous to tell him anything. Certainly finding Mom would not be on that list.

The Bells' old car, which they had loaned to me for the trip in exchange for some babysitting, chugged along the winding roads, giving me a chance to think. Going back east, admitted to NYU and excited by the hope that I might see Mom, I began to formulate a plan. I had Nana's and Granddad's number, and I knew vaguely Mom might be in Connecticut, which was one hour from them by car or train, and sixteen hours if I had to hoof it all the way from New York City. I was all in, and I had saved the money to get me there. I began to sing.

The red-brick hospital rising up before me was almost a surprise. I'd almost forgotten I was on the way to visit Dad. With its wide, old-fashioned esplanade that circled a small lake, ran back through the orchards and back up to the main house, I imagined the returning Confederates must have found it a welcome, happy sight. Perhaps Dad did too.

Inside, my heels clicked over the slick tiled floors.

It had been eight months since I'd last seen Dad, when he had vowed to have me committed, just as he had done to Lauren Rose.

The smell and the orderliness of the hospital, the military atmosphere, were familiar: home.

"Dad!" I shouted.

At the far end of the corridor, through an open door, I'd caught a glimpse of him, leaning against a bed, talking to another patient. Both men turned as I hurried in their direction, surprised to find myself running like a little girl to reach my father.

"Lil'," he said, sounding pleased and as if he had never threatened to have me committed. He gestured to his companion. "This is Private Grady Loenbee. He is ninety-two and fought in the Spanish American War in 1905."

"Practically dead now," the old man chimed in.

"Hi," I said, suddenly shy and forgetting the whole purpose of my visit.

Sitting on the red-tiled veranda, enjoying the trees and the sound of the wind whistling around the old archways, I sat with my father, as he tapped his rubber-footed walking stick.

Suddenly, he started to talk. "M hated hospitals. When she was just a kid she spent years in them, had weights attached to a plaster cast that pulled her spine straight. That's what they did in the twenties for polio. M refused to talk to me about it, but a nurse I once dated told me all about it. Clothes, toys, books were burned. Then, of course, there was boarding school."

M had polio?

"I thought her hump was from a skating accident. Or maybe dancing."

"It was pride, Lil'. Dancing mishap, skating accident, whatever sounded better than the truth – which was polio. She had a hard time, for lots of reasons. Penny and I were all she had. I know it hasn't been easy on you, all of you, and I am sorry. Really sorry."

Sorry? Is that it? I remembered hammering that red alarm at St Savior's, but this time it was this man I wanted to hit. Bloody, fucking excuse for a man. He had no idea what I'd been through, or Mags or Artie. He just thought of himself, M, what they'd been through. I decided then not to tell him about NYU, not to give one bit of my freedom, myself, to this pitiful old man.

"Yeah," I said, "I forgive you."

A white-clad nurse approached and, switching into his usual flirtatious self, he took his medication from her. She reminded me he needed to sleep.

"Do you know anything about my father?" he asked when she left.

"Nothing," I said, "other than he's dead."

"Yes, that's true, but he was a farmer, Lil', or always wanted to be one."

My father grew silent, except for the odd tap of his stick. He took in the grounds, the trees, and the few patients and visitors walking or being pushed in wheelchairs. He lit a cigarette. "He was never enough for M – did you know she divorced him? – but that's what I want to do, Lil', when I get out of here. He drank, but I liked him. I want to buy a farm. Raise cattle, maybe pigs. I am a free man now."

A gentle and efficient orderly came to retrieve his patient, reminding me it was time for Colonel Preston's nap. I agreed and accompanied them back to his room. His bedside table held water, tablets and books from the library: *Mind Over Matter, The Second Big Dream, Never Say Retired.*

"Lil'," he told me, smoothing out the sheets with busy hands, "the therapy has been a success. I'll be up and outta here in less than a week."

While that wasn't what Zach or Sara had said, I replied, "Okay, Dad, that's good news."

"You bet," he answered, before giving me his old, two-fingered salute and letting his head fall back on the pillow.

I took my time walking away, down the hospital corridor and out onto the lawn. I didn't regret my silence; I didn't want to explain or listen. I had no desire to share with him anything about NYU, Mom or my plans. The truth was he had never asked. On the veranda, I stopped, taking in the lawn, the soft white light, the apple orchard, the peacefulness, and then, without a second glance, I left.

No turning back.

FORTY-THREE

Artie called me at Diego's house. It was a pristine June day and we were toasting ourselves with iced tea by his mom's bougainvillea. I was going to NYU and he was going to the University of California at Santa Barbara. We'd be together every vacation. Could life get any better?

"Come home," Artie said over the phone.

"Why?" I asked.

"Because I have something important to tell you."

I set down my iced tea, and Diego offered to drive me. Who knew with Artie? Was it about Mom? Was she – my deepest fear – dead? Did Artie want me home to deliver the news in person? I pictured him in the kitchen of the Bells' farmhouse with its bright yellow, brown-speckled linoleum.

It wouldn't be about M. She was dead, even if it was still hard for me to believe – the woman who while alive had haunted me my whole life. She had died just a few weeks into my providential escape. The court informed the Bells, who told me Emma Preston had choked on one of her favourite cookies, the ones she kept in the tin emblazoned with the Dutch girl motif. The choking resulted in a cardiac arrest, and Aunt Penny, in order to save time and money, had her cremated before putting the Arkansas house on the market and flying back to Philadelphia.

There was no funeral, no memorial, not even a Mass. M had just melted away like the Wicked Witch of the West, screeching and cursing me for defeating her wickedness. Diego marked the moment with a rendition of 'Ding Dong, the Witch is Dead' and I felt absolutely no remorse whatsoever. M, my ostensibly ladylike and respectable grandmother, who helped to have my mother institutionalised, agitated for and paid for my parents' divorce, who had me unlawfully incarcerated in a mental institution masquerading as a school, who had attempted to have me labelled a juvenile delinquent and confined to a state penitentiary, was now officially *deceased*. This was the word I had been forced to use with my mother when I didn't believe it was true; now in the case of M, I knew it was, and I was not afraid to use it: deceased, deceased, deceased. M no longer existed, could do no further damage and I could sing 'Ding Dong' at the top of my lungs forever. I had escaped, as Diego liked to say, 'the jaws of death'.

I told Diego to drive slowly. Whatever Artie had to say would not rock my boat. I had so much to be grateful for now. I was free and beginning to stand on my own two feet. The sun warmed the car, and the beauty of the Ozark countryside, fully leafed, passed by. Caney had been right to send Artie to Zach and Sara. Artie might have a chance now, just like I had. He had already been convicted of a couple of petty crimes: stealing a Budweiser off the back of a truck, sneaking into a local restaurant and frying himself a steak at midnight.

In the front drive, I lingered, told Diego I'd see him later. I was dreading what Artie had to say.

"Hurry," he shouted from the doorway. "We have a letter from Nana and Granddad."

A vibrant light spilled through the kitchen windows, illuminating yet another translucent sweet potato vine. Artie leaned against the counter in front of the two, elbow-deep, stainless-steel sinks.

"Let me see."

"Yes," he said. "Look at this."

He spread the news clipping from the *Westport News* out over the table beside us. It was a half-page spread with one large image. There stood our mother, Lauren Rose, right in the middle, arms akimbo, wearing a gardening apron and with a mile of geraniums fanning out in the greenhouse behind her.

"Westport, Connecticut," I said.

"Yes," Artie whistled.

Mom is alive.

Of course we called Mags right away. Her response was muted, but she did ask us to keep her posted. She still believed Lauren Rose's absence was from choice, however badly our dad had behaved to her. Mags was busy finishing her degree in Library Science and under pressure to perform for her possible graduate degree at the University of Illinois, and didn't want to be distracted by anything else.

Artie lit up a cigarette, while he turned the key in the ignition of the car Zach had helped him to rebuild. I smoked one, too. We didn't speak; just drove. Then, pooling our money, we bought pizza with extra cheese and pepperoni. We drank Coca-Cola and crushed the ice with our back teeth. We didn't want to go home – not yet. We had survived, and so had Lauren Rose. We drove by M's old house, nightmare on the hill.

"Stop," I said. "You'll wake the dead."

"Or get picked up by the police."

Artie dropped me off at Diego's and put his hand over mine as I held on to his door to say goodbye.

"Where are you going?" I asked.

"Nowhere in particular," he said, shrugging his shoulders and shaking his big, blond head. "I don't know."

"Okay. I'll see you at Zach's later."

"Yes, you will, and by the way, if Sara or Zach haven't already told you, I'm filling out the application for the pre-veterinary programme at the U of A."

"No kidding?"

"No kidding, Lil'. I thought if you and Mags could read and write, maybe I could, too." He laughed, and said, "I also agreed to help the old man with his new patch of land. Learn how to milk a cow, put up a barbed-wire fence and break a thoroughbred."

FORTY-FOUR

Diego arrived early and helped me load my bags into the trunk of his car, as they didn't fit into the convertible's trunk.

"Next stop, New York?"

"Yes." I grinned.

At the airport, he took the bags out of the car. Even in his blue jeans and bleached work shirt, he was still the handsomest man anywhere. Together, we stood and watched a small passenger plane land. *How many times did I watch aeroplanes with Dad?* Then he ushered me inside the terminal.

We both felt good with me flying off to New York City, and he driving to Santa Barbara, with plans to meet over the Thanksgiving holiday.

Fayetteville's airport buzzed with morning passengers, bag handlers and ticket takers. From here, I would fly to Memphis. Finally, I was leaving. I had said goodbye to everyone. Dad, Mags, Artie. I thought of the times I had tried to keep us all together. Birthdays, zip codes, new mothers. It all flitted away. I had played mother, wife, confidante. I had come that close to being imprisoned.

Now I was free.

I checked my bag and waited, with Diego holding my hand.

"Remember," he said, "I love you. I am behind you one million per cent."

"I know."

We hugged one last time. The plane was being called for boarding.

"Write," he told me. "Write to me."

"I will."

Inside the plane, I sat over the wing because Dad always said it was the safest place.

A plane could split in two.

I looked for the nearest exit because Dad had always said to be prepared.

You never know what can happen next.

I looked for the one person I might save.

He would save the whole plane.

I spread my fingers out against the glass so Diego could see me. From the viewing platform, I could just see him waving, with that broad and wide smile I could never forget. *One million per cent.*

The plane from Memphis to New York was full of strangers. They would never know what I knew. I pressed my forehead against the window.

Thunderheads.

Rivulets scattered across the glass. The city rose up beneath me in the black of night. From the distance it looked like a snaking string of diamonds. Much closer, the threads turned into fire, and finally, moving, they spread as molten as lava.

I took a deep breath, disembarked at JFK and dove right in.

NYU didn't faze me, not even the next day's plan. I would pick up the rental car early, drive straight through – one hour and three minutes, 50.2 miles, north, on Interstate 95.

To see Mom.

293

ACKNOWLEDGEMENTS

Thank you Reader, first and foremost, for reading *Geraniums*. After you, there are many people to thank, and I apologise in advance if I have forgotten anyone. I will begin with Sara Johnson-Weyer for helping me to plow on both in the wilds of Argentina and at our Tortugas Writers Group in Buenos Aires.

Thank you to Jill Robinson and The Wimpole Street Writers Group, in London, where *Geraniums* began as *Juicy Fruit*, three, double-spaced pages at a time, one evening a week over roast chicken and other culinary delights.

Thank you to Lynn Curtis, my first editor, for saying, "Well then, let's get cracking," as well as giving Lily a backbone and the story twist and turns I had only imagined.

Thank you to Tamsin Shelton for her intense and accurate scrutiny; for helping to get a first and final draft over the line.

Thank you to L.C. for reading and for saying, "Yes!"

Thank you to Harry Coventry for mostly keeping the wheels on.

Thank you to the Hauser family.

Thank you to Paul Oberschneider for suggesting I write this in the first place.

Thank you to Christian Oberschneider, for being my inspiration every single day, since that first miraculous day when you came into our lives, and for that second magical day when you took my hand and said, "Mummy, you can write."